"ONE OF AMERICA'S FINEST NOVELISTS"

"The greatest obstacle for women who wish to accomplish something besides marriage and motherhood is the awareness that females are illegitimate in the world. Wharton's sense of this was to remain with her all her life.

"Once she had begun to take her life in her hands, however, she was prodigious . . ."

from the Introduction by
MARILYN FRENCH

Also in Berkley Editions

THE HOUSE OF MIRTH
SUMMER
THE CUSTOM OF THE COUNTRY

Coming Soon

OLD NEW YORK

Berkley books by Edith Wharton

THE CUSTOM OF THE COUNTRY
THE HOUSE OF MIRTH
ROMAN FEVER AND OTHER STORIES
SUMMER

EDITH WHARTON

WITH A NEW
INTRODUCTION BY
MARILYN FRENCH

ROMAN FEVER
AND OTHER STORIES

BERKLEY BOOKS, NEW YORK

ROMAN FEVER
AND OTHER STORIES

A Berkley Book / published by arrangement with
Charles Scribner's Sons

PRINTING HISTORY
Charles Scribner's Sons edition published in 1911
Berkley edition / October 1981

ISBN: 0-425-04609-5

A BERKLEY BOOK ® TM 757,375
Berkley Books are published by Berkley Publishing Corporation,
200 Madison Avenue, New York, New York 10016.
PRINTED IN THE UNITED STATES OF AMERICA

Contents

INTRODUCTION
by Marilyn French

I.

EDITH WHARTON is one of America's finest novelists, and during her lifetime she was highly respected, well-known, and successful. But since her death in 1937, her work has been largely neglected: only a handful of her books is still in print. Few writers of quality have suffered such an eclipse. There have been intermittent efforts, by people like Edmund Wilson and Irving Howe, to resuscitate her reputation, and indeed there has been increasing interest in Wharton's work recently. But some of the very people who have attempted to revive such interest are responsible for impeding that process, by writing essays tainted with undisguised patronization for this "lady writer," and by approaching her work negatively. That is, critics frequently direct more attention to what Wharton did not do than to what she did do. They have skirted the focusing and elucidation which is surely the first business of criticism.

But part of the reason for our long neglect of Edith Wharton may also be that without a change in certain attitudes, it was difficult to perceive what indeed her central concerns were. One of her more perceptive critics, Blake Nevius, writing in 1953, accused Wharton of a "lurking feminism." Feminist concerns do appear in her work, although she did not associate herself with the feminist movement of her time. She wrote frequently of the way in which women were educated to become ornaments, mindless and self-regarding, not persons but products. The double sexual standard chafes some of her female characters. And one of her major themes—constriction—appears most powerfully when it is linked with the rules governing the lives of women. Whether she writes about lives lived narrowly inside social constricts, or in isolation outside of them, social constrictions, Wharton is subtle, delicate, and precise. The seeming innocence of male critics about the difference between a woman's life and a man's, about the profound effects of learning to adapt the self to a small anteroom in life, has led to an impercipience about Wharton's work. She does not shout: therefore she is not heard. (Had she shouted, she would not have been published.)

She was born Edith Newbold Jones, in 1862, to an old New York family that was part of the "elite," the aristocracy almost, of this young country. This class, modeled on the British gentry had essentially bourgeois standards although gentlemen did not work except for a few who interested themselves in law, banking, or government. Ladies spoke softly and took care to be ornamental. Gentlemen sat at table after dinner drinking port or madeira while the ladies withdrew to (with-) drawing rooms which were (as Edith's mother once said, criticizing one of her early literary efforts) always tidy. Money and sex were never discussed, and ladies were not supposed even to think about them. Many other subjects were equally outside the pale.

At root, the greatest sin was feeling. Not only did one not express feeling, one did not even discuss it. People whose work was the expression of feeling—artists, writers, actors—were as déclassé as tradesmen. Strenuous exertion was acceptable only in amateur sports. Utterly secure economically, permitted to marry only within the group—thus tight and cohesive socially and sexually—this class owned its world. Any sign of need, whether it be a shabby gown or a passion for painting, was a betrayal of class. To care about anything too much was to admit that this small, isolated, independently wealthy group of people was not in fact independent, invulnerable, sufficient to itself on all occasions, superior to and untainted by the grubby concerns and seamy cravings of ordinary humanity.

This society was not without its virtues. It adhered to a high standard of probity in financial affairs; it had a clear code of manners, respect for "good" taste, and it was unpretentious and wore its opulence quietly. It maintained, for good or ill, a rigid code of sexual mores and a double standard. Above all, its stability and narrowness granted its members the pleasures of security and continuity. It also offered the pain of suffocation. In the years when Edith Wharton was weaning herself away from its values, she was frequently ill: a major symptom was the inability to breathe, a sense of stifling.

The young Edith Jones was passionate, willful, and fascinated by literature—by her own "making-up" of tales and by the books in her father's library. She was born late (her brothers were twelve and sixteen) in the life of a woman who had grown up feeling inferior, shy, and deprived, and who seems to have surrounded her daughter with a climate of cold disapproval. Her father was warmer, but remote; a gentle dilettante, he suffered from ill health as Edith grew up and he died when she was nineteen. He provided part of her knowledge of constriction and waste: in her memoir, *A Backward Glance*, she wrote, "I have wondered since [his death] what stifled cravings had once germinated in him, and what manner of man he was really meant to be. That he was a lonely one, haunted by something always unexpressed and unattained, I am sure."

Education in Wharton's class was desultory. Young men did receive formal training, and sometimes even read law, but were expected to have a smattering of knowledge about many things without strong interest in any one thing. Young women were taught the social arts and perhaps a foreign language. The Jones family was fastidious about spoken and written English, but Edith was not formally educated. The family's theory was that education should not "fatigue" the brain: concentration was as frowned upon as emotion. But the young girl read widely in the books available to her (and continued to do so, ranging into many disciplines, throughout her life), and during long periods of travel abroad with her parents, she learned several foreign languages.

She failed the standards of her world from the beginning. And they were absolute standards: drawing rooms were *always* tidy; money was *never* discussed; strong emotions were *never* expressed or discussed; passionate engagement was *always* vulgar; and sex was *never* to be thought about—not even, as Edith discovered, on the eve of one's marriage. Her powerful intelligence and nature seem to have appalled her mother. That Lucretia Jones did not believe Edith was entitled to independent existence is suggested by several biographical details, most significantly by the fact that in her announcement of her daughter's wedding, she omitted Edith's name. (This was no worse than her feelings about herself—she omitted her own name from the baptismal registry of all three of her children.)

The child's awareness that she was different (which always, for a child, is equivalent to feeling wrong), her mother's disapprobation, and her father's distance and ineffectuality combined to induce in the young girl a strong need to conform, to adhere to the standards of her society. She suffered severely from phobias. She tried hard to resist the temptation to what she called the "ecstasy" of "making up": "The call came regularly and imperiously and I . . . would struggle against it conscientiously." She learned to defer to her mother; she learned to hide or repress her interests, her sexuality, her emotions, her will, almost her very self.

When Edith was twenty-three, she married Edward ("Teddy") Wharton, an amiable thirty-three-year-old man from a suitable family. She spent the early years of her marriage attempting to be and do what a woman of her class was supposed to be and do. She dressed well, decorated a series of houses, paid visits, entertained, and travelled in Europe with her husband. In her youth she had written poetry, squirrelling away sheets of brown wrapping paper to write on because the family did not provide her with paper. But when she married, she stopped writing.

Gradually, she distanced herself from her mother, emotionally and physically. She took a Newport residence at a distance from Lucretia's; she bought a New York townhouse as far from her mother's as was respectable. Eventually, she entirely deserted Newport, the social center for summer activities, and built a mansion in Lenox, Massachusetts. Here, she threw her formidable energies into designing and decorating the house, The Mount, and its gardens.

Not until 1889, when she was twenty-seven, did she begin to write again. Her poems were immediately accepted by *Scribner's Magazine*. A year later, she wrote some short stories, which were also published by *Scribner's*. She was tremendously excited by her success in these ventures, but she later wrote, "I continued to live my old life, for my husband was as fond of society as ever, and I knew of no other existence."

She continued to write, but desultorily. She was often ill (she could not breathe) and would lapse into long silences. In 1893, Edward Burlingame of *Scribner's* suggested publishing a volume of her short stories. She was overwhelmed by the idea, and when he rejected some of her choices, she fell into a depressed silence. Again, she was ill. After a few years, she felt able to write again, but what she wrote (with co-author Ogden Codman) was *The Decoration of Houses* (1897)—an appropriate subject for a "lady". The following year she had a severe nervous breakdown. This was treated by bed rest, massage, large meals, and separation from Teddy. She recovered, and in 1899, when she was 37, her first volume of short stories, *The Greater In-*

clination, was finally published.

This publication was a turning point in Edith Wharton's life. "The publishing of *The Greater Inclination* broke the chains which had held me so long in a kind of torpor. For nearly twelve years I had tried to adjust myself to the life I had led since my marriage; but now I was overmastered by the longing to meet people who shared my interests." And she did. She reached out to other writers, thinkers, scholars; she filled her home with guests of intellect and sensibility. During her travels in Europe, she had gradually created a network of friends who were her equals; she increased this group, people with whom she could discuss art, literature, science, music. She gained confidence in herself, a sense that she could—was able to, was allowed to—write. Her first novel, *The Valley of Decision*, was published in 1902, when Edith Wharton was forty.

To this point, Edith Wharton's life sadly echoes, repeats, a pattern found in the lives of many women writers. An inadequate education made up for privately, even secretly; a painfully slow development into physical womanhood, hedged with guilt and a sense of being different; attempts to fit into social roles, resulting in illness, physical and/or emotional; attempts to break out of societal constrictions, resulting in illness, physical and/or emotional. Above all she (and many other woman writers) suffered from a deep, drenching sense of illegitimacy. Intellect and talent made them feel inadequate as women: womanhood made them feel inadequate as writers. Society offered no way out for such women: each of them had agonizingly to break the internalized mold herself, often in the face of opposition from the world around her; or let the mold break her. Critics who discuss Edith Wharton usually describe her struggle as being against the conventions of her class, but those conventions were far stricter for women than for men; her problem was one of gender as much as one of class. The greatest obstacle for women who wish to accomplish something besides marriage and motherhood is the awareness that females are illegitimate in the world. Wharton's sense of this was to remain with her all her life.

Once she had begun to take her life in her hands, however, she was prodigious. She picked it up and shaped it to her desire. She moved to Paris; she wrote daily. She surrounded herself with friends; she had a gift for friendship and knew well many of the most distinguished people of her day. She had her first love affair when she was in her mid-forties, tapping at last into her stifled, passionate nature. She created a splendid life, crowded and rich; she had her work, a huge circle of friends, brilliant discussion and argument, beautiful living quarters, beautiful clothes, devoted servants, beloved pets, and a motorcar. The motorcar was important, for Wharton lived in a flurry, impetuously gathering together some friends and motoring through the Berkshires, or down to Italy, or to England or the south of France.

In his introduction to *A Backward Glance* Louis Auchincloss writes of her that her letters in this period show a kind and conscientious woman "keeping anxious track from across the Atlantic of the fate of old servants, ordering presents for innumerable occasions, arranging that So-and-So will be looked after when he comes to Paris, seeing that her sister-in-law will have an automobile for the winter in New York." She herself wrote of this time of her life: "The core of my life was under my own roof, among my books and intimate friends. Above all it was in my work, which was growing and spreading, and absorbing more and more of my time and imagination."

From all reports, Teddy Wharton had been a sunny-natured man, a lover of society, of dogs and the outdoors, happiest when he was fishing or hunting. That the couple had no sex life did not (nor was it supposed to) disturb their mutual good manners. He does not seem at any early time actively to have impeded his strong-willed wife. He did not have to: all the weight of society was on his side. She knew her job was to adapt herself to Teddy's desires. "The people about me were so indifferent to everything I really cared for that complying with the tastes of others had become a habit.''

Once she took control of her own life, however, Teddy began to feel out of place. She had stifled in his world; now he was stifling in hers. He had odd breakdowns, as odd as hers had been. He would return to America while she was in Paris, and the couple would live apart for long periods. They had always lived mainly on her money—inherited and earned—and Teddy embezzled some of it and proceeded to live a scandalous life in Boston—scandalous, that is, for those times, in that it was openly sexual. Edith Wharton had a horror of divorce and tried for some years to keep up at least a social front but, eventually, the couple divorced. She continued to live in France, surrounded by friends and her special friend, Walter Berry (it is unclear whether or not they were ever lovers), for the rest of her life.

When the First World War broke out, Wharton threw herself into it with all her energy. She founded an *atelier* to help Frenchwomen thrown out of work by war-related events, and eventually employed a hundred of them. She established hostels for the Belgian refugees pouring into Paris hungry, sick, homeless. She helped 9000 of them in the first year alone. She visited the front lines many times, delivering supplies and ascertaining what more was needed. She organized a committee to rescue children orphaned or lost because of the war: her group bathed, clothed, fed, and solaced the young victims of violence. She opened homes for them, one for children stricken with tuberculosis. She wrote articles, arranged benefit concerts, rummage sales, art exhibitions, and pounded the doors of the rich to raise money for these undertakings. She gave so generously of her own fortune that she would have anxieties about money when the war was over. It was an extraordinary effort, and she performed it without pretension, superiority, or sniffing martyrdom; she was simply a woman doing something that had to be done. When the war was over, she was awarded the Legion of Honor by the French government.

Afterwards, she returned to her old life. She created two homes for herself, one north of Paris, one in the south of France. The post-war years were, however, tinged with sadness which increased as she aged. Beloved friends, beloved servants died. Customs and manners changed, and increasingly she felt herself a stranger in the world. Maintaining a set of dependents and her two estates with her diminished fortune was difficult, and to pay for them, she wrote more magazine stories of lesser quality. But her late novels show that she continued to try to grow, to encompass some of the changes she saw around her.

And her accomplishment is formidable. She wrote over forty books, as well as articles, reviews, and poems. Such an output is bound to be uneven, but many of her novels, books on houses and gardens, and travel books remain of lasting interest, and some are of the first rank. Whatever sorrow descended upon her, she had the serenity of knowing she had accomplished much in her life. She died of a stroke in France, in 1937, at the age of 75.

Edith Wharton created her own life—late, but many people never accomplish such a thing. She had some advantages in doing so: inherited wealth to begin with, and thus some education (something women of poorer classes could not obtain); amazing acceptance and success in the publishing world from the time of her first efforts; access to the literati in America and abroad by virtue of her elite ancestry and class; and childlessness. She went beyond some of the constrictions of her background, but not all: who can? To the end of her life, she wrote almost secretly in bed in the mornings, and spoke little about her work to her friends. She even referred to her writing as her ''secret garden,'' after *The Secret Garden*, a child's book popular in her youth—one I loved too. It had become legitimate for her to write, but

not to speak seriously about her work or even to appear
to take it seriously. In *A Backward Glance*, she included
a chapter on her writing only because the memoir would
be the merest profile without it, but she insisted, "Any
attempt to analyze work of one's own doing seems to
imply that one regards it as likely to be of lasting interest, and I wish at once to repudiate such an assumption."

She preferred the company of men to that of women
and somewhat resented the wives of her male friends:
she liked to be queen in a room full of men. She was
stubbornly uninterested in meeting accomplished
women like Virginia Woolf and Katherine Mansfield (so
were they). This characteristic is typical of slave
(illegitimate) mentalities, as diagnosed by Florynce
Kennedy and called "horizontal hostility." It was
exacerbated by the fact that men in Wharton's time
were indeed better educated and more accomplished
than women. Still, Wharton's most faithful friends were
women.

There are signs that she may not have been free from
other prejudices. She has been accused of anti-
Semitism, but the portrait of the Jew Sim Rosedale in
The House of Mirth, which begins with the curt contempt that Lily, and the New York society of which she
is a part, has towards this social climber, ends by
granting him a fuller humanity and larger stature than
any other male in the book. There seem to be traces of
prejudice against blacks in her personal correspondence. She never really understood the labor movement
and blamed it on the failure of the upper classes to exercise benevolent paternalism. She abhorred anything
bordering on socialism. She believed in the prerogatives
of wealth and class, believed in the necessity for a leisure
class, believed in the idea of legitimacy. That she did,
impeded her own development. It also impeded her in
her thinking about women. She went as far as she could.
And in her going, she created some wonderful things.

II

MOST CRITICISM of Edith Wharton declares her central concern to be the manners and mores of the old New York in which she was reared giving way slowly to a new set, those of the nouveau riche, the Vandebilts, Astors, and Whitneys—vulgar, flamboyant, and obscenely rich. She is often described as exalting the past and condemning the present.

In fact, she never exalted the old ways, although as she grew older, she came to believe there were some fine things in them. But she was never blinded to the utterly stifling quality of the old life; she never forgot not being able to breathe. She did condemn the new ways unconditionally. But she is not unusual in this: she lived to be old, and many authors, many people, who live to be old find themselves incapable of adjusting to new ways they see as crass and insensitive. In any case, the manners and mores of society never provided more than the backgrounds of her novels. They seem more emphasized because she describes them so brilliantly, with such an acute awareness of subtle distinctions.

Wharton had an intense visual awareness, especially of nature—a sensitivity she shares with many of her characters. She had an intense visual awareness of interior as well. (Edmund Wilson called her—in what spirit is not clear—the "poet of interior decoration.") She was able to conjure an entire way of life with a few concrete details. And she could do this not only with the muted, proper, good but shabby interiors of the old rich, but with the surroundings of the new rich, the very poor, and with landscape, cultivated or wilderness:

> In Mrs. Peniston's youth, fashion had returned to town in October; therefore on the tenth day of the month the blinds of her Fifth Avenue residence were drawn up, and the eyes of the Dying Gladiator in bronze who occupied the drawing room window resumed their survey of that deserted thoroughfare. [1]

*   *   *

The drawing-room walls, above their wainscoting
of highly-varnished mahogany, were hung with
salmon-pink damask and adorned with oval portraits of Marie Antoinette and the Princess de Lam-
balle. In the centre of the florid carpet a gilt table
with a top of Mexican onyx sustained a palm in a
gilt basket tied with a pink bow. But for this ornament, and a copy of "The Hound of the Basker-
villes" which lay beside it, the room showed no
traces of human use. [2]

He could see her, as Mrs. Haskett, sitting in a
"front parlour" furnished in plush, with a pianola,
and a copy of "Ben Hur" on the centre table. [3]

It was the beginning of a June afternoon. The
springlike transparent sky shed a rain of silver sun-
shine on the roofs of the village, and on the pastures
and larchwoods surrounding it. A little wind moved
among the round white clouds on the shoulders of
the hills, driving their shadows across the fields and
down the grassy road. [4]

Wharton's visual apprehension included people as
well as things. She noted vividly postures, gestures,
manners of speech, manners of walk, the tilt of a head,
the way someone held a handkerchief. She paid attention to clothes, but also to the way they were worn.
She knew that surfaces reveal values, that the depiction
of significant details creates the texture of a life, and
that the deepest beliefs of a person or a culture are perceptible in that texture:

The girl . . . noticed that he was a stranger, that he
wore city clothes, and that he was laughing with all
his teeth as the young and careless laugh at such
mishaps. [5]

He gave a little bow, like the bend of a jointed doll,

and with infinite precaution let himself down in the chair.[6]

Mr. Spragg thrust his hands into his waistcoat pockets, and began to tilt his chair till he remembered there was no wall to meet it.[7]

She had just time to take her seat before the train started; but having arranged herself in her corner with the instinctive feeling for effect which never forsook her, she glanced about in the hope of seeing some other member of the Trenors' party.[8]

In addition to her observant eye for detail, Wharton had deep empathetic currents. Very early in her writing career she wrote a story called "Bunner Sisters." It was not published until 1916, but it demonstrates that right from the outset, she was able to extend her sympathies and imagination beyond her own class. The story concerns a pair of very poor women, shopkeepers, both unmarried when the tale begins. Wharton was able to describe their surface life—what they wore, ate, how they worked or rested—but she was also able to enter their imaginative horizon believably. She has a sense of what Ann Eliza Bunner could dare to want for herself, what she would not dare to dream, and what, if she sacrificed, her sacrifice would be. In *Ethan Frome* and *Summer*, she entered fully into the dreams and fears, the sensuous texture and moral underpinnings, of people who were deprived culturally, economically, and socially. In *The Children*, she created a set of youngsters (surely one of the hardest things to do in fiction) who are ill-matched, ill-trained, and thoroughly delightful, without being sentimental idealizations. She wrote a novel set in *settecènto* Italy; she dealt with the war in *The Marne* and *A Son at the Front*; she dealt with working conditions in a factory in *The Fruit of the Tree*. About half her novels and stories are written from the perspective of a male, and of these, at least three are among her finest work—*Age of Innocence, The*

Children, and *Ethan Frome*. There are also the strong
Ralph Marvell sections of *The Custom of the Country*,
and the George Darrow section of *The Reef*.

The things I have been discussing are talents, abilities.
They allow Wharton to provide a brilliant surface for
her work, a surface which has sometimes been taken for
the theme of that work. It is not. Wharton's main
theme, her deepest concern, was the emotional/moral
life, especially in the area of sexuality. The paralysis, the
inability to move or change or affect events, that is common to her characters is located primarily in their sexual
constriction, from which arise other, subtler constrictions. For instance, in the Victorian period, it was
considered improper for a gentleman to offer a lady his
chair, since it might retain the body warmth of his but-
tocks. The proper thing was for him to rise and fetch a
fresh chair for her.

This large theme—emotional/moral experience, especially concerning or arising from sexual feeling or action—is tied to other themes. Female experience is often
central in her work. This is true sometimes even when
the focus of the story is a male. *The Touchstone*, for instance, depicts a man suffering from guilt as he
gradually shifts his contempt for himself onto his wife
because he cannot bear "the necessity of defending himself against the perpetual criticism of his wife's belief in
him." This early long story (1900) is not one of Wharton's best works, but it is acute in tracing subtly what
men do to women in their minds. Since sexual reg-
ulation was a major factor in the lives of young women,
many of the tales and novels deal with sexual constriction and the social restrictions that arose from it.

Behind the events of the works lies a set of regulations
which, although they still exist in certain pockets of
culture, seem incredible to young people of today.
Briefly, young women were protected from most of life.
They were not supposed even to think about sex, or
know anything about it. It was considered unthinkable
that they have sexual experience before marriage or, in
the age of Wharton's mother, that they have sexual ex-

perience outside of marriage. Because of the difficulty in controlling such things, other rules were brought to bear. So a young woman was not permitted to move easily about in the world, to be alone with a young man except in supervised or accepted places. Moreover, and perhaps most seriously damaging, there was a conspiracy among the older people in a young woman's life to keep silent, to keep her in ignorance about not just sex, but any deviation from the bland complacency of the social surface.

There was no need for a rule forbidding women to work; it was inconceivable that a woman of Wharton's society work. Only the lowest class of women worked outside the home; maids, factory workers, shopgirls. And since they had little education, women did not even have the option of pursuing an interest at home. They were encouraged to use their energies in choosing and wearing clothes and jewels, in going to dances and dinners, and perhaps, in archery and equestrianism. They were brought up to see themselves from the outside, as decorative objects designed to be collected and displayed by men who could afford them.

Consequently, some of the women in the early satirical stories are shallow, chameleon-like, changing themselves to fit the desires of others, finding themselves only in reflections in the eyes of others. Marriage is the only course for women. So, ambitious women marry as a way of improving their financial or social condition. Others, possessed of intelligence and sensitivity, look to marriage to free them from their emotional and (to some degree) physical bondage. For these, marriage is a transcendence, a fulfillment, a "sanctuary." That word is used frequently in Wharton's work, and in *Age of Innocence*, it is defined as "the place where one is real."

Indeed, an early short novel is entitled *Sanctuary*. Its heroine, Kate Orme, is a poignant figure who expects marriage to be the fulfillment of all her expectations from life. (*Sanctuary* is in two parts. The second part makes it clever and salable, and also makes one wonder if Wharton knew what she was really doing at that point in her life—1903. She herself did not afterward like the novel, but she must have learned from writing it. The first half, which could with a little editing stand alone, is the most exquisite and subtle description I have read of a particular female sensibility.)

The language of this tale shimmers with what cannot be spoken, cannot even be directly thought about—Kate's sensuality, her energy, her eager mind. All her enormous needs and energies, all the hopes of a growing young person, are heaped on one person—her fiancé—and one relationship—marriage. They create a weight that neither the institution nor any one person can bear. Kate's sensibility is radiant. At the same time, however, she is complacent. Ignorant about life, and aware of her ignorance, she is nevertheless unable to pierce through the veil her elders maintain about her. She has been taught that life is beautiful, peaceful, orderly, proper, and clean: she believes her life will be precisely those things. The real subject of the novel is Kate's sensibility and the shattering of her dream the golden aura with which she has endowed him. It has been remarked (and deplored, by male critics) that Wharton's men always fail their women, are always in some way ineffectual. It would be more accurate to say that Wharton depicts men as they are, and not as haloed heroes. And her emphasis is less on the mere humanness of men than on the intensity and driving need with which women of her age came to men, who provided their only access to "life."

A fuller exposition of a character like Kate Orme's, and a development of the complications resulting from such a sensibility, occurs in *The Reef* (1912). It opens with a section written from the point of view of George Darrow, a man with a gentleman's attitudes toward sex. Sex was permissible for men and certain kinds of women. George Darrow, Wharton writes, "had had a fairly varied experience of feminine types, but the women he had frequented had either been pronouncedly 'ladies' or they had not. Grateful to both for ministering to the more complex masculine nature, and disposed to assume that they had been evolved, if not designed, to that end . . . he had a contemptuous distaste for the woman who uses the privileges of one class to shelter the customs of another." Darrow meets a young girl who fits into neither category, and has an affair with her.

The young woman, Sophy Viner, a fresh and delightful character, has her own set of moral principles. She is poor and has lived on the fringes, and knows that Darrow has frequented the house of her employer, a woman of shaky respectability. Sophy has distaste for her employer, but no fear or shame about sex, or about the affair with Darrow. She feels not seduced but fulfilled by their sexual relation, and does not expect it to last more than a few days. She loves Darrow but knows he does not love her.

Darrow does love and wish to marry a character who is eminently a "lady," Anna Leath. The rest of the book belongs to Anna. She is a young, well-to-do widow with a small daughter, Effie, and a stepson, Owen. Her first marriage was deadly, and she wishes now to "live," although she only tenuously apprehends what that means. She wants experience, she wants to emerge from what Darrow calls "the deadening process of forming a 'lady.'" She is a complex figure—subtle, delicate, acute, strong; the language expressing her sensibility shimmers with the beauty and depth, the charged sexuality, of her hopes. The George Darrow she perceives is more profound and sensitive, a richer character by far than the one we have seen earlier. And she imagines marriage to him as a full sharing of joys—sexual, intellectual, sensuous, moral, and social. She believes marriage will take her to another plane of existence, and so firm is her faith that we come to believe it too.

The plot of the novel is a situation: Darrow arrives at Anna's husband's family estate to formalize their engagement, and finds there Sophy Viner, installed as governess to Effie and about to become engaged to Owen. There follows a slow, complex, emotionally

charged development as the affair between Darrow and
Sophy is gradually revealed, destroying all the relations
among the principals. Three moralities clash—Darrow's
traditional male one (which finds it easy to sacrifice
Sophy Viner); Anna's traditional female one (which
would like to sacrifice Sophy and place all blame on her,
exculpating Darrow); and Sophy's fresh, open one
(which can be perceived only through the veil of the
other two). These moralities conflict with Darrow's
sense of fairness and Anna's refusal to lie to herself.
Complicating the characters' internal struggles is the
convention of censorship, the impossibility of speaking
openly so as to discover what others feel.

The center of the novel is Anna's slow penetration
into the situation and her own feelings. She discovers
with humiliation that her desire for Darrow transcends
her moral contempt for him; that her jealousy of Sophy
leads her to distort the character of the young woman;
that her insistence on censorship and socially correct
deceit protects neither Owen from extreme anguish nor
her from his resentment. At the end, in a peculiar final
scene, Anna discovers the true root of her attitudes
—her profound sexual disgust. In this scene, Anna visits
Sophy's older sister, who lives a loose sexual life.
Anna's horror is out of proportion to what she sees;
what she is envisioning is a conclusion she finds ugly
and inevitable to Sophy's free ways. For Anna, sexual
freedom is corruption. There is no certainty at the conclusion of the novel about whether Anna will marry
George Darrow. In a sense, that is irrelevant: the novel
is concerned with the fall into experience of a "lady."
Whatever her future, it is a terrible diminishment of her
expectations. Darrow has participated with a gentleman's ease in a world Anna finds corrupt; beyond
that, he has lied to her, lied beautifully. She will never
again be able to trust him, and without trust, her vision
of marriage is impossible.

In other Wharton works, the heroines discover the
merely human in their men after marriage, and, divorce
being unthinkable, face an unalterable and bleak future.

Nevertheless, some Wharton heroines are divorced and face an equally grim future on the fringes of society, usually without much money to sustain them. There is no suggestion that work or children can fill the void created by the failure of marriage to provide full complementarity.

Ecstatic expectations of marriage, leading inevitably to disappointment, are rooted in female constriction in the world and the constriction of human sexuality. Constriction also leads to paralysis and the waste of human potential, which are themes in many Wharton novels, among them her first great one, *The House of Mirth*.

Its heroine, Lily Bart, has been trained to be a lovely flower intended for barter, an ornament for purchase by someone wealthy enough to afford her. Lily is not a strong character, but she is very taking. She continually ruins her chances for a matrimonial "catch" despite her dire need for one: she is poor and must have a rich husband if she is to survive in her society. Her errors are associated with Lawrence Selden, a man of only moderate means whom Lily loves, or would love if she had selfhood enough to conceive of personal desire (as opposed to conformity to a societal norm). Her slight motions of spontaneity and risk are not willed; rather, she drifts into them and is conscious only afterwards that she has made a *gaffe*. These motions emanate from a buried part of Lily, a part of which she is only slightly conscious—her values, her sexuality, her capacity for love.

Her progress is an alternation between motions of conformity—dressing, acting, being the beautiful ornament—and motions of genuineness with Selden. It is also a gradual descent, as she falls from favor with the "higher" strata of New York society, and finally falls out of society altogether. Her story is a tragedy of constriction: being what she is, she really has no alternatives. Selden, who holds up to her the ideal of a "republic of the spirit" for which she yearns—as if it were another version of "sanctuary"—is detached, uncharitable, and judgmental towards Lily. He too denies or evades his deeper feelings. Both Lily and Selden are paralyzed, and both are in some sense destroyed by that paralysis. Both also maintain part of themselves: Selden survives in the body; Lily becomes her real self, lives her life out before she dies.

Constriction and paralysis are the themes also of *Ethan Frome*, which is a study in paralysis of the will. The narrator, who provides the frame, is working temporarily in a small New England town, where he meets Ethan Frome, a middle-aged, crippled, and impoverished farmer. From what little gossip he is able to extract from neighbors, and his own imagination, he pieces together a story of frustrated love between the young Ethan and his wife Zenobia's young and destitute cousin, Mattie. Unable to act on their love, Ethan and Mattie attempt suicide, but survive crippled, the paralyzed Mattie tended by Zenobia. (For a fascinating analysis of this novel, see Cynthia Griffin Wolff, *A Feast of Words*.)

The physical paralysis which opens and closes the novel is merely the visible concrete symbol of the intellectual and emotional crippledness suffered by all three of the major figures, but especially Ethan and Mattie. Although Ethan has moral reasons for not acting, he never measures the moral consequences of self-denial against the world's moral standards. He never considers the consequences to Zenobia of marriage to a man who finds her physically loathsome, or the consequences to himself of denying his sexuality. His failure to consider such things seems to be caused by his insistent adherence to what the world calls "good," but it must also be related to a guilt about sex, guilt about selfhood.

Despite a clamorous attention to sex, sexual repression still exists in America and elsewhere. But it must have been far worse in the first decades of this century. Although we tend to associate this quality with the Victorian period, the art of the early twentieth century is far more anguished than Victorian art. For me, sexual repressiveness has the image of a long, rolling wave that crested at the turn of the century, reaching its peak just as it was about to collapse. Sexual repression leading to enveration of spirit underlies the work of tormented painters as different as Edward Hopper and Edvard Munch; it is a major theme in many literary works of the time, among them James Joyce's *Dubliners*. In that work, Joyce was even more oblique about the subject than Wharton is. Wharton, however, remained oblique in her treatment of sexual problems, and she was never able—as D. H. Lawrence sometimes was—to separate personal sexual need and desire from social and political institutions. Thus, she is not seen as a revolutionary writer on the subject—as both Lawrence and the later Joyce are. Yet in a sense, she is: it was revolutionary for a woman to write upon such a subject at all, and the profundity of her analyses of female attitudes toward sex has still not been recognized.

She did not directly challenge prevailing sexual norms; she also continued throughout her life to insist that sexual acts have consequences in the large outer world; but she refused, ever, to add her assent to the chorus of writers who implied, however subtly, that the ways of the Western world are for the best after all. Only Newland Archer, in *The Age of Innocence*, comes close to accepting the life he has led; the reader, however, is likely to lament his thin, half-lived life.

Archer has been hooked and reeled in by his society as a whole, but it is not just the force of convention that keeps him from Ellen Olenska. It is also his own fear of risk and nakedness, the total investment that sexual love seems to require that paralyzes him. To declare sexuality taboo is to heighten it; to declare it an act that can damn one utterly is also to suggest that it has the capacity to carry one to transcendent realms. The act of sex—like the act of marriage—cannot sustain such a burden.

Nevertheless, the reader *wants* Archer to insist on his passion for Ellen, wants him not to submit to convention. The same thing happens in *Ethan Frome*, the one of Wharton's novels that has regularly been used in high school teaching. I am sure—at least I was sure when I read it in high school—that the reason we were being taught with this book was to convince us of the danger of feeling sexual passion at all. But in fact, the novel forces the reader to rebel against the constrictions surrounding Ethan and Mattie, to wish for them less compunction, more insistence on their desire. Thus, without herself challenging prevailing sexual mores, Wharton incites such challenge in the reader.

In what I believe to be Wharton's greatest novel, *Summer*, the young heroine, Charity Royall, does have the courage to be sexual. Her act has unhappy consequences, and leads eventually to a diminished life, but it is never regretted by the heroine. She has had the world as in her time; she has known ecstasy and love, and if she is diminished, she is not frozen, dead, or paralyzed. She has life growing inside her. In one sense, *Summer* is a rethinking of *The Reef*. Charity is a child of the Mountain folk, brought up to believe that her roots lie in amorality, bestiality, savagery, although she has been raised in civilization. Her return to the Mountain, the place of her origin, is a parallel to Anna Leath's visit to Sophy's sister. But if Charity discovers horror on the Mountain, it is horror primarily caused by poverty and ignorance, not sexuality. Her unceremonialized sexual act, her illicit sexual joy, does not sever her from humanity or civilization. For Charity, unlike Anna Leath, sex itself—apart from its consequences—is not corrupt, not sin.

Percy Lubbock claimed that Wharton did not have a philosophy. But she did, insofar as any novelist can be said to have a coherent philosophy. Writing continually of constriction and paralysis, emphasizing the bleakness of lives based upon them, she pointed another direction. "Alas, I should like to get up on the house-tops and cry to all who come after us: 'Take your own life, every one of you!' " she wrote to her friend Sara Norton, who sacrificed her life to her aging famous father, Charles Eliot Norton. Wharton meant take hold of, grasp, live in accord with desire and need. Years later, she wrote to another friend, Mary Berenson, that the "real unpardonable sin" was the denial of life. And by *life*, she meant largely sexual experience, but also an existence created by the self rather than by society.

In several works, Wharton challenged what in one book she called the infliction of "sterile pain," on the self or others. Sterile pain is related to self-sacrifice. George Darrow, in *The Reef*, speaks of the "monstrousness of useless sacrifice," and Ann Eliza Bunner of the early story, thinks at her lowest moment "that to refuse the gifts of life does not insure their transmission to those for whom they have been surrendered." Wharton's challenge was directed at an American culture which still believed that suffering had value for its own sake, that self-sacrifice was the proper life for women. Kate Clephane, the heroine of a fine novel, *The Mother's Recompense*, makes a decision that is immoral by some standards in order to spare her daughter, Anne, sterile pain. Reunited with the daughter she abandoned many years before, and who offers her the love and comfort she craves, Kate discovers that Anne is in love with and wishes to marry a young man she herself has loved and with whom she had a passionate affair. Again, the central subject is sexual morality, here complicated by Kate's love for her daughter, her wish to remain in the comfortable circumstances Anne provides for her, and finally, and most devastatingly, her discovery that she still loves Chris Fenno (Anne's fiancé), and is jealous of her daughter.

The decision Kate makes is another rethinking of the problems of *The Reef*. Unlike Anna Leath, Kate does not press beyond a certain point; she injures, but does not destroy, the relation between Anne and Chris. Recognizing that whether or not she tells Anne the truth, she has lost her daughter again, and she chooses to allow Anne her happiness.

Wharton's women are always in precarious situations. Emotional well-being (and no other kind exists for them) always depends on another on whom they cannot utterly count, whom they don't fully know, and with whom they cannot talk fully and openly. The same thing is true of her male protagonists, although, since they have some sort of work or interest beyond the emotional, they seem less fragile—yet some of them are not.

This inability to speak the truth openly is one of the most painful constrictions for Wharton characters. The convention forbidding discussion of feelings, discussion of elements of life that do not conform to the bland surface, the asking of important questions, agonizes many characters. Censorship of this sort is crazy-making, in emotional life as in political. It surrounds the characters with an atmosphere of tension, terror, vulnerability, and ignorance. Immersed in a world of artificialities, their deepest need is to be themselves, but that is forbidden. It can happen, if at all, only with one other person—a spouse, friend, parent, child. When that other person turns away or fails to respond or responds with deceit (as in, for example, a fine short story, "Autres Temps") life is skimmed of any cream, the precious relation becomes as watery and thin as all others.

Wharton deals with this in a late novel, *The Children*, in which a man, Martin Boyne, is seduced away from his fiancée by a group of children. The fiancée, Rose Sellars, is a perfect "lady": she is respectable, moral, sweet, and giving. Her greatest attribute is tact. She arranges her mind, her emotions, herself, and her home to be receptive, warm, welcoming, graceful, lovely. Boyne imagines having with her the perfect sharing many Wharton heroines desire.

On shipboard, on his way to the recently widowed Rose, Boyne meets and is utterly taken by a band of dispossessed children who are rowdy, spontaneous, and boisterous. All unwanted children of divorce, they are in the care of a nanny and the oldest girl, Judith, who is fifteen. Because of their backgrounds, all of them and especially Judith are clear-eyed and know a considerable amount about human relations, sex, and money. They are realistic, and one might even say cynical, except they are usually right. They make easy declarations about forbidden subjects. Boyne is a bit embarrassed by and a tinge disapproving of their outspokenness, especially when Rose is present, but he also delights in it, it liberates him. So does their chaotic, improper behavior. In time, although he remains a correct gentleman, he comes to identify with them to the point that Rose Sellars and her standards and her tact come to seem oppressive to him. Since he cannot keep the children, and no longer wants Rose Sellars and the world she offers, he is emotionally bereft, his remaining years lonely and bleak.

This is the condition of many Wharton characters: unable to live in a new, freer world, finding the freedom somehow coarse and shallow or unsuitable, but unable to turn back to the old world, they hang in limbo. And when Wharton turns to characters who can exist in the new world, her own entrapment reveals itself. The new society in *The Children, The Mother's Recompense*, and even in the early *The House of Mirth* is painted with Wharton's broadest brush. She satirizes these people as vapid, frivolous, irresponsible, callous, tasteless, and flashy; she can find in them not a single virtue. The most important of these characters is Undine Spragg, the heroine of *The Custom of the Country*. Undine propels herself by sheer drive, exuberance, and beauty, from Apex City into the highest society, by a series of marriages. She is too extravagant for, and bored by, her fine old New York dilettante husband, Ralph Marvell; she has a somewhat scandalous love affair, then divorces him. She uses her right to custody of their son as a threat to extort money from him so that she may purchase an annulment of their marriage from the Catholic Church and marry a French nobleman. But his old aristocratic family surrounds her with a confined and bleak life, so again she extricates herself from the marriage. Finally, she marries the aspiring Elmer Moffatt, a self-made millionaire whom, we discover, she had married and quietly divorced many years before. Moffatt is Undine's alter ego, her male self.

There is no sympathy in the novel for Undine, nor are

we shown anything in her besides graspingness, the vanity of a woman who knows she is a commodity, and a willful, driving, stubborn refusal to be downed. What Wharton does grant Undine is a lack of alternative. Although she is a survivor, she is as much a victim as Lily Bart of a culture that—as Wharton (and Henry James) believed—is dominated by men who refuse to take women seriously. Indeed, Undine is Lily Bart turned inside out. Raised in a cultural desert, Undine, like her mother and American women of that period in general, has nothing to do. Her mother falls into apathy. Undine orders dresses and tries them on; she arranges herself in the mirror. A man with her drive and desire for money and power would have had other channels through which to pursue them—as Elmer Moffatt does. Wharton writes that Moffatt "used life exactly as [Undine] would have used it in his place." Undine's instrument for gaining power is her beauty: sex. She uses sex as men use money. This does not mean that she has a sexual nature. Wharton is subtle, but acute, in suggesting that people who use sex as an instrument lose a sense of sex in itself.

Wharton's strongest and most sympathetically rendered characters are women who risk: Justine Brent (*The Fruit of the Tree*), Anna Leath (*The Reef*), Charity Royall (*Summer*), and Kate Clephane (*The Mother's Recompense*). These women have moral courage, something even Wharton's most sympathetic men lack. They are not passive victims of their lives, although there is no question of their triumphing over circumstances. What they do is live their lives out fully, by feeling and thinking through whatever occurs, by refusing to blind themselves. They risk discovering their own dark sides, their sexuality, their guilt, their jealousy. Wharton's term for this process in one novel is "facing it out," confronting and dealing with troublesome emotions—their own and others'—instead of locking them away. Since all these women are confronted with serious, even insoluble difficulties, their behavior makes them large-sized, even heroic. Although all of them end with diminished expectations, with lost dreams, the subtlety, delicacy, strength, and courage of their approaches to life makes them admirable. Their lives are rich not because of what they are able to take from it but because of what they are. Thus, in a sense, all Wharton's work aims toward a definition of what constitutes full humanity: it is not victory over circumstance, but knowledge of the deepest sort, the full living of life.

A few words dealing with criticisms leveled against Wharton are in order. One, probably fostered by Wharton herself, is that she was not a serious writer. Like Emily Dickinson, Virginia Woolf, Jane Austen, the Brontes, and others, Wharton never felt legitimate enough to claim literary stature. These women were sure *in* their writing, but not sure *of* their writing. Nevertheless, she was a serious writer. Once she started, she wrote every day (with some breaks during the war years). Blake Nevius discusses the evidence in her manuscripts of painstaking revisions. And shot through all her work, like the watering through moiré, is a sense of the ennobling power of art, the enriching power of culture. Finally, there is the definitive evidence of the seriousness of the books themselves, which I hope my foregoing remarks have suggested. If all of Wharton's work is not equally good, there are good things in all of it. And she left many fine novels, novels that stand with the best America has produced. I do not know if there is a political implication in the fact that the novels I like best—and which I presume other women would find fascinating—have all been out of print for a long time: *Summer, The Reef, A Mother's Recompense*, and *The Children*. There are also the better known, and excellent, *The House of Mirth, The Age of Innocence, Ethan Frome*, and *The Custom of the Country*. Of the smaller works, I would add at least the first half of *Sanctuary*, and "Autres Temps."

Wharton is usually assumed to be a lesser Henry James, to be attempting to do precisely what James did. It is true that they were personally close, and perhaps had similar sensibilities, and that they were looking at the same world. But James, a man, emphasized the individual within society; he had a strong sense of legitimacy that strengthened and colored what he created. Wharton, a woman, was far more aware of the power of the environment over the individual, of the sapping of energy caused by a sense of illegitimacy, and of the impossibility of getting beyond the bodily and social consequences of sex. James's genius was linguistic and psychological; Wharton's was sociological and psychological. Without seeming to diminish James—who cannot be diminished—one must separate the two authors and focus on Wharton's excellences. She has a wide scope; she is more interested in the particular experience of women, and she had a profounder sense of constriction.

But this, precisely, is what most dismays critics such as Lionel Trilling and Irving Howe. Her vision is bleak; for her, life is a prison, the critics moan. She has been damned as immoral for her vision. Yet the very critics who do not like her insistence on constriction do not hesitate to castigate female characters for whom Wharton has obvious sympathy—or even Wharton herself—for having abandoned a husband, or a child, or for trying to envision fulfilled happy lives for themselves. They thereby prove the accuracy of her vision. Critics also complain that Wharton's men are either ineffectual—morally or emotionally stunted—or coarse boors. The range of her male characters is far greater than this, and many of them are sympathetic. But there are no knights on white horses in her work, as there are none in life. There are no idealizations, female or male.

Many readers may prefer novels that concentrate on the individual as author or strong co-author of his or her fate, and that diminish the overwhelming pressure of environment and inheritance. Such an attitude is moreover more pleasant and probably healthier to live with than its opposite. But the opposite is also true, a fact we are aware of at least in certain moments of life. And it is morally healthier to remember that we are small units in a large world we cannot control than to delude ourselves. There is room for both kinds of books. To condemn those which refuse to compromise, which refuse to admit that things are for the best in this best of all possible worlds, is to demand that literature be fairy tale.

Wharton had a tougher mind. She would have agreed with Aquinas' statement that "matter is never lacking privation: inasmuch as it is under one form, it is deprived of another." If Wharton concentrated on the privations attendant on a form, rather than on its fulfillment, perhaps that is because she was a woman and more aware of that side of things. It is not an accident that the most vapid and fantastic literature—romances—is written for women, who use it to escape from lives they cannot change. Henry James wrote of Wharton's work: "We move in an air purged at a stroke of the old sentimental and romantic values." Wharton forces her readers to acknowledge—and thus deal with—the fact that form is imprisonment, that any course has particular consequences, that everything costs something, that actuality is always a diminishment of the ideal, and that the richness of life lies in one's moral and emotional response to one's own situation. That is not a small accomplishment.

1. Edith Wharton, THE HOUSE OF MIRTH, New York: Berkley Publishing Corporation.
2. Edith Wharton, THE CUSTOM OF THE COUNTRY, New York: Charles Scribner's Sons.
3. Edith Wharton, "The Other Two," ROMAN FEVER AND OTHER STORIES, New York: Charles Scribner's Sons.
4. Edith Wharton, SUMMER, New York: Berkley Publishing Corporation.
5. Ibid.
6. Edith Wharton, "After Holbein," ROMAN FEVER AND OTHER STORIES, New York: Charles Scribner's Sons.
7. Edith Wharton, THE CUSTOM OF THE COUNTRY, New York: Charles Scribner's Sons.
8. Edith Wharton, THE HOUSE OF MIRTH, New York: Berkley Publishing Corporation.

ROMAN FEVER

I.

FROM THE table at which they had been lunching two American ladies of ripe but well-cared-for middle age moved across the lofty terrace of the Roman restaurant and, leaning on its parapet, looked first at each other, and then down on the outspread glories of the Palatine and the Forum, with the same expression of vague but benevolent approval.

As they leaned there a girlish voice echoed up gaily from the stairs leading to the court below. "Well, come along, then," it cried, not to them but to an invisible companion, "and let's leave the young things to their knitting"; and a voice as fresh laughed back: "Oh, look here, Babs, not actually knitting—" "Well, I mean figuratively," rejoined the first. "After all, we haven't left our poor parents much else to do . . ." and at that point the turn of the stairs engulfed the dialogue.

The two ladies looked at each other again, this time with a tinge of smiling embarrassment, and the smaller and paler one shook her head and coloured slightly.

"Barbara!" she murmured, sending an unheard rebuke after the mocking voice in the stairway.

The other lady, who was fuller, and higher in colour,

1

with a small determined nose supported by vigorous
black eyebrows, gave a good-humoured laugh. "That's
what our daughters think of us!"

Her companion replied by a deprecating gesture.
"Not of us individually. We must remember that. It's
just the collective modern idea of Mothers. And you
see—" Half guiltily she drew from her handsomely
mounted black hand-bag a twist of crimson silk run
through by two fine knitting needles. "One never
knows," she murmured. "The new system has certainly
given us a good deal of time to kill; and sometimes I get
tired just looking—even at this." Her gesture was now
addressed to the stupendous scene at their feet.

The dark lady laughed again, and they both relapsed
upon the view, contemplating it in silence, with a sort of
diffused serenity which might have been borrowed from
the spring effulgence of the Roman skies. The luncheon-
hour was long past, and the two had their end of the
vast terrace to themselves. At its opposite extremity a
few groups, detained by a lingering look at the outspread city, were gathering up guide-books and fum-
bling for tips. The last of them scattered, and the two
ladies were alone on the air-washed height.

"Well, I don't see why we shouldn't just stay here,"
said Mrs. Slade, the lady of the high colour and
energetic brows. Two derelict basketchairs stood near,
and she pushed them into the angle of the parapet, and
settled herself in one, her gaze upon the Palatine. "After all, it's still the most beautiful view in the world."

"It always will be, to me," assented her friend Mrs.
Ansley, with so slight a stress on the "me" that Mrs.
Slade, though she noticed it, wondered if it were not
merely accidental, like the random underlinings of old-
fashioned letter-writers.

"Grace Ansley was always old-fashioned," she
thought; and added aloud, with a retrospective smile:
"It's a view we've both been familiar with for a good
many years. When we first met here we were younger
than our girls are now. You remember?"

"Oh, yes, I remember," murmured Mrs. Ansley,

with the same undefinable stress.—"There's that head-waiter wondering," she interpolated. She was evidently far less sure than her companion of herself and of her rights in the world.

"I'll cure him of wondering," said Mrs. Slade, stretching her hand toward a bag as discreetly opulent-looking as Mrs. Ansley's. Signing to the head-waiter, she explained that she and her friend were old lovers of Rome, and would like to spend the end of the afternoon looking down on the view—that is, if it did not disturb the service? The head-waiter, bowing over her gratuity, assured her that the ladies were most welcome, and would be still more so if they would condescend to remain for dinner. A full moon night, they would remember . . .

Mrs. Slade's black brows drew together, as though references to the moon were out-of-place and even un-welcome. But she smiled away her frown as the head-waiter retreated. "Well, why not? We might do worse. There's no knowing. I suppose, when the girls will be back. Do you even know back from *where*? I don't!"

Mrs. Ansley again coloured slightly. "I think those young Italian aviators we met at the Embassy invited them to fly to Tarquinia for tea. I suppose they'll want to wait and fly back by moonlight."

"Moonlight—moonlight! What a part it still plays. Do you suppose they're as sentimental as we were?"

"I've come to the conclusion that I don't in the least know what they are," said Mrs. Ansley. "And perhaps we didn't know much more about each other."

"No; perhaps we didn't."

Her friend gave her a shy glance. "I never should have supposed you were sentimental, Alida."

"Well, perhaps I wasn't." Mrs. Slade drew her lids together in retrospect; and for a few moments the two ladies, who had been intimate since childhood, reflected how little they knew each other. Each one, of course, had a label ready to attach to the other's name; Mrs. Delphin Slade, for instance, would have told herself, or any one who asked her, that Mrs. Horace Ansley,

twenty-five years ago, had been exquisitely lovely—no,
you wouldn't believe it, would you? . . . though, of
course, still charming, distinguished . . . Well, as a girl
she had been exquisite; far more beautiful than her
daughter Barbara, though certainly Babs, according to
the new standards at any rate, was more effective—had
more *edge*, as they say. Funny where she got it, with
those nullities as parents. Yes; Horace Ansley was—
well, just the duplicate of his wife. Museum specimens
of old New York. Good-looking, irreproachable, exemplary. Mrs. Slade and Mrs. Ansley had lived opposite
each other—actually as well as figuratively—for years.
When the drawing-room curtains in No. 20 East 73rd
Street were renewed, No. 23, across the way, was always
aware of it. And of all the movings, buyings, travels,
anniversaries, illnesses—the tame chronicle of an
estimable pair. Little of it escaped Mrs. Slade. But she
had grown bored with it by the time her husband made
his big *coup* in Wall Street, and when they bought in upper Park Avenue had already begun to think: "I'd
rather live opposite a speak-easy for a change; at
least one might see it raided." The idea of seeing
Grace raided was so amusing that (before the move) she
launched it at a woman's lunch. It made a hit, and went
the rounds—she sometimes wondered if it had crossed
the street, and reached Mrs. Ansley. She hoped not, but
didn't much mind. Those were the days when respectability was at a discount, and it did the irreproachable
no harm to laugh at them a little.

A few years later, and not many months apart, both
ladies lost their husbands. There was an appropriate exchange of wreaths and condolences, and a brief renewal
of intimacy in the half-shadow of their mourning; and
now, after another interval, they had run across each
other in Rome, at the same hotel, each of them the
modest appendage of a salient daughter. The similarity
of their lot had again drawn them together, lending itself to mild jokes, and the mutual confession that, if in
old days it must have been tiring to "keep up" with

daughters, it was now, at times, a little dull not to.

No doubt, Mrs. Slade reflected, she felt her unemployment more than poor Grace ever would. It was a big drop from being the wife of Delphin Slade to being his widow. She had always regarded herself (with a certain conjugal pride) as his equal in social gifts, as contributing her full share to the making of the exceptional couple they were: but the difference after his death was irremediable. As the wife of the famous corporation lawyer, always with an international case or two on hand, every day brought its exciting and unexpected obligation: the impromptu entertaining of eminent colleagues from abroad, the hurried dashes on legal business to London, Paris or Rome, where the entertaining was so handsomely reciprocated; the amusement of hearing in her wake: "What, that handsome woman with the good clothes and the eyes is Mrs. Slade—*the* Slade's wife? Really? Generally the wives of celebrities are such frumps."

Yes; being *the* Slade's widow was a dullish business after that. In living up to such a husband all her faculties had been engaged; now she had only her daughter to live up to, for the son who seemed to have inherited his father's gifts had died suddenly in boyhood. She had fought through that agony because her husband was there, to be helped and to help; now, after the father's death, the thought of the boy had become unbearable. There was nothing left but to mother her daughter; and dear Jenny was such a perfect daughter that she needed no excessive mothering. "Now with Babs Ansley I don't know that I *should* be so quiet," Mrs. Slade sometimes half-enviously reflected; but Jenny, who was younger than her brilliant friend, was that rare accident, an extremely pretty girl who somehow made youth and prettiness seem as safe as their absence. It was all perplexing—and to Mrs. Slade a little boring. She wished that Jenny would fall in love—with the wrong man, even; that she might have to be watched, out-manoeuvred, rescued. And instead, it was Jenny who watched her mother, kept her out of draughts, made sure that she had taken her tonic . . .

Mrs. Ansley was much less articulate than her friend, and her mental portrait of Mrs. Slade was slighter, and drawn with fainter touches. "Alida Slade's awfully brilliant; but not as brilliant as she thinks," would have summed it up; though she would have added, for the enlightenment of strangers, that Mrs. Slade had been an extremely dashing girl; much more so than her daughter, who was pretty, of course, and clever in a way, but had none of her mother's—well, "vividness," some one had once called it. Mrs. Ansley would take up current words like this, and cite them in quotation marks, as unheard-of audacities. No; Jenny was not like her mother. Sometimes Mrs. Ansley thought Alida Slade was disappointed; on the whole she had had a sad life. Full of failures and mistakes; Mrs. Ansley had always been rather sorry for her . . .

So these two ladies visualized each other, each through the wrong end of her little telescope.

II.

FOR A long time they continued to sit side by side without speaking. It seemed as though, to both, there was a relief in laying down their somewhat futile activities in the presence of the vast Memento Mori which faced them. Mrs. Slade sat quite still, her eyes fixed on the golden slope of the Palace of the Caesars, and after a while Mrs. Ansley ceased to fidget with her bag, and she too sank into meditation. Like many intimate friends, the two ladies had never before had occasion to be silent together, and Mrs. Ansley was slightly embarrassed by what seemed, after so many years, a new stage in their intimacy, and one with which she did not yet know how to deal.

Suddenly the air was full of that deep clangour of bells which periodically covers Rome with a roof of silver. Mrs. Slade glanced at her wrist-watch. "Five o'clock already," she said, as though surprised.

Mrs. Ansley suggested interrogatively: "There's bridge at the Embassy at five." For a long time Mrs. Slade did not answer. She appeared to be lost in contemplation, and Mrs. Ansley thought the remark had escaped her. But after a while she said, as if speaking out of a dream: "Bridge, did you say? Not unless you want to . . . But I don't think I will, you know."

"Oh, no," Mrs. Ansley hastened to assure her. "I don't care to at all. It's so lovely here; and so full of old memories, as you say." She settled herself in her chair, and almost furtively drew forth her knitting. Mrs. Slade took sideway note of this activity, but her own beautifully cared-for hands remained motionless on her knee.

"I was just thinking," she said slowly, "what different things Rome stands for to each generation of travellers. To our grandmothers, Roman fever; to our mothers, sentimental dangers—how we used to be guarded!—to our daughters, no more dangers than the middle of Main Street. They don't know it—but how much they're missing!"

The long golden light was beginning to pale, and Mrs. Ansley lifted her knitting a little closer to her eyes. "Yes; how we were guarded!"

"I always used to think," Mrs. Slade continued, "that our mothers had a much more difficult job than our grandmothers. When Roman fever stalked the streets it must have been comparatively easy to gather in the girls at the danger hour; but when you and I were young, with such beauty calling us, and the spice of disobedience thrown in, and no worse risk than catching cold during the cool hour after sunset, the mothers used to be put to it to keep us in—didn't they?"

She turned again toward Mrs. Ansley, but the latter

had reached a delicate point in her knitting. "One, two, three—slip two; yes, they must have been," she assented, without looking up.

Mrs. Slade's eyes rested on her with a deepened attention. "She can knit—in the face of *this!* How like her . . ."

Mrs. Slade leaned back, brooding, her eyes ranging from the ruins which faced her to the long green hollow of the Forum, the fading glow of the church fronts beyond it, and the outlying immensity of the Colosseum. Suddenly she thought: "It's all very well to say that our girls have done away with sentiment and moonlight. But if Babs Ansley isn't out to catch that young aviator—the one who's a Marchese—then I don't know anything. And Jenny has no chance beside her. I know that too. I wonder if that's why Grace Ansley likes the two girls to go everywhere together? My poor Jenny as a foil—!" Mrs. Slade gave a hardly audible laugh, and at the sound Mrs. Ansley dropped her knitting.

"Yes—?"

"I—oh, nothing. I was only thinking how your Babs carries everything before her. That Campolieri boy is one of the best matches in Rome. Don't look so innocent, my dear—you know he is. And I was wondering, ever so respectfully, you understand . . . wondering how two such exemplary characters as you and Horace had managed to produce anything quite so dynamic." Mrs. Slade laughed again, with a touch of asperity.

Mrs. Ansley's hands lay inert across her needles. She looked straight out at the great accumulated wreckage of passion and splendour at her feet. But her small profile was almost expressionless. At length she said: "I think you overrate Babs, my dear."

Mrs. Slade's tone grew easier. "No; I don't. I appreciate her. And perhaps envy you. Oh, my girl's perfect; if I were a chronic invalid I'd—well, I think I'd rather be in Jenny's hands. There must be times . . . but there! I always wanted a brilliant daughter . . . and never quite understood why I got an angel instead."

Mrs. Ansley echoed her laugh in a faint murmur. "Babs is an angel too."

"Of course—of course! But she's got rainbow wings. Well, they're wandering by the sea with their young men; and here we sit . . . and it all brings back the past a little too acutely."

Mrs. Ansley had resumed her knitting. One might almost have imagined (if one had known her less well, Mrs. Slade reflected) that, for her also, too many memories rose from the lengthening shadows of those august ruins. But no; she was simply absorbed in her work. What was there for her to worry about? She knew that Babs would almost certainly come back engaged to the extremely eligible Campolieri. "And she'll sell the New York house, and settle down near them in Rome, and never be in their way . . . she's much too tactful. But she'll have an excellent cook, and just the right people in for bridge and cocktails . . . and a perfectly peaceful old age among her grandchildren."

Mrs. Slade broke off this prophetic flight with a recoil of self-disgust. There was no one of whom she had less right to think unkindly than of Grace Ansley. Would she never cure herself of envying her? Perhaps she had begun too long ago.

She stood up and leaned against the parapet, filling her troubled eyes with the tranquillizing magic of the hour. But instead of tranquillizing her the sight seemed to increase her exasperation. Her gaze turned toward the Colosseum. Already its golden flank was drowned in purple shadow, and above it the sky curved crystal clear, without light or colour. It was the moment when afternoon and evening hang balanced in mid-heaven.

Mrs. Slade turned back and laid her hand on her friend's arm. The gesture was so abrupt that Mrs. Ansley looked up, startled.

"The sun's set. You're not afraid, my dear?"

"Afraid—"

"Of Roman fever or pneumonia? I remember how ill you were that winter. As a girl you had a very delicate throat, hadn't you?"

"Oh, we're all right up here. Down below, in the Forum, it does get deathly cold, all of a sudden . . . but not here."

"Ah, of course you know because you had to be so careful." Mrs. Slade turned back to the parapet. She thought: "I must make one more effort not to hate her." Aloud she said: "Whenever I look at the Forum from up here, I remember that story about a great-aunt of yours, wasn't she? A dreaded wicked great-aunt?"

"Oh, yes; Great-aunt Harriet. The one who was supposed to have sent her young sister out to the Forum after sunset to gather a night-blooming flower for her album. All our great-aunts and grand-mothers used to have albums of dried flowers."

Mrs. Slade nodded. "But she really sent her because they were in love with the same man—"

"Well, that was the family tradition. They said Aunt Harriet confessed it years afterward. At any rate, the poor little sister caught the fever and died. Mother used to frighten us with the story when we were children."

"And you frightened *me* with it, that winter when you and I were here as girls. The winter I was engaged to Delphin."

Mrs. Ansley gave a faint laugh. "Oh, did I? Really frightened you? I don't believe you're easily frightened."

"Not often; but I was then. I was easily frightened because I was too happy. I wonder if you know what that means?"

"I—yes . . ." Mrs. Ansley faltered.

"Well, I suppose that was why the story of your wicked aunt made such an impression on me. And I thought: 'There's no more Roman fever, but the Forum is deathly cold after sunset—especially after a hot day. And the Colosseum's even colder and damper.' "

"The Colosseum—?"

"Yes. It wasn't easy to get in, after the gates were

locked for the night. Far from easy. Still, in those days
it could be managed; it *was* managed, often. Lovers met
there who couldn't meet elsewhere. You knew that?''

"I—I daresay. I don't remember.''

"You don't remember? You don't remember going to
visit some ruins or other one evening, just after dark,
and catching a bad chill? You were supposed to have
gone to see the moon rise. People always said that expedition was what caused your illness.''

There was a moment's silence; then Mrs. Ansley
rejoined: "Did they? It was all so long ago.''

"Yes. And you got well again—so it didn't matter.
But I suppose it struck your friends—the reason given
for your illness, I mean—because everybody knew you
were so prudent on account of your throat, and your
mother took such care of you . . . You *had* been out late
sight-seeing, hadn't you, that night?''

"Perhaps I had. The most prudent girls aren't always
prudent. What made you think of it now?''

Mrs. Slade seemed to have no answer ready. But after
a moment she broke out: "Because I simply can't bear it
any longer—!''

Mrs. Ansley lifted her head quickly. Her eyes were
wide and very pale. "Can't bear what?''

"Why—your not knowing that I've always known
why you went.''

"Why I went—?''

"Yes. You think I'm bluffing, don't you? Well, you
went to meet the man I was engaged to—and I can
repeat every word of the letter that took you there.''

While Mrs. Slade spoke Mrs. Ansley had risen unsteadily to her feet. Her bag, her knitting and gloves,
slid in a panic-stricken heap to the ground. She looked
at Mrs. Slade as though she were looking at a ghost.

"No, no—don't,'' she faltered out.

"Why not? Listen, if you don't believe me. 'My one
darling, things can't go on like this. I must see you
alone. Come to the Colosseum immediately after dark
tomorrow. There will be somebody to let you in. No one
whom you need fear will suspect'—but perhaps you've

forgotten what the letter said?''

Mrs. Ansley met the challenge with an unexpected composure. Steadying herself against the chair she looked at her friend, and replied: "No; I know it by heart too."

"And the signature? 'Only *your* D.S.' Was that it? I'm right, am I? That was the letter that took you out that evening after dark?"

Mrs. Ansley was still looking at her. It seemed to Mrs. Slade that a slow struggle was going on behind the voluntarily controlled mask of her small quiet face. "I shouldn't have thought she had herself so well in hand," Mrs. Slade reflected, almost resentfully. But at this moment Mrs. Ansley spoke. "I don't know how you knew. I burnt that letter at once."

"Yes; you would, naturally—you're so prudent!" The sneer was open now. "And if you burnt the letter you're wondering how on earth I know what was in it. That's it, isn't it?"

Mrs. Slade waited, but Mrs. Ansley did not speak.

"Well, my dear, I know what was in that letter because I wrote it!"

"You wrote it?"

"Yes."

The two women stood for a minute staring at each other in the last golden light. Then Mrs. Ansley dropped back into her chair. "Oh," she murmured, and covered her face with her hands.

Mrs. Slade waited nervously for another word or movement. None came, and at length she broke out: "I horrify you."

Mrs. Ansley's hands dropped to her knee. The face they uncovered was streaked with tears. "I wasn't thinking of you. I was thinking—it was the only letter I ever had from him!"

"And I wrote it. Yes; I wrote it! But I was the girl he was engaged to. Did you happen to remember that?"

Mrs. Ansley's head dropped again. "I'm not trying to excuse myself . . . I remembered . . ."

"And still you went?"

"Still I went."

Mrs. Slade stood looking down on the small bowed figure at her side. The flame of her wrath had already sunk, and she wondered why she had ever thought there would be any satisfaction in inflicting so purposeless a wound on her friend. But she had to justify herself.

"You do understand? I'd found out—and I hated you, hated you. I knew you were in love with Delphin—and I was afraid; afraid of you, of your quiet ways, your sweetness . . . your . . . well, I wanted you out of the way, that's all. Just for a few weeks; just till I was sure of him. So in a blind fury I wrote that letter . . . I don't know why I'm telling you now."

"I suppose," said Mrs. Ansley slowly, "it's because you're always gone on hating me."

"Perhaps. Or because I wanted to get the whole thing off my mind." She paused. "I'm glad you destroyed the letter. Of course I never thought you'd die."

Mrs. Ansley relapsed into silence, and Mrs. Slade, leaning above her, was conscious of a strange sense of isolation, of being cut off from the warm current of human communion. "You think me a monster!"

"I don't know . . . It was the only letter I had, and you say he didn't write it?"

"Ah, how you care for him still!"

"I cared for that memory," said Mrs. Ansley.

Mrs. Slade continued to look down on her. She seemed physically reduced by the blow—as if, when she got up, the wind might scatter her like a puff of dust. Mrs. Slade's jealousy suddenly leapt up again at the sight. All these years the woman had been living on that letter. How she must have loved him, to treasure the mere memory of its ashes! The letter of the man her friend was engaged to. Wasn't it she who was the monster?

"You tried your best to get him away from me, didn't you? But you failed; and I kept him. That's all."

"Yes. That's all."

"I wish now I hadn't told you. I'd no idea you'd feel about it as you do; I thought you'd be amused. It all happened so long ago, as you say; and you must do me the justice to remember that I had no reason to think you'd ever taken it seriously. How could I, when you were married to Horace Ansley two months afterward? As soon as you could get out of bed your mother rushed you off to Florence and married you. People were rather surprised—they wondered at its being done so quickly; but I thought I knew. I had an idea you did it out of *pique*—to be able to say you'd got ahead of Delphin and me. Girls have such silly reasons for doing the most serious things. And your marrying so soon convinced me that you'd never really cared."

"Yes. I suppose it would," Mrs. Ansley assented.

The clear heaven overhead was emptied of all its gold. Dusk spread over it, abruptly darkening the Seven Hills. Here and there lights began to twinkle through the foliage at their feet. Steps were coming and going on the deserted terrace—waiters looking out of the doorway at the head of the stairs, then reappearing with trays and napkins and flasks of wine. Tables were moved, chairs straightened. A feeble string of electric lights flickered out. Some vases of faded flowers were carried away, and brought back replenished. A stout lady in a dustcoat suddenly appeared, asking in broken Italian if any one had seen the elastic band which held together her tattered Baedeker. She poked with her stick under the table at which she had lunched, the waiters assisting.

The corner where Mrs. Slade and Mrs. Ansley sat was still shadowy and deserted. For a long time neither of them spoke. At length Mrs. Slade began again: "I suppose I did it as a sort of joke—"

"A joke?"

"Well, girls are ferocious sometimes, you know. Girls in love especially. And I remember laughing to myself all that evening at the idea that you were waiting around there in the dark, dodging out of sight, listening for every sound, trying to get in—. Of course I was upset when I heard you were so ill afterward."

Mrs. Ansley had not moved for a long time. But now she turned slowly toward her companion. "But I didn't wait. He'd arranged everything. He was there. We were let in at once," she said.

Mrs. Slade sprang up from her leaning position. "Delphin there? They let you in?—Ah, now you're lying!" She burst out with violence.

Mrs. Ansley's voice grew clearer, and full of surprise. "But of course he was there. Naturally he came—"

"Came? How did he know he'd find you there? You must be raving!"

Mrs. Ansley hesitated, as though reflecting. "But I answered the letter. I told him I'd be there. So he came."

Mrs. Slade flung her hands up to her face. "Oh, God—you answered! I never thought of your answering . . ."

"It's odd you never thought of it, if you wrote the letter."

"Yes. I was blind with rage."

Mrs. Ansley rose, and drew her fur scarf about her. "It is cold here. We'd better go . . . I'm sorry for you," she said, as she clasped the fur about her throat.

The unexpected words sent a pang through Mrs. Slade. "Yes; we'd better go." She gathered up her bag and cloak. "I don't know why you should be sorry for me," she muttered.

Mrs. Ansley stood looking away from her toward the dusky secret mass of the Colosseum. "Well—because I didn't have to wait that night."

Mrs. Slade gave an unquiet laugh. "Yes; I was beaten there. But I oughtn't to begrudge it to you, I suppose. At the end of all these years. After all, I had everything; I had him for twenty-five years. And you had nothing but that one letter that he didn't write."

Mrs. Ansley was again silent. At length she turned toward the door of the terrace. She took a step, and turned back, facing her companion.

"I had Barbara," she said, and began to move ahead of Mrs. Slade toward the stairway.

XINGU

I.

MRS. BALLINGER is one of the ladies who pursue Culture in bands, as though it were dangerous to meet alone. To this end she had founded the Lunch Club, an association composed of herself and several other indomitable huntresses of erudition. The Lunch Club after three or four winters of lunching and debate, had acquired such local distinction that the entertainment of distinguished strangers became one of its accepted functions; in recognition of which it duly extended to the celebrated "Osric Dane," on the day of her arrival in Hillbridge, an invitation to be present at the next meeting.

The club was to meet at Mrs. Ballinger's. The other members, behind her back, were of one voice in deploring her unwillingness to cede her rights in favor of Mrs. Plinth, whose house made a more impressive setting for the entertainment of celebrities; while, as Mrs. Leveret observed, there was always the picture-gallery to fall back on.

Mrs. Plinth made no secret of sharing this view. She had always regarded it as one of her obligations to entertain the Lunch Club's distinguished guests. Mrs.

16

Plinth was almost as proud of her obligations as she was
of her picture-gallery; she was in fact fond of implying
that the one possession implied the other, and that only
a woman of her wealth could afford to live up to a standard as high as that which she had set herself. An all-
round sense of duty, roughly adaptable to various ends,
was, in her opinion, all that Providence exacted of the
more humbly stationed; but the power which had
predestined Mrs. Plinth to keep a footman clearly intended her to maintain an equally specialized staff of
responsibilities. It was the more to be regretted that
Mrs. Ballinger, whose obligations to society were
bounded by the narrow scope of two parlour-maids,
should have been so tenacious of the right to entertain
Osric Dane.

The question of that lady's reception had for a month
past profoundly moved the members of the Lunch
Club. It was not that they felt themselves unequal to the
task, but that their sense of the opportunity plunged
them into the agreeable uncertainty of the lady who
weighs the alternatives of a well-stocked wardrobe. If
such subsidiary members as Mrs. Leveret were fluttered
by the thought of exchanging ideas with the author of
"The Wings of Death," no forebodings disturbed the
conscious adequacy of Mrs. Plinth, Mrs. Ballinger and
Miss Van Vluyck. "The Wings of Death" had, in fact,
at Miss Van Vluyck's suggestion, been chosen as the
subject of discussion at the last club meeting, and each
member had thus been enabled to express her own
opinion or to appropriate whatever sounded well in the
comments of the others.

Mrs. Roby alone had abstained from profiting by the
opportunity; but it was now openly recognised that, as a
member of the Lunch Club, Mrs. Roby was a failure.
"It all comes," as Miss Van Vluyck put it, "of accepting a woman on a man's estimation." Mrs. Roby,
returning to Hillbridge from a prolonged sojourn in ex-
otic lands—the other ladies no longer took the trouble
to remember where—had been heralded by the distinguished biologist, Professor Foreland, as the most

agreeable woman he had ever met; and the members of
the Lunch Club, impressed by an encomium that carried
the weight of a diploma, and rashly assuming that the
Professor's social sympathies would follow the line of
his professional bent, had seized the chance of annexing
a biological member. Their disillusionment was complete. At Miss Van Vluyck's first off-hand mention of
the pterodactyl Mrs. Roby had confusedly murmured:
"I know so little about metres—" and after that painful
betrayal of incompetence she had prudently withdrawn
from further participation in the mental gymnastics of
the club.

"I suppose she flattered him," Miss Van Vluyck
summed up—"or else it's the way she does her hair."

The dimensions of Miss Van Vluyck's dining-room
having restricted the membership of the club to six, the
non-conductiveness of one member was a serious obstacle to the exchange of ideas, and some wonder had
already been expressed that Mrs. Roby should care to
live, as it were, on the intellectual bounty of the others.
This feeling was increased by the discovery that she had
not yet read "The Wings of Death." She owned to having heard the name of Osric Dane; but that—incredible
as it appeared—was the extent of her acquaintance with
the celebrated novelist. The ladies could not conceal
their surprise; but Mrs. Ballinger, whose pride in the
club made her wish to put even Mrs. Roby in the best
possible light, gently insinuated that, though she had
not had time to acquaint herself with "The Wings of
Death," she must at least be familiar with its equally
remarkable predecessor, "The Supreme Instant."

Mrs. Roby wrinkled her sunny brows in a conscientious effort of memory, as a result of which she recalled
that, oh, yes, she *had* seen the book at her brother's,
when she was staying with him in Brazil, and had even
carried it off to read one day on a boating party; but
they had all got to shying things at each other in the
boat, and the book had gone overboard, so she had
never had the chance—

The picture evoked by this anecdote did not increase

Mrs. Roby's credit with the club, and there was a painful pause, which was broken by Mrs. Plinth's remarking: "I can understand that, with all your other pursuits, you should not find much time for reading; but I should have thought you might at least have *got up* 'The Wings of Death' before Osric Dane's arrival."

Mrs. Roby took this rebuke good-humouredly. She had meant, she owned, to glance through the book; but she had been so absorbed in a novel of Trollope's that—

"No one reads Trollope now," Mrs. Ballinger interrupted.

Mrs. Roby looked pained. "I'm only just beginning," she confessed.

"And does he interest you?" Mrs. Plinth enquired.

"He amuses me."

"Amusement," said Mrs. Plinth, "is hardly what I look for in my choice of books."

"Oh, certainly, 'The Wings of Death' is not amusing," ventured Mrs. Leveret, whose manner of putting forth an opinion was like that of an obliging salesman with a variety of other styles to submit if his first selection does not suit.

"Was it *meant* to be?" enquired Mrs. Plinth, who was fond of asking questions that she permitted no one but herself to answer. "Assuredly not."

"Assuredly not—that is what I was going to say," assented Mrs. Leveret, hastily rolling up her opinion and reaching for another. "It was meant to—to elevate."

Miss Van Vluyck adjusted her spectacles as though they were the black cap of condemnation. "I hardly see," she interposed, "how a book steeped in the bitterest pessimism can be said to elevate, however much it may instruct."

"I meant of course, to instruct," said Mrs. Leveret, flurried by the unexpected distinction between two terms which she had supposed to be synonymous. Mrs. Leveret's enjoyment of the Lunch Club was frequently marred by such surprise; and not knowing her own value to the other ladies as a mirror for their mental

complacency she was sometimes troubled by a doubt of
her worthiness to join in their debates. It was only the
fact of having a dull sister who thought her clever that
saved her from a sense of hopeless inferiority.

"Do they get married in the end?" Mrs. Roby interposed.

"They—who?" the Lunch Club collectively exclaimed.

"Why, the girl and man. It's a novel, isn't it? I always
think that's the one thing that matters. If they're parted
it spoils my dinner."

Mrs. Plinth and Mrs. Ballinger exchanged scandalised
glances, and the latter said: "I should hardly advise you
to read 'The Wings of Death' in that spirit. For my part,
when there are so many books one *has* to read, I wonder
how any one can find time for those that are merely
amusing."

"The beautiful part of it," Laura Glyde murmured,
"is surely just this—that no one can tell *how* 'The
Wings of Death' ends. Osric Dane, overcome by the
awful significance of her own meaning, has mercifully
veiled it—perhaps even from herself—as Apelles, in
representing the sacrifice of Iphigenia, veiled the face of
Agamemnon."

"What's that? Is it poetry?" whispered Mrs. Leveret
to Mrs. Plinth, who, disdaining a definite reply, said
coldly: "You should look it up. I always make it a point
to look things up." Her tone added—"though I might
easily have it done for me by the footman."

"I was about to say," Miss Van Vluyck resumed,
"that it must always be a question whether a book *can*
instruct unless it elevates."

"Oh—" murmured Mrs. Leveret, now feeling herself hopelessly astray.

"I don't know," said Mrs. Ballinger, scenting in Miss
Van Vluyck's tone a tendency to depreciate the coveted
distinction of entertaining Osric Dane; "I don't know
that such a question can seriously be raised as to a book
which has attracted more attention among thoughtful

people than any novel since 'Robert Elsmere.' "

"Oh, but don't you see," exclaimed Laura Glyde, "that it's just the dark hopelessness of it all—the wonderful tone-scheme of black on black—that makes it such an artistic achievement? It reminded me when I read it of Prince Rupert's *manière noire* . . . the book is etched, not painted, yet one feels the colour-values so intensely. . . ."

"Who is *he*?" Mrs. Leveret whispered to her neighbour. "Some one she's met abroad?"

"The wonderful part of the book," Mrs. Ballinger conceded, "is that it may be looked at from so many points of view. I hear that as a study of determinism Professor Lupton ranks it with 'The Data of Ethics.' "

"I'm told that Osric Dane spent ten years in preparatory studies before beginning to write it," said Mrs. Plinth. "She looks up everything—verifies everything. It has always been my principle, as you know. Nothing would induce me, now, to put aside a book before I'd finished it, just because I can buy as many more as I want."

"And what do *you* think of 'The Wings of Death'?" Mrs. Roby abruptly asked her.

It was the kind of question that might be termed out of order, and the ladies glanced at each other as though disclaiming any share in such a breach of discipline. They all knew there was nothing Mrs. Plinth so much disliked as being asked her opinion of a book. Books were written to read; if one read them what more could be expected? To be questioned in detail regarding the contents of a volume seemed to her as great an outrage as being searched for smuggled laces at the Custom House. The club had always respected this idiosyncrasy of Mrs. Plinth's. Such opinions as she had were imposing and substantial: her mind, like her house, was furnished with monumental "pieces" that were not meant to be disarranged; and it was one of the unwritten rules of the Lunch Club that, within her own province, each member's habits of thought should be respected.

The meeting therefore closed with an increased sense, on the part of the other ladies, of Mrs. Roby's hopeless unfitness to be one of them.

II.

MRS. LEVERET, on the eventful day, arrived early at Mrs. Ballinger's, her volume of Appropriate Allusions in her pocket.

It always flustered Mrs. Leveret to be late at the Lunch Club: she liked to collect her thoughts and gather a hint, as the others assembled, of the turn the conversation was likely to take. Today, however, she felt herself completely at a loss; and even the familiar contact of Appropriate Allusions, which stuck into her as she sat down, failed to give her any reassurance. It was an admirable little volume, compiled to meet all the social emergencies; so that, whether on the occasion of Anniversaries, joyful or melancholy (as the classification ran), of Banquets, social or municipal, or of Baptisms, Church of England or sectarian, its student need never be at a loss for a pertinent reference. Mrs. Leveret, though she had for years devoutly conned its pages, valued it, however, rather for its moral support than for its practical services; for though in the privacy of her own room she commanded an army of quotations, these invariably deserted her at the critical moment, and the only phrase she retained—*Canst thou draw out leviathan with a hook?*—was one she had never yet found occasion to apply.

To-day she felt that even the complete mastery of the volume would hardly have insured her self-possession; for she thought it probable that, even if she *did*, in some miraculous way, remember an Allusion, it would be only to find that Osric Dane used a different volume (Mrs. Leveret was convinced that literary people always carried them), and would consequently not recognise her quotations.

Mrs. Leveret's sense of being adrift was intensified by the appearance of Mrs. Ballinger's drawing-room. To a careless eye its aspect was unchanged; but those acquainted with Mrs. Ballinger's way of arranging her books would instantly have detected the marks of recent perturbation. Mrs. Ballinger's province, as a member of the Lunch Club, was the Book of the Day. On that, whatever it was, from a novel to a treatise on experimental psychology, she was confidently, authoritatively "up." What became of last year's books, or last week's even; what she did with the "subjects" she had previously professed with equal authority; no one had ever yet discovered. Her mind was an hotel where facts came and went like transient lodgers, without leaving their address behind, and frequently without paying for their board. It was Mrs. Ballinger's boast that she was "abreast with the Thought of the Day," and her pride that this advanced position should be expressed by the books on her table. These volumes, frequently renewed, and almost always damp from the press, bore names generally unfamiliar to Mrs. Leveret, and giving her, as she furtively scanned them, a disheartened glimpse of new fields of knowledge to be breathlessly traversed in Mrs. Ballinger's wake. But to-day a number of maturer-looking volumes were adroitly mingled with the *primeurs* of the press—Karl Marx jostled Professor Bergson, and the "Confessions of St. Augustine" lay beside the last work on "Mendelism"; so that even to Mrs. Leveret's fluttered perceptions it was clear that Mrs. Ballinger didn't in the least know what Osric Dane was likely to talk about, and had taken measures to be prepared for anything. Mrs. Leveret felt like a passenger on an ocean steamer who is told that there is no immediate danger, but that she had better put on her life-belt.

It was a relief to be roused from those forebodings by Miss Van Vluyck's arrival.

"Well, my dear," the new-comer briskly asked her hostess, "what subjects are we to discuss to-day?"

Mrs. Ballinger was furtively replacing a volume of Wordsworth by a copy of Verlaine. "I hardly know," she said, somewhat nervously. "Perhaps we had better leave that to circumstances."

"Circumstances?" said Miss Van Vluyck drily. "That means, I suppose, that Laura Glyde will take the floor as usual, and we shall be deluged with literature."

Philanthropy and statistics were Miss Van Vluyck's province, and she resented any tendency to divert their guest's attention from these topics.

Mrs. Plinth at this moment appeared.

"Literature?" she protested in a tone of remonstrance. "But this is perfectly unexpected. I understood we were to talk of Osric Dane's novel."

Mrs. Ballinger winced at the discrimination, but let it pass. "We hardly make that our chief subject—at least not *too* intentionally," she suggested. "Of course we can let our talk *drift* in that direction, but we ought to have some other topic as an introduction, and that is what I wanted to consult you about. The fact is, we know so little of Osric Dane's tastes and interests that it is difficult to make any special preparation."

"It may be difficult," said Mrs. Plinth with decision, "but it is necessary. I know what that happy-go-lucky principle leads to. As I told one of my nieces the other day, there are certain emergencies for which a lady should always be prepared. It's in shocking taste to wear colours when one pays a visit of condolence, or a last year's dress when there are reports that one's husband is on the wrong side of the market; and so it is with conversation. All I ask is that I should know beforehand what is to be talked about; then I feel sure of being able to say the proper thing."

"I quite agree with you," Mrs. Ballinger assented: "but—"

And at that instant, heralded by the fluttered parlour-maid, Osric Dane appeared upon the threshold.

Mrs. Leveret told her sister afterward that she had known at a glance what was coming. She saw that Osric Dane was not going to meet them half way. That distinguished personage had indeed entered with an air of compulsion not calculated to promote the easy exercise of hospitality. She looked as though she were about to be photographed for a new edition of her books.

The desire to propitiate a divinity is generally in inverse ratio to its responsiveness, and the sense of discouragement produced by Osric Dane's entrance visibly increased the Lunch Club's eagerness to please her. Any lingering idea that she might consider herself under an obligation to her entertainers was at once dispelled by her manner: as Mrs. Leveret said afterward to her sister, she had a way of looking at you that made you feel as if there was something wrong with your hat. This evidence of greatness produced such an immediate impression on the ladies that a shudder of awe ran through them when Mrs. Roby, as their hostess led the great personage into the dining-room, turned back to whisper to the others: "What a brute she is!"

The hour about the table did not tend to revise this verdict. It was passed by Osric Dane in the silent deglutition of Mrs. Ballinger's menu, and by the members of the club in the emission of tentative platitudes which their guest seemed to swallow as perfunctorily as the successive courses of the luncheon.

Mrs. Ballinger's reluctance to fix a topic had thrown the club into a mental disarray which increased with the return to the drawing-room, where the actual business of discussion was to open. Each lady waited for the other to speak; and there was a general shock of disappointment when their hostess opened the conversation by the painfully commonplace enquiry: "Is this your first visit to Hillbridge?"

Even Mrs. Leveret was conscious that this was a bad beginning; and a vague impulse of deprecation made Miss Glyde interject: "It is a very small place indeed."

Mrs. Plinth bristled. "We have a great many representative people," she said, in the tone of one who speaks for her order.

Osric Dane turned to her. "What do they represent?" she asked.

Mrs. Plinth's constitutional dislike to being questioned was intensified by her sense of unpreparedness; and her reproachful glance passed the question on to Mrs. Ballinger.

"Why," said that lady, glancing in turn at the other members, "as a community I hope it is not too much to say that we stand for culture."

"For art—" Miss Glyde interjected.

"For art and literature," Mrs. Ballinger emended.

"And for sociology, I trust," snapped Miss Van Vluyck.

"We have a standard," said Mrs. Plinth, feeling herself suddenly secure on the vast expanse of a generalisation; and Mrs. Leveret, thinking there must be room for more than one on so broad a statement, took courage to murmur: "Oh, certainly; we have a standard."

"The object of our little club," Mrs. Ballinger continued, "is to concentrate the highest tendencies of Hillbridge—to centralise and focus its intellectual effort."

This was felt to be so happy that the ladies drew an almost audible breath of relief.

"We aspire," the President went on, "to be in touch with whatever is highest in art, literature and ethics."

Osric Dane again turned to her. "What ethics?" she asked.

A tremor of apprehension encircled the room. None of the ladies required any preparation to pronounce on a question of morals; but when they were called ethics it was different. The club, when fresh from the "Encyclopaedia Britannica," the "Reader's Handbook" or Smith's "Classical Dictionary," could deal confidently with any subject; but when taken unawares it had been known to define agnosticism as a heresy of the Early Church and Professor Froude as a distinguished histologist; and such minor members as Mrs. Leveret still secretly regarded ethics as something vaguely pagan.

Even to Mrs. Ballinger, Osric Dane's question was unsettling, and there was a general sense of gratitude when Laura Glyde leaned forward to say, with her most sympathetic accent: "You must excuse us, Mrs. Dane, for not being able, just at present, to talk of anything but 'The Wings of Death.'"

"Yes," said Miss Van Vluyck, with a sudden resolve to carry the war into the enemy's camp. "We are so anxious to know the exact purpose you had in mind in writing your wonderful book."

"You will find," Mrs. Plinth interposed, "that we are not superficial readers."

"We are eager to hear from you," Miss Van Vluyck continued, "if the pessimistic tendency of the book is an expression of your own convictions or—"

"Or merely," Miss Glyde thrust in, "a sombre background brushed in to throw your figures into more vivid relief. *Are* you not primarily plastic?"

"*I* have always maintained," Mrs. Ballinger interposed, "that you represent the purely objective method—"

Osric Dane helped herself critically to coffee. "How do you define objective?" she then enquired.

There was a flurried pause before Laura Glyde intensely murmured: "In reading *you* we don't define, we feel."

Osric Dane smiled. "The cerebellum," she remarked, "is not infrequently the seat of the literary emotions." And she took a second lump of sugar.

The sting that this remark was vaguely felt to conceal was almost neutralised by the satisfaction of being addressed in such technical language.

"Ah, the cerebellum," said Miss Van Vluyck complacently. "The club took a course in psychology last winter."

"Which psychology?" asked Osric Dane.

There was an agonising pause, during which each member of the club secretly deplored the distressing inefficiency of the others. Only Mrs. Roby went on placidly sipping her chartreuse. At last Mrs. Ballinger said, with an attempt at a high tone: "Well, really, you know, it was last year that we took psychology, and this winter we have been so absorbed in—"

She broke off, nervously trying to recall some of the club's discussions; but her faculties seemed to be paralysed by the petrifying stare of Osric Dane. What *had* the club been absorbed in? Mrs. Ballinger, with a vague purpose of gaining time, repeated slowly: "We've been so intensely absorbed in—"

Mrs. Roby put down her liqueur glass and drew near the group with a smile.

"In Xingu?" she gently prompted.

A thrill ran through the other members. They exchanged confused glances, and then, with one accord, turned a gaze of mingled relief and interrogation on their rescuer. The expression of each denoted a different phase of the same emotion. Mrs. Plinth was the first to compose her features to an air of reassurance: after a moment's hasty adjustment her look almost implied that it was she who had given the word to Mrs. Ballinger.

"Xingu, of course!" exclaimed the latter with her accustomed promptness, while Miss Van Vluyck and Laura Glyde seemed to be plumbing the depths of memory, and Mrs. Leveret, feeling apprehensively for Appropriate Allusions, was somehow reassured by the uncomfortable pressure of its bulk against her person.

Osric Dane's change of countenance was no less striking than that of her entertainers. She too put down her coffee-cup, but with a look of distinct annoyance; she too wore, for a brief moment, what Mrs. Roby afterward described as the look of feeling for something in the back of her head; and before she could dissemble these momentary signs of weakness, Mrs. Roby, turning to her with a deferential smile, had said: "And we've been so hoping that to-day you would tell us just what you think of it."

Osric Dane received the homage of the smile as a

matter of course; but the accompanying question obviously embarrassed her, and it became clear to her observers that she was not quick at shifting her facial scenery. It was as though her countenace had so long been set in an expression of unchallenged superiority that the muscles had stiffened, and refused to obey her orders.

"Xingu—" she said, as if seeking in her turn to gain time.

Mrs. Roby continued to press her. "Knowing how engrossing the subject is, you will understand how it happens that the club has let everything else go to the wall for the moment. Since we took up Xingu I might almost say—were it not for your books—that nothing else seems to us worth remembering."

Osric Dane's stern features were darkened rather than lit up by an uneasy smile. "I am glad to hear that you make one exception," she gave out between narrowed lips.

"Oh, of course," Mrs. Roby said prettily; "but as you have shown us that—so very naturally!—you don't care to talk of your own things, we really can't let you off from telling us exactly what you think about Xingu; especially," she added, with a still more persuasive smile, "as some people say that one of your last books was saturated with it."

It was an *it*, then—the assurance sped like fire through the parched minds of the other members. In their eagerness to gain the least little clue to Xingu they almost forgot the joy of assisting at the discomfiture of Mrs. Dane.

The latter reddened nervously under her antagonist's challenge. "May I ask," she faltered out, "to which of my books you refer?"

Mrs. Roby did not falter. "That's just what I want you to tell us; because, though I was present, I didn't actually take part."

"Present at what?" Mrs. Dane took her up; and for an instant the trembling members of the Lunch Club thought that the champion Providence had raised up for them had lost a point. But Mrs. Roby explained herself gaily: "At the discussion, of course. And so we're dreadfully anxious to know just how it was that you went into the Xingu."

There was a portentous pause, a silence so big with incalculable dangers that the members with one accord checked the words on their lips, like soldiers dropping their arms to watch a single combat between their leaders. Then Mrs. Dane gave expression to their inmost dread by saying sharply: "Ah—you say *the* Xingu, do you?"

Mrs. Roby smiled undauntedly. "It *is* a shade pedantic, isn't it? Personally, I always drop the article; but I don't know how the other members feel about it."

The other members looked as though they would willingly have dispensed with this appeal to their opinion, and Mrs. Roby, after a bright glance about the group, went on: "They probably think, as I do, that nothing really matters except the thing itself—except Xingu."

No immediate reply seemed to occur to Mrs. Dane, and Mrs. Ballinger gathered courage to say: "Surely every one must feel that about Xingu."

Mrs. Plinth came to her support with a heavy murmur of assent, and Laura Glyde sighed out emotionally: "I have known cases where it has changed a whole life."

"It has done me worlds of good," Mrs. Leveret interjected, seeming to herself to remember that she had either taken it or read it the winter before.

"Of course," Mrs. Roby admitted, "the difficulty is that one must give up so much time to it. It's very long."

"I can't imagine," said Miss Van Vluyck, "grudging the time given to such a subject."

"And deep in places," Mrs. Roby pursued; (so then it was a book!) "And it isn't easy to skip."

"I never skip," said Mrs. Plinth dogmatically.

"Ah, it's dangerous to, in Xingu. Even at the start there are places where one can't. One must just wade through."

"I should hardly call it *wading*," said Mrs. Ballinger sarcastically.

Mrs. Roby sent her a look of interest. "Ah—you always found it went swimmingly?"

Mrs. Ballinger hesitated. "Of course there are difficult passages," she conceded.

"Yes; some are not at all clear—even," Mrs. Roby added, "if one is familiar with the original."

"As I suppose you are?" Osric Dane interposed, suddenly fixing her with a look of challenge.

Mrs. Roby met it by a deprecating gesture. "Oh, it's really not difficult up to a certain point; though some of the branches are very little known, and it's almost impossible to get at the source."

"Have you ever tried?" Mrs. Plinth enquired, still distrustful of Mrs. Roby's thoroughness.

Mrs. Roby was silent for a moment; then she replied with lowered lids: "No—but a friend of mine did; a very brilliant man; and he told me it was best for women—not to. . . ."

A shudder ran around the room. Mrs. Leveret coughed so that the parlour-maid, who was handing the cigarettes, should not hear; Miss Van Vluyck's face took on a nauseated expression, and Mrs. Plinth looked as if she were passing some one she did not care to bow to. But the most remarkable result of Mrs. Roby's words was the effect they produced on the Lunch Club's distinguished guest. Osric Dane's impassive features suddenly softened to an expression of the warmest human sympathy, and edging her chair toward Mrs. Roby's she asked: "Did he really? And—did you find he was right?"

Mrs. Ballinger, in whom annoyance at Mrs. Roby's unwonted assumption of prominence was beginning to displace gratitude for the aid she had rendered, could not consent to her being allowed, by such dubious means, to monopolise the attention of their guest. If Osric Dane had not enough self-respect to resent Mrs. Roby's flippancy, at least the Lunch Club would do so in the person of its President.

Mrs. Ballinger laid her hand on Mrs. Roby's arm. "We must not forget," she said with a frigid amiability, "that absorbing as Xingu is to *us*, it may be less interesting to—"

"Oh, no, on the contrary, I assure you," Osric Dane intervened.

"—to others," Mrs. Ballinger finished firmly; "and we must not allow our little meeting to end without persuading Mrs. Dane to say a few words to us on a subject which, to-day, is much more present in all our thoughts. I refer, of course, to 'The Wings of Death.' "

The other members, animated by various degrees of the same sentiment, and encouraged by the humanised mien of their redoubtable guest, repeated after Mrs. Ballinger: "Oh, yes, you really *must* talk to us a little about your book."

Osric Dane's expression became as bored, though not as haughty, as when her work had been previously mentioned. But before she could respond to Mrs. Ballinger's request, Mrs. Roby had risen from her seat, and was pulling down her veil over her frivolous nose.

"I'm so sorry," she said, advancing toward her hostess with outstretched hand, "but before Mrs. Dane begins I think I'd better run away. Unluckily, as you know, I haven't read her books, so I should be at a terrible disadvantage among you all, and besides, I've an engagement to play bridge."

If Mrs. Roby had simply pleaded her ignorance of Osric Dane's works as a reason for withdrawing, the Lunch Club, in view of her recent prowess, might have approved such evidence of discretion; but to couple this excuse with the brazen announcement that she was foregoing the privilege for the purpose of joining a bridge-party was only one more instance of her deplorable lack of discrimination.

The ladies were disposed, however, to feel that her departure—now that she had performed the sole service she was ever likely to render them—would probably make for greater order and dignity in the impending discussion, besides relieving them of the sense of self-distrust which her presence always mysteriously produced. Mrs. Ballinger therefore restricted herself to a formal murmur of regret, and the other members were just grouping themselves comfortably about Osric Dane when the latter, to their dismay, started up from the sofa on which she had been seated.

"Oh wait—do wait, and I'll go with you!" she called out to Mrs. Roby; and, seizing the hands of the disconcerted members, she administered a series of farewell pressures with the mechanical haste of a railway-conductor punching tickets.

"I'm so sorry—I'd quite forgotten—" she flung back at them from the threshold; and as she joined Mrs. Roby, who had turned in surprise at her appeal, the other ladies had the mortification of hearing her say, in a voice which she did not take the pains to lower: "If you'll let me walk a little way with you, I should so like to ask you a few more questions about Xingu . . ."

III.

THE INCIDENT had been so rapid that the door closed on the departing pair before the other members had time to understand what was happening. Then a sense of the indignity put upon them by Osric Dane's unceremonious desertion began to contend with the confused feeling that they had been cheated out of their due without exactly knowing how or why.

There was a silence, during which Mrs. Ballinger, with a perfunctory hand, rearranged the skilfully grouped literature at which her distinguished guest had not so much as glanced; then Miss Van Vluyck tartly pronounced: "Well, I can't say that I consider Osric Dane's departure a great loss."

This confession crystallised the resentment of the other members, and Mrs. Leveret exclaimed: "I do believe she came on purpose to be nasty!"

It was Mrs. Plinth's private opinion that Osric Dane's attitude toward the Lunch Club might have been very different had it welcomed her in the majestic setting of the Plinth drawing-rooms; but not liking to reflect on the inadequacy of Mrs. Ballinger's establishment she sought a roundabout satisfaction in depreciating her lack of foresight.

"I said from the first that we ought to have had a subject ready. It's what always happens when you're unprepared. Now if we'd only got up Xingu—"

The slowness of Mrs. Plinth's mental processes was always allowed for by the club; but this instance of it was too much for Mrs. Ballinger's equanimity.

"Xingu!" she scoffed. "Why, it was the fact of our knowing so much more about it than she did—unprepared though we were—that made Osric Dane so furious. I should have thought that was plain enough to everybody!"

This retort impressed even Mrs. Plinth, and Laura Glyde, moved by an impulse of generosity, said: "Yes, we really ought to be grateful to Mrs. Roby for introducing the topic. It may have made Osric Dane furious, but at least it made her civil."

"I am glad we were able to show her," added Miss Van Vluyck, "that a broad and up-to-date culture is not confined to the great intellectual centres."

This increased the satisfaction of the other members, and they began to forget their wrath against Osric Dane in the pleasure of having contributed to her discomfiture.

Miss Van Vluyck thoughtfully rubbed her spectacles. "What surprised me most," she continued, "was that Fanny Roby should be so up on Xingu."

This remark threw a slight chill on the company, but Mrs. Ballinger said with an air of indulgent irony: "Mrs. Roby always has the knack of making a little go a long way; still, we certainly owe her a debt for hap-

pening to remember that she'd heard of Xingu." And
this was felt by the other members to be a graceful way
of cancelling once for all the club's obligation to Mrs.
Roby.

Even Mrs. Leveret took courage to speed a timid
shaft of irony. "I fancy Osric Dane hardly expected to
take a lesson in Xingu at Hillbridge!"

Mrs. Ballinger smiled. "When she asked me what we
represented—do you remember?—I wish I'd simply said
we represented Xingu!"

All the ladies laughed appreciatively at this sally, except Mrs. Plinth, who said, after a moment's deliberation: "I'm not sure it would have been wise to do
so."

Mrs. Ballinger, who was already beginning to feel as
if she had launched at Osric Dane the retort which had
just occurred to her, turned ironically on Mrs. Plinth.
"May I ask why?" she enquired.

Mrs. Plinth looked grave. "Surely," she said, "I understood from Mrs. Roby herself that the subject was
one it was as well not to go into too deeply?"

Miss Van Vluyck rejoined with precision: "I think
that applied only to an investigation of the origin of
the—of the—"; and suddenly she found that her usually
accurate memory had failed her. "It's a part of the subject I never studied myself," she concluded.

"Nor I," said Mrs. Ballinger.

Laura Glyde bent toward them with widened eyes.
"And yet it seems—doesn't it?—the part that is fullest
of an esoteric fascination?"

"I don't know on what you base that," said Miss Van
Vluyck argumentatively.

"Well, didn't you notice how intensely interested
Osric Dane became as soon as she heard what the brilliant foreigner—he *was* a foreigner, wasn't he?—had
told Mrs. Roby about the origin—the origin of the rite
—or whatever you call it?"

Mrs. Plinth looked disapproving, and Mrs. Ballinger
visibly wavered. Then she said: "It may not be desirable
to touch on the—on that part of the subject in general

conversation; but, from the importance it evidently has to a woman of Osric Dane's distinction, I feel as if we ought not to be afraid to discuss it among our-selves—without gloves—though with closed doors, if necessary.''

''I'm quite of your opinion,'' Miss Van Vluyck came briskly to her support; ''on condition, that is, that all grossness of language is avoided.''

''Oh, I'm sure we shall understand without that,'' Mrs. Leveret tittered; and Laura Glyde added sig-nificantly: ''I fancy we can read between the lines,'' while Mrs. Ballinger rose to assure herself that the doors were really closed.

Mrs. Plinth had not yet given her adhesion. ''I hardly see,'' she began, ''what benefit is to be derived from in-vestigating such peculiar customs—''

But Mrs. Ballinger's patience had reached the extreme limit of tension. ''This at least,'' she returned; ''that we shall not be placed again in the humiliating position of finding ourselves less up on our own subjects than Fanny Roby!''

Even to Mrs. Plinth this argument was conclusive. She peered furtively about the room and lowered her commanding tones to ask: ''Have you got a copy?''

''A—a copy?'' stammered Mrs. Ballinger. She was aware that the other members were looking at her ex-pectantly, and that this answer was inadequate, so she supported it by asking another question. ''A copy of what?''

Her companions bent their expectant gaze on Mrs. Plinth, who, in turn, appeared less sure of herself than usual. ''Why, of—of—the book,'' she explained.

''What book?'' snapped Miss Van Vluyck, almost as sharply as Osric Dane.

Mrs. Ballinger looked at Laura Glyde, whose eyes were interrogatively fixed on Mrs. Leveret. The fact of being deferred to was so new to the latter that it filled her with an insane temerity. ''Why, Xingu, of course!'' she exclaimed.

A profound silence followed this challenge to the resources of Mrs. Ballinger's library, and the latter, after glancing nervously toward the Books of the Day, returned with dignity: "It's not a thing one cares to leave about."

"I should think *not!*" exclaimed Mrs. Plinth.

"It *is* a book, then?" said Miss Van Vluyck.

This again threw the company into disarray, and Mrs. Ballinger, with an impatient sigh, rejoined: "Why—there *is* a book—naturally. . . ."

"Then why did Miss Glyde call it a religion?"

Laura Glyde started up. "A religion? I never—"

"Yes, you did," Miss Van Vluyck insisted; "you spoke of rites; and Mrs. Plinth said it was a custom."

Miss Glyde was evidently making a desperate effort to recall her statement; but accuracy of detail was not her strongest point. At length she began in a deep murmur: "Surely they used to do something of the kind at the Eleusinian mysteries—"

"Oh—" said Miss Van Vluyck, on the verge of disapproval; and Mrs. Plinth protested: "I understood there was to be no indelicacy!"

Mrs. Ballinger could not control her irritation. "Really, it is too bad that we should not be able to talk the matter over quietly among ourselves. Personally, I think that if one goes into Xingu at all—"

"Oh, so do I!" cried Miss Glyde.

"And I don't see how one can avoid doing so, if one wishes to keep up with the Thought of the Day—"

Mrs. Leveret uttered an exclamation of relief. "There—that's it!" she interposed.

"What's it?" the President took her up.

"Why—it's a—a Thought: I mean a philosophy."

This seemed to bring a certain relief to Mrs. Ballinger and Laura Glyde, but Miss Van Vluyck said: "Excuse me if I tell you that you're all mistaken. Xingu happens to be a language."

"A language!" the Lunch Club cried.

"Certainly. Don't you remember Fanny Roby's

saying that there were several branches, and that some were hard to trace? What could that apply to but dialects?"

Mrs. Ballinger could no longer restrain a contemptuous laugh. "Really, if the Lunch Club has reached such a pass that it has to go to Fanny Roby for instruction on a subject like Xingu, it had almost better cease to exist!"

"It's really her fault for not being clearer," Laura Glyde put in.

"Oh, clearness and Fanny Roby!" Mrs. Ballinger shrugged. "I daresay we shall find she was mistaken on almost every point."

"Why not look it up?" said Mrs. Plinth.

As a rule this recurrent suggestion of Mrs. Plinth's was ignored in the heat of discussion, and only resorted to afterward in the privacy of each member's home. But on the present occasion the desire to ascribe their own confusion of thought to the vague and contradictory nature of Mrs. Roby's statements caused the members of the Lunch Club to utter a collective demand for a book of reference.

At this point the production of her treasured volume gave Mrs. Leveret, for a moment, the unusual experience of occupying the centre front; but she was not able to hold it long, for Appropriate Allusions contained no mention of Xingu.

"Oh, that's not the kind of thing we want!" exclaimed Miss Van Vluyck. She cast a disparaging glance over Mrs. Ballinger's assortment of literature, and added impatiently: "Haven't you any useful books?"

"Of course I have," replied Mrs. Ballinger indignantly; "I keep them in my husband's dressing-room."

From this region, after some difficulty and delay, the parlour-maid produced the W-Z volume of an Encyclopaedia and, in deference to the fact that the demand for it had come from Miss Van Vluyck, laid the ponderous tome before her.

There was a moment of painful suspense while Miss

Van Vluyck rubbed her spectacles, adjusted them, and turned to Z; and a murmur of surprise when she said: "It isn't here."

"I suppose," said Mrs. Plinth, "it's not fit to be put in a book of reference."

"Oh, nonsense!" exclaimed Mrs. Ballinger. "Try X."

Miss Van Vluyck turned back through the volume, peering short-sightedly up and down the pages, till she came to a stop and remained motionless, like a dog on a point.

"Well, have you found it?" Mrs. Ballinger enquired after a considerable delay.

"Yes. I've found it," said Miss Van Vluyck in a queer voice.

Mrs. Plinth hastily interposed: "I beg you won't read it aloud if there's anything offensive."

Miss Van Vluyck, without answering, continued her silent scrutiny.

"Well, what *is* it?" exclaimed Laura Glyde excitely.

"*Do* tell us!" urged Mrs. Leveret, feeling that she would have something awful to tell her sister.

Miss Van Vluyck pushed the volume aside and turned slowly toward the expectant group.

"It's a river."

"A *river*?"

"Yes: in Brazil. Isn't that where she's been living?"

"Who? Fanny Roby? Oh, but you must be mistaken. You've been reading the wrong thing," Mrs. Ballinger exclaimed, leaning over her to seize the volume.

"It's the only *Xingu* in the Encyclopaedia; and she *has* been living in Brazil," Miss Van Vluyck persisted.

"Yes: her brother has a consulship there," Mrs. Leveret interposed.

"But it's too ridiculous! I—we—why we *all* remember studying Xingu last year—or the year before last," Mrs. Ballinger stammered.

"I thought I did when *you* said so," Laura Glyde avowed.

"*I* said so?" cried Mrs. Ballinger.

"Yes. You said it had crowded everything else out of your mind."

"Well *you* said it had changed your whole life!"

"For that matter, Miss Van Vluyck said she had never grudged the time she'd given it."

Mrs. Plinth interposed: "I made it clear that I knew nothing whatever of the original."

Mrs. Ballinger broke off the dispute with a groan. "Oh, what does it all matter if she's been making fools of us? I believe Miss Van Vluyck's right—she was talking of the river all the while!"

"How could she? It's too preposterous," Miss Glyde exclaimed.

"Listen." Miss Van Vluyck had repossessed herself of the Encyclopaedia, and restored her spectacles to a nose reddened by excitement. " 'The Xingu, one of the principal rivers of Brazil, rises on the plateau of Mato Grosso, and flows in a northerly direction for a length of no less than one thousand one hundred and eighteen miles, entering the Amazon near the mouth of the latter river. The upper course of the Xingu is auriferous and fed by numerous branches. Its source was first discovered in 1884 by the German explorer von den Steinen, after a difficult and dangerous expedition through a region inhabited by tribes still in the Stone Age of culture.' "

The ladies received this communication in a state of stupefied silence from which Mrs. Leveret was the first to rally. "She certainly *did* speak of its having branches."

The word seemed to snap the last thread of their incredulity. "And of its great length," gasped Mrs. Ballinger.

"She said it was awfully deep, and you couldn't skip—you just had to wade through," Miss Glyde added.

The idea worked its way more slowly through Mrs. Plinth's compact resistances. "How could there be anything improper about a river?" she enquired.

"Improper?"

"Why, what she said about the source—that it was corrupt?"

"Not corrupt, but hard to get at," Laura Glyde corrected. "Some one who'd been there had told her so. I daresay it was the explorer himself—doesn't it say the expedition was dangerous?"

" 'Difficult and dangerous,' " read Miss Van Vluyck.

Mrs. Ballinger pressed her hands to her throbbing temples. "There's nothing she said that wouldn't apply to a river—to this river!" She swung about excitedly to the other members. "Why, do you remember her telling us that she hadn't read 'The Supreme Instant' because she'd taken it on a boating party while she was staying with her brother, and some one had 'shied' it overboard—'shied' of course was her own expression."

The ladies breathlessly signified that the expression had not escaped them.

"Well—and then didn't she tell Osric Dane that one of her books was simply saturated with Xingu? Of course it was, if one of Mrs. Roby's rowdy friends had thrown it into the river!"

This surprising reconstruction of the scene in which they had just participated left the members of the Lunch Club inarticulate. At length, Mrs. Plinth, after visibly labouring with the problem, said in a heavy tone: "Osric Dane was taken in too."

Mrs. Leveret took courage at this. "Perhaps that's what Mrs. Roby did it for. She said Osric Dane was a brute, and she may have wanted to give her a lesson."

Miss Van Vluyck frowned. "It was hardly worth while to do it at our expense."

"At least," said Miss Glyde with a touch of bitterness, "she succeeded in interesting her, which was more than we did."

"What chance had we?" rejoined Mrs. Ballinger. "Mrs. Roby monopolised her from the first. And *that*, I've no doubt, was her purpose—to give Osric Dane a false impression of her own standing in the club. She would hesitate at nothing to attract attention: we all know how she took in poor Professor Foreland."

"She actually makes him give bridge-teas every Thursday," Mrs. Leveret piped up.

Laura Glyde struck her hands together. "Why, this is Thursday, and it's *there* she's gone, of course; and taken Osric with her!"

"And they're shrieking over us at this moment," said Mrs. Ballinger between her teeth.

This possibility seemed too preposterous to be admitted. "She would hardly dare," said Miss Van Vluyck, "confess the imposture to Osric Dane."

"I'm not so sure: I thought I saw her make a sign as she left. If she hadn't made a sign, why should Osric Dane have rushed out after her?"

"Well, you know, we'd all been telling her how wonderful Xingu was, and she said she wanted to find out more about it," Mrs. Leveret said, with a tardy impulse of justice to the absent.

This reminder, far from mitigating the wrath of the other members, gave it a stronger impetus.

"Yes—and that's exactly what they're both laughing over now," said Laura Glyde ironically.

Mrs. Plinth stood up and gathered her expensive furs about her monumental form. "I have no wish to criticise," she said; "but unless the Lunch Club can protect its members against the recurrence of such—such unbecoming scenes, I for one—"

"Oh, so do I!" agreed Miss Glyde, rising also.

Miss Van Vluyck closed the Encyclopaedia and proceeded to button herself into her jacket. "My time is really too valuable—" she began.

"I fancy we are all of one mind," said Mrs. Ballinger, looking searchingly at Mrs. Leveret, who looked at the others.

"I always deprecate anything like a scandal—" Mrs. Plinth continued.

"She has been the cause of one to-day!" exclaimed Miss Glyde.

Mrs. Leveret moaned: "I don't see how she *could*!" and Miss Van Vluyck said, picking up her note-book: "Some women stop at nothing."

"—but if," Mrs. Plinth took up her argument impressively, "anything of the kind had happened in *my* house" (it never would have, her tone implied), "I should have felt that I owed it to myself either to ask for Mrs. Roby's resignation—or to offer mine."

"Oh, Mrs. Plinth—" gasped the Lunch Club.

"Fortunately for me," Mrs. Plinth continued with an awful magnanimity, "the matter was taken out of my hands by our President's decision that the right to entertain distinguished guests was a privilege vested in her office; and I think the other members will agree that, as she was alone in this opinion, she ought to be alone in deciding on the best way of effacing its—its really deplorable consequences."

A deep silence followed this outbreak of Mrs. Plinth's long-stored resentment.

"I don't see why *I* should be expected to ask her to resign—" Mrs. Ballinger at length began; but Laura Glyde turned back to remind her: "You know she made you say that you'd got on swimmingly in Xingu."

An ill-timed giggle escaped from Mrs. Leveret, and Mrs. Ballinger energetically continued "—but you needn't think for a moment that I'm afraid to!"

The door of the drawing-room closed on the retreating backs of the Lunch Club, and the President of that distinguished association, seating herself at her writing-table, and pushing away a copy of "The Wings of Death" to make room for her elbow, drew forth a sheet of the club's note-paper, on which she began to write: "My dear Mrs. Roby—"

THE OTHER TWO

I.

WAYTHORN, ON the drawing-room hearth, waited for his wife to come down to dinner.

It was their first night under his own roof, and he was surprised at his thrill of boyish agitation. He was not so old, to be sure—his glass gave him little more than the five-and-thirty years to which his wife confessed—but he had fancied himself already in the temperate zone; yet here he was listening for her step with a tender sense of all it symbolised, with some old trail of verse about the garlanded nuptial door-posts floating through his enjoyment of the pleasant room and the good dinner just beyond it.

They had been hastily recalled from their honeymoon by the illness of Lily Haskett, the child of Mrs. Waythorn's first marriage. The little girl, at Waythorn's desire, had been transferred to his house on the day of her mother's wedding, and the doctor, on their arrival, broke the news that she was ill with typhoid, but declared that all the symptoms were favourable. Lily could show twelve years of unblemished health, and the case promised to be a light one. The nurse spoke as reassuringly, and after a moment of alarm Mrs.

Waythorn had adjusted herself to the situation. She was very fond of Lily—her affection for the child had perhaps been her decisive charm in Waythorn's eyes—but she had the perfectly balanced nerves which her little girl had inherited, and no woman ever wasted less tissue in unproductive worry. Waythorn was therefore quite prepared to see her come in presently, a little late because of a last look at Lily, but as serene and well-appointed as if her goodnight kiss had been laid on the brow of health. Her composure was restful to him; it acted as ballast to his somewhat unstable sensibilities. As he pictured her bending over the child's bed he thought how soothing her presence must be in illness: her very step would prognosticate recovery.

His own life had been a gray one, from temperament rather than circumstance, and he had been drawn to her by the unperturbed gaiety which kept her fresh and elastic at an age when most women's activities are growing either slack or febrile. He knew what was said about her; for, popular as she was, there had always been a faint undercurrent of detraction. When she had appeared in New York, nine or ten years earlier, as the pretty Mrs. Haskett whom Gus Varick had unearthed somewhere—was it in Pittsburgh or Utica?—society, while promptly accepting her, had reserved the right to cast a doubt on its own indiscrimination. Enquiry, however, established her undoubted connection with a socially reigning family, and explained her recent divorce as the natural result of a runaway match at seventeen; and as nothing was known of Mr. Haskett it was easy to believe the worst of him.

Alice Haskett's remarriage with Gus Varick was a passport to the set whose recognition she coveted, and for a few years the Varicks were the most popular couple in town. Unfortunately, the alliance was brief and stormy, and this time the husband had his champions. Still, even Varick's staunchest supporters admitted that he was not meant for matrimony, and Mrs. Varick's grievances were of a nature to bear the inspection of the New York courts. A New York divorce is in itself a diploma of virture, and in the semi-widowhood of this second separation Mrs. Varick took on an air of sanctity, and was allowed to confide her wrongs to some of the most scrupulous ears in town. But when it was known that she was to marry Waythorn there was a momentary reaction. Her best friends would have preferred to see her remain in the rôle of the injured wife, which was as becoming to her as crape to a rosy complexion. True, a decent time had elapsed, and it was not even suggested that Waythorn had supplanted his predecessor. People shook their heads over him, however, and one grudging friend, to whom he affirmed that he took the step with his eyes open, replied oracularly: "Yes—and with your ears shut."

Waythorn could afford to smile at these innuendoes. In the Wall Street phrase, he had "discounted" them. He knew that society has not yet adapted itself to the consequences of divorce, and that till the adaptation takes place every woman who uses the freedom the law accords her must be her own social justification. Waythorn had an amused confidence in his wife's ability to justify herself. His expectations were fulfilled, and before the wedding took place Alice Varick's group had rallied openly to her support. She took it all imperturbably: she had a way of surmounting obstacles without seeming to be aware of them, and Waythorn looked back with wonder at the trivialities over which he had worn his nerves thin. He had the sense of having found refuge in a richer, warmer nature than his own, and his satisfaction, at the moment, was humorously summed up in the thought that his wife, when she had done all she could for Lily, would not be ashamed to come down and enjoy a good dinner.

The anticipation of such enjoyment was not, however, the sentiment expressed by Mrs. Waythorn's charming face when she presently joined him. Though she had put on her most engaging tea-gown she had neglected to assume the smile that went with it, and Waythorn thought he had never seen her look so nearly worried.

"What is it?" he asked. "Is anything wrong with Lily?"

"No; I've just been in and she's still sleeping." Mrs. Waythorn hesitated. "But something tiresome has happened."

He had taken her two hands, and now perceived that he was crushing a paper between them.

"This letter?"

"Yes—Mr. Haskett has written—I mean his lawyer has written."

Waythorn felt himself flush uncomfortably. He dropped his wife's hands.

"What about?"

"About seeing Lily. You know the courts—"

"Yes, yes," he interrupted nervously.

Nothing was known about Haskett in New York. He was vaguely supposed to have remained in the outer darkness from which his wife had been rescued, and Waythorn was one of the few who were aware that he had given up his business in Utica and followed her to New York in order to be near his little girl. In the days of his wooing, Waythorn had often met Lily on the doorstep, rosy and smiling, on her way "to see papa."

"I am so sorry," Mrs. Waythorn murmured.

He roused himself. "What does he want?"

"He wants to see her. You know she goes to him once a week."

"Well—he doesn't expect her to go to him now, does he?"

"No—he has heard of her illness; but he expects to come here."

"*Here?*"

Mrs. Waythorn reddened under his gaze. They looked away from each other.

"I'm afraid he has the right. . . . You'll see. . . ." She made a proffer of the letter.

Waythorn moved away with a gesture of refusal. He stood staring about the softly lighted room, which a moment before had seemed so full of bridal intimacy.

"I'm so sorry," she repeated. "If Lily could have been moved—"

"That's out of the question," he returned impatiently.

"I suppose so."

Her lip was beginning to tremble, and he felt himself a brute.

"He must come, of course," he said. "When is—his day?"

"I'm afraid—to-morrow."

"Very well. Send a note in the morning."

The butler entered to announce dinner.

Waythorn turned to his wife. "Come—you must be tired. It's beastly, but try to forget about it," he said, drawing her hand through his arm.

"You're so good, dear. I'll try," she whispered back.

Her face cleared at once, and as she looked at him across the flowers, between the rosy candle-shades, he saw her lips waver back into a smile.

"How pretty everything is!" she sighed luxuriously.

He turned to the butler. "The champagne at once, please. Mrs. Waythorn is tired."

In a moment or two their eyes met above the sparkling glasses. Her own were quite clear and untroubled: he saw that she had obeyed his injunction and forgotten.

II.

WAYTHORN, THE next morning, went down town earlier than usual. Haskett was not likely to come till the afternoon, but the instinct of flight drove him forth. He meant to stay away all day—he had thoughts of dining at his club. As his door closed behind him he reflected that before he opened it again it would have admitted another man who had as much right to enter it as himself, and the thought filled him with a physical repugnance.

He caught the "elevated" at the employees' hour, and found himself crushed between two layers of pendulous humanity. At Eighth Street the man facing him wriggled out, and another took his place. Waythorn glanced up and saw that it was Gus Varick. The men were so close together that it was impossible to ignore the smile of recognition on Varick's handsome overblown face. And after all—why not? They had always been on good terms, and Varick had been divorced before Waythorn's attentions to his wife began. The two exchanged a word on the perennial grievance of the congested trains, and when a seat at their side was miraculously left empty the instinct of self-preservation made Waythorn slip into it after Varick.

The latter drew the stout man's breath of relief. "Lord—I was beginning to feel like a pressed flower." He leaned back, looking unconcernedly at Waythorn. "Sorry to hear that Sellers is knocked out again."

"Sellers?" echoed Waythorn, starting at his partner's name.

Varick looked surprised. "You didn't know he was laid up with the gout?"

"No. I've been away—I only got back last night." Waythorn felt himself reddening in anticipation of the other's smile.

"Ah—yes; to be sure. And Sellers's attack came on two days ago. I'm afraid he's pretty bad. Very awkward for me, as it happens, because he was just putting through a rather important thing for me."

"Ah?" Waythorn wondered vaguely since when Varick had been dealing in "important things." Hitherto he had dabbled only in the shallow pools of speculation, with which Waythorn's office did not usually concern itself.

It occurred to him that Varick might be talking at random, to relieve the strain of their propinquity. That strain was becoming momentarily more apparent to Waythorn, and when, at Cortlandt Street, he caught sight of an acquaintance and had a sudden vision of the picture he and Varick must present to an initiated eye, he jumped up with a muttered excuse.

"I hope you'll find Sellers better," said Varick civilly, and he stammered back: "If I can be of any use to you—" and let the departing crowd sweep him to the platform.

At his office he heard that Sellers was in fact ill with the gout, and would probably not be able to leave the house for some weeks.

"I'm sorry it should have happened so, Mr. Waythorn," the senior clerk said with affable significance. "Mr. Sellers was very much upset at the idea of giving you such a lot of extra work just now."

"Oh, that's no matter," said Waythorn hastily. He secretly welcomed the pressure of additional business, and was glad to think that, when the day's work was over, he would have to call at his partner's on the way home.

He was late for luncheon, and turned in at the nearest restaurant instead of going to his club. The place was full, and the waiter hurried him to the back of the room to capture the only vacant table. In the cloud of cigar-smoke Waythorn did not at once distinguish his neighbours; but presently, looking about him, he saw Varick seated a few feet off. This time, luckily, they were too far apart for conversation, and Varick, who faced another way, had probably not even seen him; but there was an irony in their renewed nearness.

Varick was said to be fond of good living, and as Waythorn sat despatching his hurried luncheon he looked across half enviously at the other's leisurely degustation of his meal. When Waythorn first saw him he had been helping himself with critical deliberation to a bit of Camembert at the ideal point of liquefaction, and now, the cheese removed, he was just pouring his *café double* from its little two-storied earthen pot. He poured slowly, his ruddy profile bent above the task, and one beringed white hand steadying the lid of the coffee-pot; then he stretched his other hand to the decanter of cognac at his elbow, filled a liqueur-glass, took a tentative sip, and poured the brandy into his coffee-cup.

Waythorn watched him in a kind of fascination. What was he thinking of—only of the flavour of the coffee and the liqueur? Had the morning's meeting left no more trace in his thoughts than on his face? Had his wife so completely passed out of his life that even this odd encounter with her present husband, within a week after her remarriage, was no more than an incident in his day? And as Waythorn mused, another idea struck him: had Haskett ever met Varick as Varick and he had just met? The recollection of Haskett perturbed him, and he rose and left the restaurant, taking a circuitous way out to escape the placid irony of Varick's nod.

It was after seven when Waythorn reached home. He thought the footman who opened the door looked at him oddly.

"How is Miss Lily?" he asked in haste.

"Doing very well, sir. A gentleman—"

"Tell Barlow to put off dinner for half an hour," Waythorn cut him off, hurrying upstairs.

He went straight to his room and dressed without seeing his wife. When he reached the drawing-room she was there, fresh and radiant. Lily's day had been good; the doctor was not coming back that evening.

At dinner Waythorn told her of Seller's illness and of the resulting complications. She listened sympathetically, adjuring him not to let himself be overworked, and asking vague feminine questions about the routine of the office. Then she gave him the chronicle of Lily's day; quoted the nurse and doctor, and told him who had called to inquire. He had never seen her more serene and unruffled. It struck him, with a curious pang, that she was very happy in being with him, so happy that she found a childish pleasure in rehearsing the trivial incidents of her day.

After dinner they went to the library, and the servant

put the coffee and liqueurs on a low table before her and
left the room. She looked singularly soft and girlish in
her rosy pale dress, against the dark leather of one of his
bachelor armchairs. A day earlier the contrast would
have charmed him.

He turned away now, choosing a cigar with affected
deliberation.

"Did Haskett come?" he asked, with his back to her.

"Oh, yes—he came."

"You didn't see him, of course?"

She hesitated a moment. "I let the nurse see him."

That was all. There was nothing more to ask. He
swung round toward her, applying a match to his cigar.
Well, the thing was over for a week, at any rate. He
would try not to think of it. She looked up at him, a
trifle rosier than usual, with a smile in her eyes.

"Ready for your coffee, dear?"

He leaned against the mantelpiece, watching her as
she lifted the coffee-pot. The lamplight struck a gleam
from her bracelets and tipped her soft hair with brightness. How light and slender she was, and how each
gesture flowed into the next! She seemed a creature all
compact of harmonies. As the thought of Haskett
receded, Waythorn felt himself yielding again to the joy
of possessorship. They were his, those white hands with
their flitting motions, his the light haze of hair, the lips
and eyes. . . .

She set down the coffee-pot, and reaching for the
decanter of cognac, measured off a liqueur-glass and
poured it into his cup.

Waythorn uttered a sudden exclamation.

"What is the matter?" she said, startled.

"Nothing; only—I don't take cognac in my coffee."

"Oh, how stupid of me," she cried.

Their eyes met, and she blushed a sudden agonised
red.

III.

TEN DAYS later, Mr. Sellers, still house-bound, asked Waythorn to call on his way down town.

The senior partner, with his swaddled foot propped up by the fire, greeted his associate with an air of embarrassment.

"I'm sorry, my dear fellow; I've got to ask you to do an awkward thing for me."

Waythorn waited, and the other went on, after a pause apparently given to the arrangement of his phrases: "The fact is, when I was knocked out I had just gone into a rather complicated piece of business for—Gus Varick."

"Well?" said Waythorn, with an attempt to put him at his ease.

"Well—it's this way: Varick came to me the day before my attack. He had evidently had an inside tip from somebody, and had made about a hundred thousand. He came to me for advice, and I suggested his going in with Vanderlyn."

"Oh, the deuce!" Waythorn exclaimed. He saw in a flash what had happened. The investment was an alluring one, but required negotiation. He listened quietly while Sellers put the case before him, and, the statement ended, he said: "You think I ought to see Varick?"

"I'm afraid I can't as yet. The doctor is obdurate. And this thing can't wait. I hate to ask you, but no one else in the office knows the ins and outs of it."

Waythorn stood silent. He did not care a farthing for the success of Varick's venture, but the honour of the office was to be considered, and he could hardly refuse to oblige his partner.

"Very well," he said, "I'll do it."

That afternoon, apprised by telephone, Varick called at the office. Waythorn, waiting in his private room, wondered what the others thought of it. The newspapers, at the time of Mrs. Waythorn's marriage, had

acquainted their readers with every detail of her
previous matrimonial ventures, and Waythorn could
fancy the clerks smiling behind Varick's back as he was
ushered in.

Varick bore himself admirably. He was easy without
being undignified, and Waythorn was conscious of cut-
ting a much less impressive figure. Varick had no experience of business, and the talk prolonged itself for
nearly an hour while Waythorn set forth with scrupulous precision the details of the proposed transaction.

"I'm awfully obliged to you," Varick said as he rose.
"The fact is I'm not used to having much money to look
after, and I don't want to make an ass of myself—" He
smiled, and Waythorn could not help noticing that there
was something pleasant about his smile. "It feels uncommonly queer to have enough cash to pay one's bills.
I'd have sold my soul for it a few years ago!"

Waythorn winced at the allusion. He had heard it
rumoured that a lack of funds had been one of the
determining causes of the Varick separation, but it did
not occur to him that Varick's words were intentional.
It seemed more likely that the desire to keep clear of embarrassing topics had fatally drawn him into one.
Waythorn did not wish to be outdone in civility.

"We'll do the best we can for you," he said. "I think
this is a good thing you're in."

"Oh, I'm sure it's immense. It's awfully good of
you—" Varick broke off, embarrassed. "I suppose the
thing's settled now—but if—"

"If anything happens before Sellers is about, I'll see
you again," said Waythorn quietly. He was glad, in the
end, to appear the more self-possessed of the two.

.   .   .   .

The course of Lily's illness ran smooth, and as the
days passed Waythorn grew used to the idea of
Haskett's weekly visit. The first time the day came
round, he stayed out late, and questioned his wife as to

the visit on his return. She replied at once that Haskett had merely seen the nurse downstairs, as the doctor did not wish any one in the child's sick-room till after the crisis.

The following week Waythorn was again conscious of the recurrence of the day, but had forgotten it by the time he came home to dinner. The crisis of the disease came a few days later, with a rapid decline of fever, and the little girl was pronounced out of danger. In the rejoicing which ensued the thought of Haskett passed out of Waythorn's mind, and one afternoon, letting himself into the house with a latchkey, he went straight to his library without noticing a shabby hat and umbrella in the hall.

In the library he found a small effaced-looking man with a thinnish gray beard sitting on the edge of a chair. The stranger might have been a piano-tuner, or one of those mysteriously efficient persons who are summoned in emergencies to adjust some detail of the domestic machinery. He blinked at Waythorn through a pair of gold-rimmed spectacles and said mildly: "Mr. Waythorn, I presume? I am Lily's father."

Waythorn flushed. "Oh—" he stammered uncomfortably. He broke off, disliking to appear rude. Inwardly he was trying to adjust the actual Haskett to the image of him projected by his wife's reminiscences. Waythorn had been allowed to infer that Alice's first husband was a brute.

"I am sorry to intrude," said Haskett, with his over-the-counter politeness.

"Don't mention it," returned Waythorn, collecting himself. "I suppose the nurse has been told?"

"I presume so. I can wait," said Haskett. He had a resigned way of speaking, as though life had worn down his natural powers of resistance.

Waythorn stood on the threshold, nervously pulling off his gloves.

"I'm sorry you've been detained. I will send for the nurse," he said; and as he opened the door he added with an effort: "I'm glad we can give you a good report of Lily." He winced as the *we* slipped out, but Haskett seemed not to notice it.

"Thank you, Mr. Waythorn. It's been an anxious time for me."

"Ah, well, that's past. Soon she'll be able to go to you." Waythorn nodded and passed out.

In his own room he flung himself down with a groan. He hated the womanish sensibility which made him suffer so acutely from the grotesque chances of life. He had known when he married that his wife's former husbands were both living, and that amid the multiplied contacts of modern existence there were a thousand chances to one that he would run against one or the other, yet he found himself as much disturbed by his brief encounter with Haskett as though the law had not obligingly removed all difficulties in the way of their meeting.

Waythorn sprang up and began to pace the room nervously. He had not suffered half as much from his two meetings with Varick. It was Haskett's presence in his own house that made the situation so intolerable. He stood still, hearing steps in the passage.

"This way, please," he heard the nurse say. Haskett was being taken upstairs, then: not a corner of the house but was open to him. Waythorn dropped into another chair, staring vaguely ahead of him. On his dressing-table stood a photograph of Alice, taken when he had first known her. She was Alice Varick then—now fine and exquisite he had thought her! Those were Varick's pearls about her neck. At Waythorn's instance they had been returned before her marriage. Had Haskett ever given her any trinkets—and what had become of them, Waythorn wondered? He realised suddenly that he knew very little of Haskett's past or present situation; but from the man's appearance and manner of speech he could reconstruct with curious precision the surroundings of Alice's first marriage. And it startled him to think that she had, in the background of her life, a phase of existence so different from anything with which he had connected her. Varick, whatever his faults, was a gentleman, in the conventional, traditional sense of the term: the sense which at that moment seemed, oddly enough, to have most meaning to Waythorn. He and Varick had the same social habits, spoke the same language, understood the same allusions. But this other man . . . it was grotesquely uppermost in Waythorn's mind that Haskett had worn a made-up tie attached with an elastic. Why should that ridiculous detail symbolise the whole man? Waythorn was exasperated by his own paltriness, but the fact of the tie expanded, forced itself on him, became as it were the key to Alice's past. He could see her, as Mrs. Haskett, sitting in a "front parlour" furnished in plush, with a pianola, and a copy of "Ben Hur" on the centre-table. He could see her going to the theatre with Haskett—or perhaps even to a "Church Sociable"—she in a "picture hat" and Haskett in a black frock-coat, a little creased, with the made-up tie on an elastic. On the way home they would stop and look at the illuminated shop-windows, lingering over the photographs of New York actresses. On Sunday afternoons Haskett would take her for a walk, pushing Lily ahead of them in a white enamelled perambulator, and Waythorn had a vision of the people they would stop and talk to. He could fancy how pretty Alice must have looked, in a dress adroitly constructed from the hints of a New York fashion-paper, and how she must have looked down on the other women, chafing at her life, and secretly feeling that she belonged in a bigger place.

For the moment his foremost thought was one of wonder at the way in which she had shed the phase of existence which her marriage with Haskett implied. It was as if her whole aspect, every gesture, every inflection, every allusion, were a studied negation of that period of her life. If she had denied being married to Haskett she could hardly have stood more convicted of duplicity than in this obliteration of the self which had been his wife.

Waythorn started up, checking himself in the analysis

of her motives. What right had he to create a fantastic effigy of her and then pass judgment on it? She had spoken vaguely of her first marriage as unhappy, had hinted, with becoming reticence, that Haskett had wrought havoc among her young illusions. . . . It was a pity for Waythorn's peace of mind that Haskett's very inoffensiveness shed a new light on the nature of those illusions. A man would rather think that his wife has been brutalised by her first husband than that the process has been reversed.

IV.

"MR. WAYTHORN, I don't like that French governess of Lily's."

Haskett, subdued and apologetic, stood before Waythorn in the library, revolving his shabby hat in his hand.

Waythorn, surprised in his armchair over the evening paper, stared back perplexedly at his visitor.

"You'll excuse my asking to see you," Haskett continued. "But this is my last visit, and I thought if I could have a word with you it would be a better way than writing to Mrs. Waythorn's lawyer."

Waythorn rose uneasily. He did not like the French governess either; but that was irrelevant.

"I am not so sure of that," he returned stiffly; "but since you wish it I will give your message to—my wife." He always hesitated over the possessive pronoun in addressing Haskett.

The latter sighed. "I don't know as that will help much. She didn't like it when I spoke to her."

Waythorn turned red. "When did you see her?" he asked.

"Not since the first day I came to see Lily—right after she was taken sick. I remarked to her then that I didn't like the governess."

Waythorn made no answer. He remembered distinctly that, after that first visit, he had asked his wife if she had seen Haskett. She had lied to him then, but she had respected his wishes since; and the incident cast a curious light on her character. He was sure she would not have seen Haskett that first day if she had divined that Waythorn would object, and the fact that she did not divine it was almost as disagreeable to the latter as the discovery that she had lied to him.

"I don't like the woman," Haskett was repeating with mild persistency. "She ain't straight, Mr. Waythorn—she'll teach the child to be underhand. I've noticed a change in Lily—she's too anxious to please—and she don't always tell the truth. She used to be the straightest child, Mr. Waythorn—" He broke off, his voice a little thick. "Not but what I want her to have a stylish education," he ended.

Waythorn was touched. "I'm sorry, Mr. Haskett; but frankly, I don't quite see what I can do."

Haskett hesitated. Then he laid his hat on the table, and advanced to the hearth-rug, on which Waythorn was standing. There was nothing aggressive in his manner, but he had the solemnity of a timid man resolved on a decisive measure.

"There's just one thing you can do, Mr. Waythorn," he said. "You can remind Mrs. Waythorn that, by the decree of the courts, I am entitled to have a voice in Lily's bringing up." He paused, and went on more deprecatingly: "I'm not the kind to talk about enforcing my rights, Mr. Waythorn. I don't know as I think a man is entitled to rights he hasn't known how to hold on to; but this business of the child is different. I've never let go there—and I never mean to."

.   .   .   .

The scene left Waythorn deeply shaken. Shame-

facedly, in indirect ways, he had been finding out about
Haskett; and all that he had learned was favourable.
The little man, in order to be near his daughter, had sold
out his share in a profitable business in Utica, and accepted a modest clerkship in a New York manufacturing
house. He boarded in a shabby street and had few
acquaintances. His passion for Lily filled his life.
Waythorn felt that this exploration of Haskett was like
groping about with a dark-lantern in his wife's past; but
he saw now that there were recesses his lantern had not
explored. He had never enquired into the exact circumstances of his wife's first matrimonial rupture. On
the surface all had been fair. It was she who had ob-
tained the divorce, and the court had given her the child.
But Waythorn knew how many ambiguities such a verdict might cover. The mere fact that Haskett retained a
right over his daughter implied an unsuspected compromise. Waythorn was an idealist. He always refused
to recognise unpleasant contingencies till he found himself confronted with them, and then he saw them
followed by a spectral train of consequences. His next
days were thus haunted, and he determined to try to lay
the ghosts by conjuring them up in his wife's presence.

When he repeated Haskett's request a flame of anger
passed over her face; but she subdued it instantly and
spoke with a slight quiver of outraged motherhood.

"It is very ungentlemanly of him," she said.

The word grated on Waythorn. "That is neither here
nor there. It's a bare question of rights."

She murmured: "It's not as if he could ever be a help
to Lily—"

Waythorn flushed. This was even less to his taste.
"The question is," he repeated, "what authority has he
over her?"

She looked downward, twisting herself a little in her
seat. "I am willing to see him—I thought you objected," she faltered.

In a flash he understood that she knew the extent of
Haskett's claims. Perhaps it was not the first time she
had resisted them.

"My objecting has nothing to do with it," he said coldly; "if Haskett has a right to be consulted you must consult him."

She burst into tears, and he saw that she expected him to regard her as a victim.

Haskett did not abuse his rights. Waythorn had felt miserably sure that he would not. But the governess was dismissed, and from time to time the little man demanded an interview with Alice. After the first outburst she accepted the situation with her usual adaptability. Haskett had once reminded Waythorn of the piano-tuner, and Mrs. Waythorn, after a month or two, appeared to class him with that domestic familiar. Waythorn could not but respect the father's tenacity. At first he had tried to cultivate the suspicion that Haskett might be "up to" something, that he had an object in securing a foothold in the house. But in his heart Waythorn was sure of Haskett's single-mindedness; he even guessed in the latter a mild contempt for such advantages as his relation with the Waythorns might offer. Haskett's sincerity of purpose made him invulnerable, and his successor had to accept him as a lien on the property.

. . . .

Mr. Sellers was sent to Europe to recover from his gout, and Varick's affairs hung on Waythorn's hands. The negotiations were prolonged and complicated; they necessitated frequent conferences between the two men, and the interests of the firm forbade Waythorn's suggesting that his client should transfer his business to another office.

Varick appeared well in the transaction. In moments of relaxation his coarse streak appeared, and Waythorn dreaded his geniality; but in the office he was concise and clear-headed, with a flattering deference to Waythorn's judgment. Their business relations being so affably established, it would have been absurd for the two men to ignore each other in society. The first time they met in a drawing-room, Varick took up their intercourse in the same easy key, and his hostess's grateful glance obliged Waythorn to respond to it. After that they ran across each other frequently, and one evening at a ball Waythorn, wandering through the remoter rooms, came upon Varick seated beside his wife. She coloured a little, and faltered in what she was saying; but Varick nodded to Waythorn without rising, and the latter strolled on.

In the carriage, on the way home, he broke out nervously: "I didn't know you spoke to Varick."

Her voice trembled a little. "It's the first time—he happened to be standing near me; I didn't know what to do. It's so awkward, meeting everywhere—and he said you had been very kind about some business."

"That's different," said Waythorn.

She paused a moment. "I'll do just as you wish," she returned pliantly. "I thought it would be less awkward to speak to him when we meet."

Her pliancy was beginning to sicken him. Had she really no will of her own—no theory about her relation to these men? She had accepted Haskett—did she mean to accept Varick? It was "less awkward," as she had said, and her instinct was to evade difficulties or to circumvent them. With sudden vividness Waythorn saw how the instinct had developed. She was "as easy as an old shoe"—a shoe that too many feet had worn. Her elasticity was the result of tension in too many different directions. Alice Haskett—Alice Varick—Alice Waythorn—she had been each in turn, and had left hanging to each name a little of her privacy, a little of her personality, a little of the inmost self where the unknown god abides.

"Yes—it's better to speak to Varick," said Waythorn wearily.

V.

THE WINTER wore on, and society took advantage of the Waythorns' acceptance of Varick. Harassed hostesses were grateful to them for bridging over a social difficulty, and Mrs. Waythorn was held up as a miracle of good taste. Some experimental spirits could not resist the diversion of throwing Varick and his former wife together, and there were those who thought he found a zest in the propinquity. But Mrs. Waythorn's conduct remained irreproachable. She neither avoided Varick nor sought him out. Even Waythorn could not but admit that she had discovered the solution of the newest social problem.

He had married her without giving much thought to that problem. He had fancied that a woman can shed her past like a man. But now he saw that Alice was bound to hers both by the circumstances which forced her into continued relation with it, and by the traces it had left on her nature. With grim irony Waythorn compared himself to a member of a syndicate. He held so many shares in his wife's personality and his predecessors were his partners in the business. If there had been any element of passion in the transaction he would have felt less deteriorated by it. The fact that Alice took her change of husbands like a change of weather reduced the situation to mediocrity. He could have forgiven her for blunders, for excesses; for resisting Haskett, for yielding to Varick; for anything but her acquiescence and her tact. She reminded him of a juggler tossing knives; but the knives were blunt and she knew they would never cut her.

And then, gradually, habit formed a protecting surface for his sensibilities. If he paid for each day's comfort with the small change of his illusions, he grew daily to value the comfort more and set less store upon the coin. He had drifted into a dulling propinquity with Haskett and Varick and he took refuge in the cheap revenge of satirising the situation. He even began to reckon up the advantages which accrued from it, to ask himself if it were not better to own a third of a wife who knew how to make a man happy than a whole one who had lacked opportunity to acquire the art. For it *was* an art, and made up, like all others, of concessions, eliminations and embellishments; of lights judiciously thrown and shadows skilfully softened. His wife knew exactly how to manage the lights, and he knew exactly to what training she owed her skill. He even tried to trace the source of his obligations, to discriminate between the influences which had combined to produce his domestic happiness: he perceived that Haskett's commonness had made Alice worship good breeding, while Varick's liberal construction of the marriage bond had taught her to value the conjugal virtues; so that he was directly indebted to his predecessors for the devotion which made his life easy if not inspiring.

From this phase he passed into that of complete acceptance. He ceased to satirise himself because time dulled the irony of the situation and the joke lost its humour with its sting. Even the sight of Haskett's hat on the hall table had ceased to touch the springs of epigram. The hat was often seen there now, for it had been decided that it was better for Lily's father to visit her than for the little girl to go to his boarding-house. Waythorn, having acquiesced in this arrangement, had been surprised to find how little difference it made. Haskett was never obtrusive, and the few visitors who met him on the stairs were unaware of his identity. Waythorn did not know how often he saw Alice, but with himself Haskett was seldom in contact.

One afternoon, however, he learned on entering that Lily's father was waiting to see him. In the library he found Haskett occupying a chair in his usual provisional way. Waythorn always felt grateful to him for not leaning back.

"I hope you'll excuse me, Mr. Waythorn," he said rising. "I wanted to see Mrs. Waythorn about Lily, and your man asked me to wait here till she came in."

"Of course," said Waythorn, remembering that a

sudden leak had that morning given over the drawing-room to the plumbers.

He opened his cigar-case and held it out to his visitor, and Haskett's acceptance seemed to mark a fresh stage in their intercourse. The spring evening was chilly, and Waythorn invited his guest to draw up his chair to the fire. He meant to find an excuse to leave Haskett in a moment; but he was tired and cold, and after all the little man no longer jarred on him.

The two were enclosed in the intimacy of their blended cigar-smoke when the door opened and Varick walked into the room. Waythorn rose abruptly. It was the first time that Varick had come to the house, and the surprise of seeing him, combined with the singular inopportuneness of his arrival, gave a new edge to Waythorn's blunted sensibilities. He stared at his visitor without speaking.

Varick seemed too preoccupied to notice his host's embarrassment.

"My dear fellow," he exclaimed in his most expansive tone, "I must apologise for tumbling in on you in this way, but I was too late to catch you down town, and so I thought—"

He stopped short, catching sight of Haskett, and his sanguine colour deepened to a flush which spread vividly under his scant blond hair. But in a moment he recovered himself and nodded slightly. Haskett returned the bow in silence, and Waythorn was still groping for speech when the footman came in carrying a tea-table.

The intrusion offered a welcome vent to Waythorn's nerves. "What the deuce are you bringing this here for?" he said sharply.

"I beg your pardon, sir, but the plumbers are still in the drawing-room, and Mrs. Waythorn said she would have tea in the library." The footman's perfectly respectful tone implied a reflection on Waythorn's reasonableness.

"Oh, very well," said the latter resignedly, and the footman proceeded to open the folding tea-table and set out its complicated appointments. While this in-

terminable process continued the three men stood
motionless, watching it with a fascinated stare, till
Waythorn, to break the silence, said to Varick: "Won't
you have a cigar?"

He held out the case he had just tendered to Haskett,
and Varick helped himself with a smile. Waythorn
looked about for a match, and finding none, proffered
a light from his own cigar. Haskett, in the background,
held his ground mildly, examining his cigar-tip now and
then, and stepping forward at the right moment to
knock its ashes into the fire.

The footman at last withdrew, and Varick immediately began: "If I could just say half a word to you
about this business—"

"Certainly," stammered Waythorn; "in the dining-
room—"

But as he placed his hand on the door it opened from
without, and his wife appeared on the threshold.

She came in fresh and smiling, in her street dress and
hat, shedding a fragrance from the boa which she
loosened in advancing.

"Shall we have tea in here, dear?" she began; and
then she caught sight of Varick. Her smile deepened,
veiling a slight tremor of surprise.

"Why, how do you do?" she said with a distinct note
of pleasure.

As she shook hands with Varick she saw Haskett
standing behind him. Her smile faded for a moment,
but she recalled it quickly, with a scarcely perceptible
side-glance at Waythorn.

"How do you do, Mr. Haskett?" she said, and shook
hands with him a shade less cordially.

The three men stood awkwardly before her, till
Varick, always the most self-possessed, dashed into an
explanatory phrase.

"We—I had to see Waythorn a moment on business," he stammered, brick-red from chin to nape.

Haskett stepped forward with his air of mild obstinacy. "I am sorry to intrude; but you appointed five

o'clock"—he directed his resigned glance to the timepiece on the mantel.

She swept aside their embarrassment with a charming gesture of hospitality.

"I'm so sorry—I'm always late; but the afternoon was so lovely." She stood drawing off her gloves, propitiatory and graceful, diffusing about her a sense of ease and familiarity in which the situation lost its grotesqueness. "But before talking business," she added brightly, "I'm sure every one wants a cup of tea."

She dropped into her low chair by the tea-table, and the two visitors, as if drawn by her smile, advanced to receive the cups she held out.

She glanced about for Waythorn, and he took the third cup with a laugh.

SOULS BELATED

I.

THEIR RAILWAY-CARRIAGE had been full when the train left Bologna; but at the first station beyond Milan their only remaining companion—a courtly person who ate garlic out of a carpet-bag—had left his crumb-strewn seat with a bow.

Lydia's eye regretfully followed the shiny broadcloth of his retreating back till it lost itself in the cloud of touts and cab-drivers hanging about the station; then she glanced across at Gannett and caught the same regret in his look. They were both sorry to be alone.

"*Par-ten-za!*" shouted the guard. The train vibrated to a sudden slamming of doors; a waiter ran along the platform with a tray of fossilized sandwiches; a belated porter flung a bundle of shawls and band-boxes into a third-class carriage; the guard snapped out a brief *Partenza!* which indicated the purely ornamental nature of his first shout; and the train swung out of the station.

The direction of the road had changed, and a shaft of sunlight struck across the dusty red velvet seats into Lydia's corner. Gannett did not notice it. He had returned to his *Revue de Paris*, and she had to rise and lower the shade of the farther window. Against the vast

68

horizon of their leisure such incidents stood out sharply.

Having lowered the shade, Lydia sat down, leaving the length of the carriage between herself and Gannett. At length he missed her and looked up.

"I moved out of the sun," she hastily explained.

He looked at her curiously: the sun was beating on her through the shade.

"Very well," he said pleasantly; adding, "You don't mind?" as he drew a cigarette-case from his pocket.

It was a refreshing touch, relieving the tension of her spirit with the suggestion that, after all, if he could *smoke*—! The relief was only momentary. Her experience of smokers was limited (her husband had disapproved of the use of tobacco) but she knew from hearsay that men sometimes smoked to get away from things; that a cigar might be the masculine equivalent of darkened windows and a headache. Gannett, after a puff or two, returned to his review.

It was just as she had foreseen; he feared to speak as much as she did. It was one of the misfortunes of their situation that they were never busy enough to necessitate, or even to justify, the postponement of unpleasant discussions. If they avoided a question it was obviously, unconcealably because the question was disagreeable. They had unlimited leisure and an accumulation of mental energy to devote to any subject that presented itself; new topics were in fact at a premium. Lydia sometimes had premonitions of a famine-stricken period when there would be nothing left to talk about, and she had already caught herself doling out piecemeal what, in the first prodigality of their confidences, she would have flung to him in a breath. Their silence therefore might simply mean that they had nothing to say; but it was another disadvantage of their position that it allowed infinite opportunity for the classification of minute differences. Lydia had learned to distinguish between real and factitious silences; and under Gannett's she now detected a hum of speech to which her own thoughts made breathless answer.

How could it be otherwise, with that thing between

them? She glanced up at the rack overhead. The *thing* was there, in her dressing-bag, symbolically suspended over her head and his. He was thinking of it now, just as she was; they had been thinking of it in unison ever since they had entered the train. While the carriage had held other travellers they had screened her from his thoughts; but now that he and she were alone she knew exactly what was passing through his mind; she could almost hear him asking himself what he should say to her. . . .

The thing had come that morning, brought up to her in an innocent-looking envelope with the rest of their letters, as they were leaving the hotel at Bologna. As she tore it open, she and Gannett were laughing over some ineptitude of the local guide-book—they had been driven, of late, to make the most of such incidental humors of travel. Even when she had unfolded the document she took it for some unimportant business paper sent abroad for her signature, and her eye travelled inattentively over the curly *Whereases* of the preamble until a word arrested her:—Divorce. There it stood, an impassable barrier, between her husband's name and hers.

She had been prepared for it, of course, as healthy people are said to be prepared for death, in the sense of knowing it must come without in the least expecting that it will. She had known from the first that Tillotson meant to divorce her—but what did it matter? Nothing mattered, in those first days of supreme deliverance, but the fact that she was free; and not so much (she had begun to be aware) that freedom had released her from Tillotson as that it had given her to Gannett. This discovery had not been agreeable to her self-esteem. She had preferred to think that Tillotson had himself embodied all her reasons for leaving him; and those he represented had seemed cogent enough to stand in no need of reinforcement. Yet she had not left him till she met Gannett. It was her love for Gannett that had made life with Tillotson so poor and incomplete a business. If she had never, from the first, regarded her marriage as a full cancelling of her claims upon life, she had at least, for a number of years, accepted it as a provisional compensation,—she had made it "do." Existence in the commodious Tillotson mansion in Fifth Avenue—with Mrs. Tillotson senior commanding the approaches from the second-story front windows—had been reduced to a series of purely automatic acts. The moral atmosphere of the Tillotson interior was as carefully screened and curtained as the house itself: Mrs. Tillotson senior dreaded ideas as much as a draught on her back. Prudent people liked an even temperature; and to do anything unexpected was as foolish as going out in the rain. One of the chief advantages of being rich was that one need not be exposed to unforeseen contingencies: by the use of ordinary firmness and common sense one could make sure of doing exactly the same thing every day at the same hour. These doctrines, reverentially imbibed with his mother's milk, Tillotson (a model son who had never given his parents an hour's anxiety) complacently expounded to his wife, testifying to his sense of their importance by the regularity with which he wore goloshes on damp days, his punctuality at meals, and his elaborate precautions against burglars and contagious diseases. Lydia, coming from a smaller town, and entering New York life through the portals of the Tillotson mansion, had mechanically accepted this point of view as inseparable from having a front pew in church and a parterre box at the opera. All the people who came to the house revolved in the same small circle of prejudices. It was the kind of society in which, after dinner, the ladies compared the exorbitant charges of their children's teachers, and agreed that, even with the new duties on French clothes, it was cheaper in the end to get everything from Worth; while the husbands, over their cigars, lamented municipal corruption, and decided that the men to start a reform were those who had no private interests at stake.

To Lydia this view of life had become a matter of course, just as lumbering about in her mother-in-law's landau had come to seem the only possible means of

locomotion, and listening every Sunday to a fashionable
Presbyterian divine the inevitable atonement for having
thought oneself bored on the other six days of the week.
Before she met Gannett her life had seemed merely dull:
his coming made it appear like one of those dismal
Cruikshank prints in which the people are all ugly and
all engaged in occupations that are either vulgar or
stupid.

It was natural that Tillotson should be the chief suf-
ferer from this readjustment of focus. Gannett's nearness had made her husband ridiculous, and a part of the
ridicule had been reflected on herself. Her tolerance laid
her open to a suspicion of obtuseness from which she
must, at all costs, clear herself in Gannett's eyes.

She did not understand this until afterwards. At the
time she fancied that she had merely reached the limits
of endurance. In so large a charter of liberties as the
mere act of leaving Tillotson seemed to confer, the
small question of divorce or no divorce did not count. It
was when she saw that she had left her husband only to
be with Gannett that she perceived the significance of
anything affecting their relations. Her husband, in
casting her off, had virtually flung her at Gannett: it
was thus that the world viewed it. The measure of
alacrity with which Gannett would receive her would be
the subject of curious speculation over afternoon-tea
tables and in club corners. She knew what would be
said—she had heard it so often of others! The recollection bathed her in misery. The men would probably
back Gannett to "do the decent thing"; but the ladies'
eyebrows would emphasize the worthlessness of such
enforced fidelity; and after all, they would be right. She
had put herself in a position where Gannett "owed" her
something; where, as a gentleman, he was bound to
"stand the damage." The idea of accepting such compensation had never crossed her mind; the so-called
rehabilitation of such a marriage had always seemed to
her the only real disgrace. What she dreaded was the
necessity of having to explain herself; of having to combat his arguments; of calculating, in spite of herself, the

exact measure of insistence with which he pressed them. She knew not whether she most shrank from his insisting too much or too little. In such a case the nicest sense of proportion might be at fault; and how easy to fall into the error of taking her resistance for a test of his sincerity! Whichever way she turned, an ironical implication confronted her: she had the exasperated sense of having walked into the trap of some stupid practical joke.

Beneath all these preoccupations lurked the dread of what he was thinking. Sooner or later, of course, he would have to speak; but that, in the meantime, he should think, even for a moment, that there was any use in speaking, seemed to her simply unendurable. Her sensitiveness on this point was aggravated by another fear, as yet barely on the level of consciousness; the fear of unwillingly involving Gannett in the trammels of her dependence. To look upon him as the instrument of her liberation; to resist in herself the least tendency to a wifely taking possession of his future; had seemed to Lydia the one way of maintaining the dignity of their relation. Her view had not changed, but she was aware of a growing inability to keep her thoughts fixed on the essential point—the point of parting with Gannett. It was easy to face as long as she kept it sufficiently far off: but what was this act of mental postponement but a gradual encroachment on his future? What was needful was the courage to recognize the moment when, by some word or look, their voluntary fellowship should be transformed into a bondage the more wearing that it was based on none of those common obligations which make the most imperfect marriage in some sort a centre of gravity.

When the porter, at the next station, threw the door open, Lydia drew back, making way for the hoped-for intruder, but none came, and the train took up its leisurely progress through the spring wheat-fields and budding copses. She now began to hope that Gannett would speak before the next station. She watched him furtively, half-disposed to return to the seat opposite his, but there was an artificiality about his absorption that restrained her. She had never before seen him read with so conspicuous an air of warding off interruption. What could he be thinking of? Why should he be afraid to speak? Or was it her answer that he dreaded?

The train paused for the passing of an express, and he put down his book and leaned out of the window. Presently he turned to her with a smile.

"There's a jolly old villa out here," he said.

His easy tone relieved her, and she smiled back at him as she crossed over to his corner.

Beyond the embankment, through the opening in a mossy wall, she caught sight of the villa, with its broken balustrades, its stagnant fountains, and the stone satyr closing the perspective of a dusky grass-walk.

"How should you like to live there?" he asked as the train moved on.

"There?"

"In some such place, I mean. One might do worse, don't you think so? There must be at least two centuries of solitude under those yew-trees. Shouldn't you like it?"

"I—I don't know," she faltered. She knew now that he meant to speak.

He lit another cigarette. "We shall have to live somewhere, you know," he said as he bent above the match.

Lydia tried to speak carelessly. *"Je n'en vois pas la nécessité!* Why not live everywhere, as we have been doing?"

"But we can't travel forever, can we?"

"Oh, forever's a long word," she objected, picking up the review he had thrown aside.

"For the rest of our lives then," he said, moving nearer.

She made a slight gesture which caused his hand to slip from hers.

"Why should we make plans? I thought you agreed with me that it's pleasanter to drift."

He looked at her hesitatingly. "It's been pleasant,

certainly; but I suppose I shall have to get at my work again some day. You know I haven't written a line since—all this time," he hastily emended.

She flamed with sympathy and self-reproach. "Oh, if you mean *that*—if you want to write—of course we must settle down. How stupid of me not to have thought of it sooner! Where shall we go? Where do you think you could work best? We oughtn't to lose any more time."

He hesitated again. "I had thought of a villa in these parts. It's quiet; we shouldn't be bothered. Should you like it?"

"Of course I should like it." She paused and looked away. "But I thought—I remember your telling me once that your best work had been done in a crowd—in big cities. Why should you shut yourself up in a desert?"

Gannett, for a moment, made no reply. At length he said, avoiding her eye as carefully as she avoided his: "It might be different now; I can't tell, of course, till I try. A writer ought not to be dependent on his *milieu*; it's a mistake to humor oneself in that way; and I thought that just at first you might prefer to be—"

She faced him. "To be what?"

"Well—quiet. I mean—"

"What do you mean by 'at first'?" she interrupted.

He paused again. "I mean after we are married."

She thrust up her chin and turned toward the window. "Thank you!" she tossed back at him.

"Lydia!" he exclaimed blankly; and she felt in every fibre of her averted person that he had made the inconceivable, the unpardonable mistake of anticipating her acquiescence.

The train rattled on and he groped for a third cigarette. Lydia remained silent.

"I haven't offended you?" he ventured at length, in the tone of a man who feels his way.

She shook her head with a sigh. "I thought you understood," she moaned. Their eyes met and she moved back to his side.

"Do you want to know how not to offend me? By

taking it for granted, once for all, that you've said your say on this odious question and that I've said mine, and that we stand just where we did this morning before that—that hateful paper came to spoil everything between us!''

"To spoil everything between us? What on earth do you mean? Aren't you glad to be free?''

"I was free before.''

"Not to marry me,'' he suggested.

"But I don't *want* to marry you!'' she cried.

She saw that he turned pale. "I'm obtuse, I suppose,'' he said slowly. "I confess I don't see what you're driving at. Are you tired of the whole business? Or was I simply a—an excuse for getting away? Perhaps you didn't care to travel alone? Was that it? And now you want to chuck me?'' His voice had grown harsh. "You owe me a straight answer, you know; don't be tenderhearted!''

Her eyes swam as she leaned to him. "Don't you see it's because I care—because I care so much? Oh, Ralph! Can't you see how it would humiliate me? Try to feel it as a woman would! Don't you see the misery of being made your wife in this way? If I'd known you as a girl—that would have been a real marriage! But now—this vulgar fraud upon society—and upon a society we despised and laughed at—this sneaking back into a position that we're voluntarily forfeited: don't you see what a cheap compromise it is? We neither of us believe in the abstract 'sacredness' of marriage; we both know that no ceremony is needed to consecrate our love for each other; what object can we have in marrying, except the secret fear of each that the other may escape, or the secret longing to work our way back gradually—oh, very gradually—into the esteem of the people whose conventional morality we have always ridiculed and hated? And the very fact that, after a decent interval, these same people would come and dine with us—the women who talk about the indissolubility of marriage, and who would let me die in a gutter to-day because I am 'leading a life of sin'—doesn't that disgust you more than their turning their backs on us now? I can stand being cut by them, but I couldn't stand their coming to call and asking what I meant to do about visiting that unfortunate Mrs. So-and-so!"

She paused, and Gannett maintained a perplexed silence.

"You judge things too theoretically," he said at length, slowly. "Life is made up of compromises."

"The life we ran away from—yes! If we had been willing to accept them"—she flushed—"we might have gone on meeting each other at Mrs. Tillotson's dinners."

He smiled slightly. "I didn't know that we ran away to found a new system of ethics. I suppose it was because we loved each other."

"Life is complex, of course; isn't it the very recognition of that fact that separates us from the people who see it *tout d'une pièce*? If *they* are right—if marriage is sacred in itself and the individual must always be sacrificed to the family—then there can be no real marriage between us, since our—our being together is a protest against the sacrifice of the individual to the family." She interrupted herself with a laugh. "You'll say now that I'm giving you a lecture on sociology! Of course one acts as one can—as one must, perhaps—pulled by all sorts of invisible threads; but at least one needn't pretend, for social advantages, to subscribe to a creed that ignores the complexity of human motives—that classifies people by arbitrary signs, and puts it in everybody's reach to be on Mrs. Tillotson's visiting-list. It may be necessary that the world should be ruled by conventions—but if we believed in them, why did we break through them? And if we don't believe in them, is it honest to take advantage of the protection they afford?"

Gannett hesitated. "One may believe in them or not; but as long as they do rule the world it is only by taking advantage of their protection that one can find a *modus vivendi*."

"Do outlaws need a *modus vivendi*?"

He looked at her hopelessly. Nothing is more perplexing to man than the mental process of a woman who
reasons her emotions.

She thought she had scored a point and followed it up
passionately. "You do understand, don't you? You see
how the very thought of the thing humiliates me! We are
together to-day because we choose to be—don't let us
look any farther than that!" She caught his hands.
"*Promise* me you'll never speak of it again; promise me
you'll never *think* of it even," she implored, with a tear-
ful prodigality of italics.

Through what followed—his protests, his arguments,
his final unconvinced submission to her wishes—she
had a sense of his but half-discerning all that, for her,
had made the moment so tumultuous. They had reached
that memorable point in every heart-history when, for
the first time, the man seems obtuse and the woman
irrational. It was the abundance of his intentions that
consoled her, on reflection, for what they lacked in
quality. After all, it would have been worse, in-
calculably worse, to have detected any overreadiness to
understand her.

II.

WHEN THE train at night-fall brought them to their
journey's end at the edge of one of the lakes, Lydia was
glad that they were not, as usual, to pass from one
solitude to another. Their wanderings, during the year
had indeed been like the flight of outlaws: through
Sicily, Dalmatia, Transylvania and Southern Italy they
had persisted in their tacit avoidance of their kind.
Isolation, at first, had deepened the flavor of their happiness, as night intensifies the scent of certain flowers;

but in the new phase on which they were entering, Lydia's chief wish was that they should be less abnormally exposed to the action of each other's thoughts.

She shrank, nevertheless, as the brightly-looming bulk of the fashionable Anglo-American hotel on the water's brink began to radiate toward their advancing boat its vivid suggestion of social order, visitors' lists, Church services, and the bland inquisition of the *table-d' hôte*. The mere fact that in a moment or two she must take her place on the hotel register as Mrs. Gannett seemed to weaken the springs of her resistance.

They had meant to stay for a night only, on their way to a lofty village among the glaciers of Monte Rosa; but after the first plunge into publicity, when they entered the dining-room, Lydia felt the relief of being lost in a crowd, of ceasing for a moment to be the centre of Gannett's scrutiny; and in his face she caught the reflection of her feeling. After dinner, when she went upstairs, he strolled into the smoking-room, and an hour or two later, sitting in the darkness of her window, she heard his voice below and saw him walking up and down the terrace with a companion cigar at his side. When he came up he told her he had been talking to the hotel chaplain—a very good sort of fellow.

"Queer little microcosms, these hotels! Most of these people live here all summer and then migrate to Italy or the Riviera. The English are the only people who can lead that kind of life with dignity—those soft-voiced old ladies in Shetland shawls somehow carry the British Empire under their caps. *Civis Romanus sum.* It's a curious study—there might be some good things to work up here."

He stood before her with the vivid preoccupied stare of the novelist on the trail of a "subject." With a relief that was half painful she noticed that, for the first time since they had been together, he was hardly aware of her presence.

"Do you think you could write here?"

"Here? I don't know." His stare dropped. "After being out of things so long one's first impressions are bound to be tremendously vivid, you know. I see a dozen threads already that one might follow—"

He broke off with a touch of embarrassment.

"Then follow them. We'll stay," she said with sudden decision.

"Stay here?" He glanced at her in surprise, and then, walking to the window, looked out upon the dusky slumber of the garden.

"Why not?" she said at length, in a tone of veiled irritation.

"The place is full of old cats in caps who gossip with the chaplain. Shall you like—I mean, it would be different if—"

She flamed up.

"Do you suppose I care? It's none of their business."

"Of course not; but you won't get them to think so."

"They may think what they please."

He looked at her doubtfully.

"It's for you to decide."

"We'll stay," she repeated.

Gannett, before they met, had made himself known as a successful writer of short stories and of a novel which had achieved the distinction of being widely discussed. The reviewers called him "promising," and Lydia now accused herself of having too long interfered with the fulfilment of his promise. There was a special irony in the fact, since his passionate assurances that only the stimulus of her companionship could bring out his latent faculty had almost given the dignity of a "vocation" to her course: there had been moments when she had felt unable to assume, before posterity, the responsibility of thwarting his career. And, after all, he had not written a line since they had been together: his first desire to write had come from renewed contact with the world! Was it all a mistake then? Must the most intelligent choice work more disastrously than the blundering combinations of chance? Or was there a still more humiliating answer to her perplexities? His sudden impulse of activity so exactly coincided with her own wish to withdraw, for a time, from the range of his observation, that she wondered if he too were not seeking sanctuary from intolerable problems.

"You must begin to-morrow!" she cried, hiding a tremor under the laugh with which she added, "I wonder if there's any ink in the inkstand?"

Whatever else they had at the Hotel Bellosguardo, they had, as Miss Pinsent said, "a certain tone." It was to Lady Susan Condit that they owed this inestimable benefit; an advantage ranking in Miss Pinsent's opinion above even the lawn tennis courts and the resident chaplain. It was the fact of Lady Susan's annual visit that made the hotel what it was. Miss Pinsent was certainly the last to underrate such a privilege:—"It's so important, my dear, forming as we do a little family, that there should be some one to give *the tone*; and no one could do it better than Lady Susan—an earl's daughter and a person of such determination. Dear Mrs. Ainger now—who really *ought*, you know, when Lady Susan's away—absolutely refuses to assert herself." Miss Pinsent sniffed derisively. "A bishop's niece!—my dear, I saw her once actually give in to some South Americans—and before us all. She gave up her seat at table to oblige them—such a lack of dignity! Lady Susan spoke to her very plainly about it afterwards."

Miss Pinsent glanced across the lake and adjusted her auburn front.

"But of course I don't deny that the stand Lady Susan takes is not always easy to live up to—for the rest of us, I mean. Monsieur Grossart, our good proprietor, finds it trying at times, I know—he has said as much, privately, to Mrs. Ainger and me. After all, the poor man is not to blame for wanting to fill his hotel, is he? And Lady Susan is so difficult—so very difficult—about new people. One might almost say that she disapproves of them beforehand, on principle. And yet she's had warnings—she very nearly made a dreadful mistake once with the Duchess of Levens, who dyed her hair and—well, swore and smoked. One would have thought that might have been a lesson to Lady Susan."

Miss Pinsent resumed her knitting with a sigh. "There are exceptions, of course. She took at once to you and Mr. Gannett—it was quite remarkable, really. Oh, I don't mean that either—of course not! It was perfectly natural—we *all* thought you so charming and interesting from the first day—we knew at once that Mr. Gannett was intellectual, by the magazines you took in; but you know what I mean. Lady Susan is so very—well, I won't say prejudiced, as Mrs. Ainger does—but so prepared *not* to like new people, that her taking to you in that way was a surprise to us all, I confess."

Miss Pinsent sent a significant glance down the long laurustinus alley from the other end of which two people—a lady and gentleman—were strolling toward them through the smiling neglect of the garden.

"In this case, of course, it's very different; that I'm willing to admit. Their looks are against them; but, as Mrs. Ainger says, one can't exactly tell them so."

"She's very handsome," Lydia ventured, with her eyes on the lady, who showed, under the dome of a vivid sunshade, the hour-glass figure and superlative coloring of a Christmas chromo.

"That's the worst of it. She's too handsome."

"Well, after all, she can't help that."

"Other people manage to," said Miss Pinsent skeptically.

"But isn't it rather unfair of Lady Susan—considering that nothing is known about them?"

"But, my dear, that's the very thing that's against them. It's infinitely worse than any actual knowledge."

Lydia mentally agreed that, in the case of Mrs. Linton, it possibly might be.

"I wonder why they came here?" she mused.

"That's against them too. It's always a bad sign when loud people come to a quiet place. And they've brought van-loads of boxes—her maid told Mrs. Ainger's that they meant to stop indefinitely."

"And Lady Susan actually turned her back on her in the *salon*?"

"My dear, she said it was for our sakes; that makes it

so unanswerable! But poor Grossart *is* in a way! The Lintons have taken his most expensive *suite*, you know—the yellow damask drawing-room above the portico—and they have champagne with every meal!"

They were silent as Mr. and Mrs. Linton sauntered by; the lady with tempestuous brows and challenging chin; the gentleman, a blond stripling, trailing after her, head downward, like a reluctant child dragged by his nurse.

"What does your husband think of them, my dear?" Miss Pinsent whispered as they passed out of earshot.

Lydia stooped to pick a violet in the border.

"He hasn't told me."

"Of your speaking to them, I mean. Would he approve of that? I know how very particular nice Americans are. I think your action might make a difference; it would certainly carry weight with Lady Susan."

"Dear Miss Pinsent, you flatter me!"

Lydia rose and gathered up her book and sunshade.

"Well, if you're asked for an opinion—if Lady Susan asks you for one—I think you ought to be prepared," Miss Pinsent admonished her as she moved away.

III.

LADY SUSAN held her own. She ignored the Lintons, and her little family, as Miss Pinsent phrased it, followed suit. Even Mrs. Ainger agreed that it was obligatory. If Lady Susan owed it to the others not to speak to the Lintons, the others clearly owed it to Lady Susan to back her up. It was generally found expedient, at the Hotel Bellosguardo, to adopt this form of reasoning.

Whatever effect this combined action may have had upon the Lintons, it did not at least have that of driving them away. Monsieur Grossart, after a few days of suspense, had the satisfaction of seeing them settle down in his yellow damask *premier* with what looked like a permanent installation of palm-trees and silk sofa-cushions, and a gratifying continuance in the consumption of champagne. Mrs. Linton trailed her Doucet draperies up and down the garden with the same challenging air, while her husband, smoking innumerable cigarettes, dragged himself dejectedly in her wake; but neither of them, after the first encounter with Lady Susan, made any attempt to extend their acquaintance. They simply ignored their ignorers. As Miss Pinsent resentfully observed, they behaved exactly as though the hotel were empty.

It was therefore a matter of surprise, as well as of displeasure, to Lydia, to find, on glancing up one day from her seat in the garden, that the shadow which had fallen across her book was that of the enigmatic Mrs. Linton.

"I want to speak to you," that lady said, in a rich hard voice that seemed the audible expression of her gown and her complexion.

Lydia started. She certainly did not want to speak to Mrs. Linton.

"Shall I sit down here?" the latter continued, fixing her intensely-shaded eyes on Lydia's face, "or are you afraid of being seen with me?"

"Afraid?" Lydia colored. "Sit down, please. What is it that you wish to say?"

Mrs. Linton, with a smile, drew up a garden-chair and crossed one open-work ankle above the other.

"I want you to tell me what my husband said to your husband last night."

Lydia turned pale.

"My husband—to yours?" she faltered, staring at the other.

"Didn't you know they were closeted together for hours in the smoking-room after you went upstairs? My man didn't get to bed until nearly two o'clock and when he did I couldn't get a word out of him. When he wants to be aggravating I'll back him against anybody living!'' Her teeth and eyes flashed persuasively upon Lydia. ''But you'll tell me what they were talking about, won't you? I know I can trust you—you look so awfully kind. And it's for his own good. He's such a precious donkey and I'm so afraid he's got into some beastly scrape or other. If he'd only trust his own old woman! But they're always writing to him and setting him against me. And I've got nobody to turn to.'' She laid her hand on Lydia's with a rattle of bracelets. ''You'll help me, won't you?''

Lydia drew back from the smiling fierceness of her brows.

''I'm sorry—but I don't think I understand. My husband has said nothing to me of—of yours.''

The great black crescents above Mrs. Linton's eyes met angrily. ''I say—is that true?'' she demanded.

Lydia rose from her seat.

''Oh, look here, I didn't mean that, you know—you mustn't take one up so! Can't you see how rattled I am?''

Lydia saw that, in fact, her beautiful mouth was quivering beneath softened eyes.

''I'm beside myself!'' the splendid creature wailed, dropping into her seat.

''I'm so sorry,'' Lydia repeated, forcing herself to speak kindly; ''but how can I help you?''

Mrs. Linton raised her head sharply.

''By finding out—there's a darling!''

''Finding what out?''

''What Trevenna told him.''

''Trevenna—?'' Lydia echoed in bewilderment.

Mrs. Linton clapped her hand to her mouth.

''Oh, Lord—there, it's out! What a fool I am! But I supposed of course you knew; I supposed everybody knew.'' She dried her eyes and bridled. ''Didn't you know that he's Lord Trevenna? I'm Mrs. Cope.''

Lydia recognized the names. They had figured in a

flamboyant elopement which had thrilled fashionable London some six months earlier.

"Now you see how it is—you understand, don't you?" Mrs. Cope continued on a note of appeal. "I knew you would—that's the reason I came to you. I suppose *he* felt the same thing about your husband; he's not spoken to another soul in the place." Her face grew anxious again. "He's awfully sensitive, generally—he feels our position, he says—as if it wasn't *my* place to feel that! But when he does get talking there's no knowing what he'll say. I know he's been brooding over something lately, and I *must* find out what it is—it's to his interest that I should. I always tell him that I think only of his interest; if he'd only trust me! But he's been so odd lately—I can't think what he's plotting. You will help me, dear?"

Lydia, who had remained standing, looked away uncomfortably.

"If you mean by finding out what Lord Trevenna has told my husband, I'm afraid it's impossible."

"Why impossible?"

"Because I infer that it was told in confidence."

Mrs. Cope stared incredulously.

"Well, what of that? Your husband looks such a dear—any one can see he's awfully gone on you. What's to prevent your getting it out of him?"

Lydia flushed.

"I'm not a spy!" she exclaimed.

"A spy—a spy? How dare you?" Mrs. Cope flamed out. "Oh, I don't mean that either! Don't be angry with me—I'm so miserable." She essayed a softer note. "Do you call that spying—for one woman to help out another? I do need help so dreadfully! I'm at my wits' end with Trevenna, I am indeed. He's such a boy—a mere baby, you know; he's only two-and-twenty." She dropped her orbed lids. "He's younger than me—only fancy! a few months younger. I tell him he ought to listen to me as if I was his mother; oughtn't he now? But he won't, he won't! All his people are at him, you see—oh, I know *their* little game! Trying to get him away from me before I can get my divorce—that's what they're up to. At first he wouldn't listen to them; he used to toss their letters over to me to read; but now he reads them himself, and answers 'em too, I fancy; he's always shut up in his room, writing. If I only knew what his plan is I could stop him fast enough—he's such a simpleton. But he's dreadfully deep too—at times I can't make him out. But I know he's told your husband everything—I knew that last night the minute I laid eyes on him. And I *must* find out—you must help me—I've got no one else to turn to!"

She caught Lydia's fingers in a stormy pressure.

"Say you'll help me—you and your husband."

Lydia tried to free herself.

"What you ask is impossible; you must see that it is. No one could interfere in—in the way you ask."

Mrs. Cope's clutch tightened.

"You won't, then? You won't?"

"Certainly not. Let me go, please."

Mrs. Cope released her with a laugh.

"Oh, go by all means—pray don't let me detain you! Shall you go and tell Lady Susan Condit that there's a pair of us—or, shall I save you the trouble of enlightening her?"

Lydia stood still in the middle of the path, seeing her antagonist through a mist of terror. Mrs. Cope was still laughing.

"Oh, I'm not spiteful by nature, my dear; but you're a little more than flesh and blood can stand! It's impossible, is it? Let you go, indeed! You're too good to be mixed up in my affairs, are you? Why, you little fool, the first day I laid eyes on you I saw that you and I were both in the same box—that's the reason I spoke to you."

She stepped nearer, her smile dilating on Lydia like a lamp through a fog.

"You can take your choice, you know; I always play fair. If you'll tell I'll promise not to. Now then, which is it to be?"

Lydia, involuntarily, had begun to move away from

the pelting storm of words; but at this she turned and sat down again.

"You may go," she said simply. "I shall stay here."

IV.

SHE STAYED there for a long time, in the hypnotized contemplation, not of Mrs. Cope's present, but of her own past. Gannett, early that morning, had gone off on a long walk—he had fallen into the habit of taking these mountain-tramps with various fellow-lodgers; but even had he been within reach she could not have gone to him just then. She had to deal with herself first. She was surprised to find how, in the last months, she had lost the habit of introspection. Since their coming to the Hotel Bellosguardo she and Gannett had tacitly avoided themselves and each other.

She was aroused by the whistle of the three o'clock steamboat as it neared the landing just beyond the hotel gates. Three o'clock! Then Gannett would soon be back—he had told her to expect him before four. She rose hurriedly, her face averted from the inquisitorial facade of the hotel. She could not see him just yet; she could not go indoors. She slipped through one of the overgrown garden-alleys and climbed a steep path to the hills.

It was dark when she opened their sitting-room door. Gannett was sitting on the window-ledge smoking a cigarette. Cigarettes were now his chief resource: he had not written a line during the two months they had spent at the Hotel Bellosguardo. In that respect, it had turned out not to be the right *milieu* after all.

He started up at Lydia's entrance.

"Where have you been? I was getting anxious."

She sat down in a chair near the door.

"Up the mountain," she said wearily.

"Alone?"

"Yes."

Gannett threw away his cigarette: the sound of her voice made him want to see her face.

"Shall we have a little light?" he suggested.

She made no answer and he lifted the globe from the lamp and put a match to the wick. Then he looked at her.

"Anything wrong? You look done up."

She sat glancing vaguely about the little sitting-room, dimly lit by the pallid-globed lamp, which left in twilight the outlines of the furniture, of his writing-table heaped with books and papers, of the tea-roses and jasmine drooping on the mantel-piece. How like home it had all grown—how like home!

"Lydia, what is wrong?" he repeated.

She moved away from him, feeling for her hatpins and turning to lay her hat and sunshade on the table.

Suddenly she said: "That woman has been talking to me."

Gannett stared.

"That woman? What woman?"

"Mrs. Linton—Mrs. Cope."

He gave a start of annoyance, still, as she perceived, not grasping the full import of her words.

"The deuce! She told you—?"

"She told me everything."

Gannett looked at her anxiously.

"What impudence! I'm so sorry that you should have been exposed to this, dear."

"Exposed!" Lydia laughed.

Gannett's brow clouded and they looked away from each other.

"Do you know *why* she told me? She had the best of reasons. The first time she laid eyes on me she saw that we were both in the same box."

"Lydia!"

"So it was natural, of course, that she should turn to me in a difficulty."

"What difficulty?"

"It seems she has reason to think that Lord Trevenna's people are trying to get him away from her before she gets her divorce—"

"Well?"

"And she fancied he had been consulting with you last night as to—as to the best way of escaping from her."

Gannett stood up with an angry forehead.

"Well—what concern of yours was all this dirty business? Why should she go to you?"

"Don't you see? It's so simple. I was to wheedle his secret out of you."

"To oblige that woman?"

"Yes; or, if I was unwilling to oblige her, then to protect myself."

"To protect yourself? Against whom?"

"Against her telling everyone in the hotel that she and I are in the same box."

"She threatened that?"

"She left me the choice of telling it myself or of doing it for me."

"The beast!"

There was a long silence. Lydia had seated herself on the sofa, beyond the radius of the lamp, and he leaned against the window. His next question surprised her.

"When did this happen? At what time, I mean?"

She looked at him vaguely.

"I don't know—after luncheon, I think. Yes, I remember; it must have been at about three o'clock."

He stepped into the middle of the room and as he approached the light she saw that his brow had cleared.

"Why do you ask?" she said.

"Because when I came in, at about half-past three, the mail was just being distributed, and Mrs. Cope was waiting as usual to pounce on her letters; you know she was always watching for the postman. She was standing so close to me that I couldn't help seeing a big official-looking envelope that was handed to her. She tore it open, gave one look at the inside, and rushed off up-stairs like a whirlwind, with the director shouting after her that she had left all her other letters behind. I don't believe she ever thought of you again after that paper was put into her hand."

"Why?"

"Because she was too busy. I was sitting in the window, watching for you, when the five o'clock boat left, and who should go on board, bag and baggage, valet and maid, dressing-bags and poodle, but Mrs. Cope and Trevenna. Just an hour and a half to pack up in! And you should have seen her when they started. She was radiant—shaking hands with everybody—waving her handkerchief from the deck—distributing bows and smiles like an empress. If ever a woman got what she wanted just in the nick of time that woman did. She'll be Lady Trevenna within a week, I'll wager."

"You think she has her divorce?"

"I'm sure of it. And she must have got it just after her talk with you."

Lydia was silent.

At length she said, with a kind of reluctance, "She was horribly angry when she left me. It wouldn't have taken long to tell Lady Susan Condit."

"Lady Susan Condit has not been told."

"How do you know?"

"Because when I went downstairs half an hour ago I met Lady Susan on the way—"

He stopped, half smiling.

"Well?"

"And she stopped to ask if I thought you would act as patroness to a charity concert she is getting up."

In spite of themselves they both broke into a laugh. Lydia's ended in sobs and she sank down with her face hidden. Gannett bent over her, seeking her hands.

"That vile woman—I ought to have warned you to

keep away from her; I can't forgive myself! But he spoke to me in confidence; and I never dreamed—well, it's all over now.''

Lydia lifted her head.

"Not for me. It's only just beginning."

"What do you mean?"

She put him gently aside and moved in her turn to the window. Then she went on, with her face turned toward the shimmering blackness of the lake, "You see of course that it might happen again at any moment."

"What?"

"This—this risk of being found out. And we could hardly count again on such a lucky combination of chances, could we?"

He sat down with a groan.

Still keeping her face toward the darkness, she said, "I want you to go and tell Lady Susan—and the others."

Gannett, who had moved towards her, paused a few feet off.

"Why do you wish me to do this?" he said at length, with less surprise in his voice than she had been prepared for.

"Because I've behaved basely, abominably, since we came here: letting these people believe we were married—lying with every breath I drew—"

"Yes, I've felt that too," Gannett exclaimed with sudden energy.

The words shook her like a tempest: all her thoughts seemed to fall about her in ruins.

"You—you've felt so?"

"Of course I have." He spoke with low-voiced vehemence. "Do you suppose I like playing the sneak any better than you do? It's damnable."

He had dropped on the arm of a chair, and they stared at each other like blind people who suddenly see.

"But you have liked it here," she faltered.

"Oh, I've liked it—I've liked it." He moved impatiently. "Haven't you?"

"Yes," she burst out; "that's the worst of it—that's

what I can't bear. I fancied it was for your sake that I
insisted on staying—because you thought you could
write here; and perhaps just at first that really was the
reason. But afterwards I wanted to stay myself—I loved
it." She broke into a laugh. "Oh, do you see the full
derision of it? These people—the very prototypes of the
bores you took me away from, with the same fenced-in
view of life, the same keep-off-the-grass morality, the
same little cautious virtues and the same little frightened
vices—well, I've clung to them, I've delighted in them,
I've done my best to please them. I've toadied Lady
Susan, I've gossiped with Miss Pinsent, I've pretended
to be shocked with Mrs. Ainger. Respectability! It was
the one thing in life that I was sure I didn't care about,
and it's grown so precious to me that I've stolen it
because I couldn't get it in any other way."

She moved across the room and returned to his side
with another laugh.

"I who used to fancy myself unconventional! I must
have been born with a card-case in my hand. You
should have seen me with that poor woman in the garden. She came to me for help, poor creature, because
she fancied that, having 'sinned,' as they call it, I might
feel some pity for others who had been tempted in the
same way. Not I! She didn't know me. Lady Susan
would have been kinder, because Lady Susan wouldn't
have been afraid. I hated the woman—my one thought
was not to be seen with her—I could have killed her for
guessing my secret. The one thing that mattered to me at
that moment was my standing with Lady Susan!"

Gannett did not speak.

"And you—you've felt it too!" she broke out ac-
cusingly. "You've enjoyed being with these people as
much as I have; you've let the chaplain talk to you by
the hour about 'The Reign of Law' and Professor
Drummond. When they asked you to hand the plate in
church I was watching you—*you wanted to accept.*"

She stepped close, laying her hand on his arm.

"Do you know, I begin to see what marriage is for.
It's to keep people away from each other. Sometimes I

think that two people who love each other can be saved from madness only by the things that come between them—children, duties, visits, bores, relations—the things that protect married people from each other. We've been too close together—that has been our sin. We've seen the nakedness of each other's souls.''

She sank again on the sofa, hiding her face in her hands.

Gannett stood above her perplexedly: he felt as though she were being swept away by some implacable current while he stood helpless on its bank.

At length he said, ''Lydia, don't think me a brute— but don't you see yourself that it won't do?''

''Yes, I see it won't do,'' she said without raising her head.

His face cleared.

''Then we'll go to-morrow.''

''Go—where?''

''To Paris; to be married.''

For a long time she made no answer; then she asked slowly, ''Would they have us here if we were married?''

''Have us here?''

''I mean Lady Susan—and the others.''

''Have us here? Of course they would.''

''Not if they knew—at least, not unless they could pretend not to know.''

He made an impatient gesture.

''We shouldn't come back here, of course; and other people needn't know—no one need know.''

She sighed. ''Then it's only another form of deception and a meaner one. Don't you see that?''

''I see that we're not accountable to any Lady Susans on earth!''

''Then why are you ashamed of what we are doing here?''

''Because I'm sick of pretending that you're my wife when you're not—when you won't be.''

She looked at him sadly.

''If I were your wife you'd have to go on pretending. You'd have to pretend that I'd never been—anything else. And our friends would have to pretend that they believed what you pretended."

Gannett pulled off the soft-tassel and flung it away.

"You're impossible," he groaned.

"It's not I—it's our being together that's impossible. I only want you to see that marriage won't help it."

"What will help it then?"

She raised her head.

"My leaving you."

"Your leaving me?" He sat motionless, staring at the tassel which lay at the other end of the room. At length some impulse of retaliation for the pain she was inflicting made him say deliberately:

"And where would you go if you left me?"

"Oh!" she cried, wincing.

He was at her side in an instant.

"Lydia—Lydia—you know I didn't mean it; I couldn't mean it! But you've driven me out of my senses; I don't know what I'm saying. Can't you get out of this labyrinth of self-torture? It's destroying us both."

"That's why I must leave you."

"How easily you say it!" He drew her hands down and made her face him. "You're very scrupulous about yourself—and others. But have you thought of me? You have no right to leave me unless you've ceased to care—"

"It's because I care—"

"Then I have a right to be heard. If you love me you can't leave me."

Her eyes defied him.

"Why not?"

He dropped her hands and rose from her side.

"Can you?" he said sadly.

The hour was late and the lamp flickered and sank. She stood up with a shiver and turned toward the door of her room.

V.

AT DAYLIGHT a sound in Lydia's room woke Gannett
from a troubled sleep. He sat up and listened. She was
moving about softly, as though fearful of disturbing
him. He heard her push back one of the creaking shut-
ters; then there was a moment's silence, which seemed
to indicate that she was waiting to see if the noise had
roused him.

Presently she began to move again. She had spent a
sleepless night, probably, and was dressing to go down
to the garden for a breath of air. Gannett rose also; but
some undefinable instinct made his movements as
cautious as hers. He stole to his window and looked out
through the slats of the shutter.

It had rained in the night and the dawn was gray and
lifeless. The cloud-muffled hills across the lake were
reflected in its surface as in a tarnished mirror. In the
garden, the birds were beginning to shake the drops
from the motionless laurustinus-boughs.

An immense pity for Lydia filled Gannett's soul. Her
seeming intellectual independence had blinded him for a
time to the feminine cast of her mind. He had never
thought of her as a woman who wept and clung: there
was a lucidity in her intuitions that made them appear to
be the result of reasoning. Now he saw the cruelty he
had committed in detaching her from the normal conditions of life; he felt, too, the insight with which she
had hit upon the real cause of their suffering. Their life
was "impossible," as she had said—and its worst
penalty was that it had made any other life impossible
for them. Even had his love lessened, he was bound to
her now by a hundred ties of pity and self-reproach; and
she, poor child! must turn back to him as Latude returned to his cell . . .

A new sound startled him: it was the stealthy closing
of Lydia's door. He crept to his own and heard her foot-
steps passing down the corridor. Then he went back to
the window and looked out.

A minute or two later he saw her go down the steps of the porch and enter the garden. From his post of observation her face was invisible, but something about her appearance struck him. She wore a long travelling cloak and under its folds he detected the outline of a bag or bundle. He drew a deep breath and stood watching her.

She walked quickly down the laurustinus alley toward the gate; there she paused a moment, glancing about the little shady square. The stone benches under the trees were empty, and she seemed to gather resolution from the solitude about her, for she crossed the square to the steam-boat landing, and he saw her pause before the ticket-office at the head of the wharf. Now she was buying her ticket. Gannett turned his head a moment to look at the clock: the boat was due in five minutes. He had time to jump into his clothes and overtake her—

He made no attempt to move; an obscure reluctance restrained him. If any thought emerged from the tumult of his sensations, it was that he must let her go if she wished it. He had spoken last night of his rights: what were they? At the last issue, he and she were two separate beings, not made one by the miracle of common forebearances, duties, abnegations, but bound together in a *noyade* of passion that left them resisting yet clinging as they went down.

After buying her ticket, Lydia had stood for a moment looking out across the lake; then he saw her seat herself on one of the benches near the landing. He and she, at that moment, were both listening for the same sound: the whistle of the boat as it rounded the nearest promontory. Gannett turned again to glance at the clock: the boat was due now.

Where would she go? What would her life be when she had left him? She had no near relations and few friends. There was money enough . . . but she asked so much of life, in ways so complex and immaterial. He thought of her as walking barefooted through a stony waste. No one would understand her—no one would pity her—and he, who did both, was powerless to come to her aid . . .

He saw that she had risen from the bench and walked toward the edge of the lake. She stood looking in the direction from which the steamboat was to come; then she turned to the ticket-office, doubtless to ask the cause of the delay. After that she went back to the bench and sat down with bent head. What was she thinking of?

The whistle sounded; she started up, and Gannett involuntarily made a movement toward the door. But he turned back and continued to watch her. She stood motionless, her eyes on the trail of smoke that preceded the appearance of the boat. Then the little craft rounded the point, a dead-white object on the leaden water: a minute later it was puffing and backing at the wharf.

The few passengers who were waiting—two or three peasants and a snuffy priest—were clustered near the ticket-office. Lydia stood apart under the trees.

The boat lay alongside now; the gang-plank was run out and the peasants went on board with their baskets of vegetables, followed by the priest. Still Lydia did not move. A bell began to ring querulously; there was a shriek of steam, and someone must have called to her that she would be late, for she started forward, as though in answer to a summons. She moved waveringly, and at the edge of the wharf she paused. Gannett saw a sailor beckon to her; the bell rang again and she stepped upon the gang-plank.

Half-way down the short incline to the deck she stopped again; then she turned and ran back to the land. The gang-plank was drawn in, the bell ceased to ring, and the boat backed out into the lake. Lydia, with slow steps, was walking toward the garden . . .

As she approached the hotel she looked up furtively and Gannett drew back into the room. He sat down beside a table; a Bradshaw lay at his elbow, and mechanically, without knowing what he did, he began looking out the trains to Paris . . .

THE ANGEL AT THE
GRAVE

I.

THE HOUSE stood a few yards back from the elm-shaded village street, in that semi-publicity sometimes cited as a democratic protest against old-world standards of domestic exclusiveness. This candid exposure to the public eye is more probably a result of the gregariousness which, in the New England bosom, oddly coexists with a shrinking from direct social contact; most of the inmates of such houses preferring that furtive intercourse which is the result of observations through shuttered windows and a categorical acquaintance with the neighboring clothes-lines. The House, however, faced its public with a difference. For sixty years it had written itself with a capital letter, had self-consciously squared itself in the eye of an admiring nation. The most searching inroads of village intimacy hardly counted in a household that opened on the universe; and a lady whose door-bell was at any moment liable to be rung by visitors from London or Vienna was not likely to flutter up-stairs when she observed a neighbor "stepping over."

The solitary inmate of the Anson House owed this induration of the social texture to the most conspicuous accident in her annals: the fact that she was the only granddaughter of the great Orestes Anson. She had been born, as it were, into a museum, and cradled in a glass case with a label; the first foundations of her consciousness being built on the rock of her grandfather's celebrity. To a little girl who acquires her earliest knowledge of literature through a *Reader* embellished with fragments of her ancestor's prose, that personage necessarily fills an heroic space in the foreground of life. To communicate with one's past through the impressive medium of print, to have, as it were, a footing in every library in the country, and an acknowledged kinship with that world-diffused clan, the descendants of the great, was to be pledged to a standard of manners that amazingly simplified the lesser relations of life. The village street on which Paulina Anson's youth looked out led to all the capitals of Europe; and over the roads of intercommunication unseen caravans bore back to the elm-shaded House the tribute of an admiring world.

Fate seemed to have taken a direct share in fitting Paulina for her part as the custodian of this historic dwelling. It had long been secretly regarded as a "visitation" by the great man's family that he had left no son and that his daughters were not "intellectual." The ladies themselves were the first to lament their deficiency, to own that nature had denied them the gift of making the most of their opportunities. A profound veneration for their parent and an unswerving faith in his doctrines had not amended their congenital incapacity to understand what he had written. Laura, who had her moments of mute rebellion against destiny, had sometimes thought how much easier it would have been if their progenitor had been a poet; for she could recite, with feeling, portions of *The Culprit Fay* and of the poems of Mrs. Hemans; and Phoebe, who was more conspicuous for memory than imagination, kept an album filled with "selections." But the great man was a philosopher; and to both daughters respiration was difficult on the cloudy heights of metaphysic. The situation would have been intolerable but for the fact that, while

Phoebe and Laura were still at school, their father's fame had passed from the open ground of conjecture to the chill privacy of certitude. Dr. Anson had in fact achieved one of those anticipated immortalities not uncommon at a time when people were apt to base their literary judgments on their emotions, and when to affect plain food and despise England went a long way toward establishing a man's intellectual pre-eminence. Thus, when the daughters were called on to strike a filial attitude about their parent's pedestal, there was little to do but to pose gracefully and point upward; and there are spines to which the immobility of worship is not a strain. A legend had by this time crystallized about the great Orestes, and it was of more immediate interest to the public to hear what brand of tea he drank, and whether he took off his boots in the hall, than to rouse the drowsy echo of his dialectic. A great man never draws so near his public as when it has become unnecessary to read his books and is still interesting to know what he eats for breakfast.

As recorders of their parent's domestic habits, as pious scavengers of his waste-paper basket, the Misses Anson were unexcelled. They always had an interesting anecdote to impart to the literary pilgrim, and the tact with which, in later years, they intervened between the public and the growing inaccessibility of its idol, sent away many an enthusiast satisfied to have touched the veil before the sanctuary. Still it was felt, especially by old Mrs. Anson, who survived her husband for some years, that Phoebe and Laura were not worthy of their privileges. There had been a third daughter so unworthy of hers that she had married a distant cousin, who had taken her to live in a new Western community where the *Works of Orestes Anson* had not yet become a part of the civic consciousness; but of this daughter little was said, and she was tacitly understood to be excluded from the family heritage of fame. In time, however, it appeared that the traditional penny with which she had been cut off had been invested to unexpected advantage; and the interest on it, when she died, returned to the Anson House in the shape of a granddaughter who was at once felt to be what Mrs. Anson called a "compensation." It was Mrs. Anson's firm belief that the remotest operations of nature were governed by the centripetal force of her husband's greatness and that Paulina's exceptional intelligence could be explained only on the ground that she was designed to act as the guardian of the family temple.

The House, by the time Paulina came to live in it, had already acquired the publicity of a place of worship; not the perfumed chapel of a romantic idolatry but the cold clean empty meeting-house of ethical enthusiasms. The ladies lived on its outskirts, as it were, in cells that left the central fane undisturbed. The very position of the furniture had come to have a ritual significance: the sparse ornaments were the offerings of kindred intellects, the steel engravings by Raphael Morghen marked the Via Sacra of a European tour, and the black-walnut desk with its bronze inkstand modelled on the Pantheon was the altar of this bleak temple of thought.

To a child compact of enthusiasms, and accustomed to pasture them on the scanty herbage of a new social soil, the atmosphere of the old house was full of floating nourishment. In the compressed perspective of Paulina's outlook it stood for a monument of ruined civilizations, and its white portico opened on legendary distances. Its very aspect was impressive to eyes that had first surveyed life from the jig-saw "residence" of a raw-edged Western town. The high-ceilinged rooms, with their panelled walls, their polished mahogany, their portraits of triple-stocked ancestors and of ringleted "females" in crayon, furnished the child with the historic scenery against which a young imagination constructs its vision of the past. To other eyes the cold spotless thinly-furnished interior might have suggested the shuttered mind of a maiden-lady who associates fresh air and sunlight with dust and discoloration; but it is the eye which supplies the coloring-matter, and Paulina's brimmed with the richest hues.

Nevertheless, the House did not immediately dominate her. She had her confused out-reachings toward other centres of sensation, her vague intuition of a heliocentric system; but the attraction of habit, the steady pressure of example, gradually fixed her roving allegiance and she bent her neck to the yoke. Vanity had a share in her subjugation; for it had early been discovered that she was the only person in the family who could read her grandfather's works. The fact that she had perused them with delight at an age when (even presupposing a metaphysical bias) it was impossible for her to understand them, seemed to her aunts and grandmother sure evidence of predestination. Paulina was to be the interpreter of the oracle, and the philosophic fumes so vertiginous to meaner minds would throw her into the needed condition of clairvoyance. Nothing could have been more genuine than the emotion on which this theory was based. Paulina, in fact, delighted in her grandfather's writings. His sonorous periods, his mystic vocabulary, his bold flights into the rarefied air of the abstract, were thrilling to a fancy unhampered by the need of definitions. This purely verbal pleasure was supplemented later by the excitement of gathering up crumbs of meaning from the rhetorical board. What could have been more stimulating than to construct the theory of a girlish world out of the fragments of this Titanic cosmogony? Before Paulina's opinions had reached the stage when ossification sets in their form was fatally predetermined.

The fact that Dr. Anson had died and that his apotheosis had taken place before his young priestess's induction to the temple, made her ministrations easier and more inspiring. There were no little personal traits—such as the great man's manner of helping himself to salt, or the guttural cluck that started the wheels of speech—to distract the eye of young veneration from the central fact of his divinity. A man whom one knows only through a crayon portrait and a dozen yellowing tomes on freewill and intuition is at least secure from the belittling effects of intimacy.

Paulina thus grew up in a world readjusted to the fact of her grandfather's greatness; and as each organism draws from its surroundings the kind of nourishment most needful to its growth, so from this somewhat colorless conception she absorbed warmth, brightness and variety. Paulina was the type of woman who transmutes thought into sensation and nurses a theory in her bosom like a child.

In due course Mrs. Anson "passed away"—no one died in the Anson vocabulary—and Paulina became more than ever the foremost figure of the commemorative group. Laura and Phoebe, content to leave their father's glory in more competent hands, placidly lapsed into needlework and fiction, and their niece stepped into immediate prominence as the chief "authority" on the great man. Historians who were "getting up" the period wrote to consult her and to borrow documents; ladies with inexplicable yearnings begged for an interpretation of phrases which had "influenced" them, but which they had not quite understood; critics applied to her to verify some doubtful citation or to decide some disputed point in chronology; and the great tide of thought and investigation kept up a continuous murmur on the quiet shores of her life.

An explorer of another kind disembarked there one day in the shape of a young man to whom Paulina was primarily a kissable girl, with an after-thought in the shape of a grandfather. From the outset it had been impossible to fix Hewlett Winsloe's attention on Dr. Anson. The young man behaved with the innocent profanity of infants sporting on a tomb. His excuse was that he came from New York, a Cimmerian outskirt which survived in Paulina's geography only because Dr. Anson had gone there once or twice to lecture. The curious thing was that she should have thought it worth while to find excuses for young Winsloe. The fact that she did so had not escaped the attention of the village; but people, after a gasp of awe, said it was the most natural thing in the world that a girl like Paulina Anson

should think of marrying. It would certainly seem a little odd to see a man in the House, but young Winsloe
would of course understand that the Doctor's books
were not to be disturbed, and that he must go down to
the orchard to smoke—. The village had barely framed
this *modus vivendi* when it was convulsed by the announcement that young Winsloe declined to live in the
House on any terms. Hang going down to the orchard
to smoke! He meant to take his wife to New York. The
village drew its breath and watched.

Did Persephone, snatched from the warm fields of
Enna, peer half-consentingly down the abyss that
opened at her feet? Paulina, it must be owned, hung a
moment over the black gulf of temptation. She would
have found it easy to cope with a deliberate disregard of
her grandfather's rights; but young Winsloe's un-
consciousness of that shadowy claim was as much a
natural function as the falling of leaves on a grave. His
love was an embodiment of the perpetual renewal which
to some tender spirits seems a crueller process than
decay.

On women of Paulina's mould this piety toward im-
plicit demands, toward the ghosts of dead duties
walking unappeased among usurping passions, has a
stronger hold than any tangible bond. People said that
she gave up young Winsloe because her aunts disapproved of her leaving them; but such disapproval as
reached her was an emanation from the walls of the
House, from the bare desk, the faded portraits, the
dozen yellowing tomes that no hand but hers ever lifted
from the shelf.

II.

AFTER THAT the House possessed her. As if conscious of its victory, it imposed a conqueror's claims. It had once been suggested that she should write a life of her grandfather, and the task from which she had shrunk as from a too-oppressive privilege now shaped itself into a justification of her course. In a burst of filial pantheism she tried to lose herself in the vast ancestral consciousness. Her one refuge from scepticism was a blind faith in the magnitude and the endurance of the idea to which she had sacrificed her life, and with a passionate instinct of self-preservation she labored to fortify her position.

The preparations for the *Life* led her through byways that the most scrupulous of the previous biographers had left unexplored. She accumulated her material with a blind animal patience unconscious of fortuitous risks. The years stretched before her like some vast blank page spread out to receive the record of her toil; and she had a mystic conviction that she would not die till her work was accomplished.

The aunts, sustained by no such high purpose, withdrew in turn to their respective divisions of the Anson "plot," and Paulina remained alone with her task. She was forty when the book was completed. She had travelled little in her life, and it had become more and more difficult to her to leave the House even for a day; but the dread of entrusting her document to a strange hand made her decide to carry it herself to the publisher. On the way to Boston she had a sudden vision of the loneliness to which this last parting condemned her. All her youth, all her dreams, all her renunciations lay in that neat bundle on her knee. It was not so much her grandfather's life as her own that she had written; and the knowledge that it would come back to her in all the glorification of print was of no more help than, to a mother's grief, the assurance that the lad she must part with will return with epaulets.

She had naturally addressed herself to the firm which had published her grandfather's works. Its founder, a personal friend of the philosopher's, had survived the Olympian group of which he had been a subordinate member, long enough to bestow his octogenarian approval on Paulina's pious undertaking. But he had died soon afterward; and Miss Anson found herself confronted by his grandson, a person with a brisk commercial view of his trade, who was said to have put "new blood" into the firm.

This gentleman listened attentively, fingering her manuscript as though literature were a tactile substance; then, with a confidential twist of his revolving chair, he emitted the verdict: "We ought to have had this ten years sooner."

Miss Anson took the words as an allusion to the repressed avidity of her readers. "It has been a long time for the public to wait," she solemnly assented.

The publisher smiled. "They haven't waited," he said.

She looked at him strangely. "Haven't waited?"

"No—they've gone off; taken another train. Literature's like a big railway-station now, you know: there's a train starting every minute. People are not going to hang round the waiting-room. If they can't get to a place when they want to they go somewhere else."

The application of this parable cost Miss Anson several minutes of throbbing silence. At length she said: "Then I am to understand that the public is no longer interested in—in my grandfather?" She felt as though heaven must blast the lips that risked such a conjecture.

"Well, it's this way. He's a name still, of course. People don't exactly want to be caught not knowing who he is; but they don't want to spend two dollars finding out, when they can look him up for nothing in any biographical dictionary."

Miss Anson's world reeled. She felt herself adrift among mysterious forces, and no more thought of prolonging the discussion than of opposing an earthquake with argument. She went home carrying the manuscript like a wounded thing. On the return journey she found herself travelling straight toward a fact that had lurked for months in the background of her life, and that now seemed to await her on the very threshold: the fact that fewer visitors came to the House. She owned to herself that for the last four or five years the number had steadily diminished. Engrossed in her work, she had noted the change only to feel thankful that she had fewer interruptions. There had been a time when, at the travelling season, the bell rang continuously, and the ladies of the House lived in a chronic state of "best silks" and expectancy. It would have been impossible then to carry on any consecutive work; and she now saw that the silence which had gathered round her task had been the hush of death.

Not of *his* death! The very walls cried out against the implication. It was the world's enthusiasm, the world's faith, the world's loyalty that had died. A corrupt generation that had turned aside to worship the brazen serpent. Her heart yearned with a prophetic passion over the lost sheep straying in the wilderness. But all great glories had their interlunar period; and in due time her grandfather would once more flash full-orbed upon a darkling world.

The few friends to whom she confided her adventure reminded her with tender indignation that there were other publishers less subject to the fluctuations of the market; but much as she had braved for her grandfather she could not again brave that particular probation. She found herself, in fact, incapable of any immediate effort. She had lost her way in a labyrinth of conjecture where her worst dread was that she might put her hand upon the clue.

She locked up the manuscript and sat down to wait. If a pilgrim had come just then the priestess would have fallen on his neck; but she continued to celebrate her rites alone. It was a double solitude; for she had always thought a great deal more of the people who came to see the House than of the people who came to see her. She fancied that the neighbors kept a keen eye on the path to the House; and there were days when the figure of a stranger strolling past the gate seemed to focus upon her the scorching sympathies of the village. For a time she thought of travelling; of going to Europe, or even to Boston; but to leave the House now would have seemed like deserting her post. Gradually her scattered energies centred themselves in the fierce resolve to understand what had happened. She was not the woman to live long in an unmapped country or to accept as final her private interpretation of phenomena. Like a traveller in unfamiliar regions she began to store for future guidance the minutest natural signs. Unflinchingly she noted the accumulating symptoms of indifference that marked her grandfather's descent toward posterity. She passed from the heights on which he had been grouped with the sages of his day to the lower level where he had come to be "the friend of Emerson," "the correspondent of Hawthorne," or (later still) "the Dr. Anson" mentioned in their letters. The change had taken place as slowly and imperceptibly as a natural process. She could not say that any ruthless hand had stripped the leaves from the tree: it was simply that, among the evergreen glories of his group, her grandfather's had proved deciduous.

She had still to ask herself why. If the decay had been a natural process, was it not the very pledge of renewal? It was easier to find such arguments than to be convinced by them. Again and again she tried to drug her solicitude with analogies; but at last she saw that such expedients were but the expression of a growing incredulity. The best way of proving her faith in her grandfather was not to be afraid of critics. She had no notion where these shadowy antagonists lurked; for she had never heard of the great man's doctrine being directly combated. Oblique assaults there must have been, however, Parthian shots at the giant that none dared face; and she thirsted to close with such assailants. The difficulty was to find them. She began by re-reading the

Works; thence she passed to the writers of the same school, those whose rhetoric bloomed perennial in *First Readers* from which her grandfather's prose had long since faded. Amid that clamor of far-off enthusiasms she detected no controversial note. The little knot of Olympians held their views in common with an early-Christian promiscuity. They were continually proclaiming their admiration for each other; the public joining as chorus in this guileless antiphon of praise; and she discovered no traitor in their midst.

What then had happened? Was it simply that the main current of thought had set another way? Then why did the others survive? Why were they still marked down as tributaries to the philosophic stream? This question carried her still farther afield, and she pressed on with the passion of a champion whose reluctance to know the worst might be construed into a doubt of his cause. At length—slowly but inevitably—an explanation shaped itself. Death had overtaken the doctrines about which her grandfather had draped his cloudy rhetoric. They had disintegrated and been reabsorbed, adding their little pile to the dust drifted about the mute lips of the Sphinx. The great man's contemporaries had survived not by reason of what they taught, but of what they were; and he, who had been the mere mask through which they mouthed their lesson, the instrument on which their tune was played, lay buried deep among the obsolete tools of thought.

The discovery came to Paulina suddenly. She looked up one evening from her reading and it stood before her like a ghost. It had entered her life with stealthy steps, creeping close before she was aware of it. She sat in the library, among the carefully-tended books and portraits; and it seemed to her that she had been walled alive into a tomb hung with the effigies of dead ideas. She felt a desperate longing to escape into the outer air, where people toiled and loved, and living sympathies went hand in hand. It was the sense of wasted labor that oppressed her; of two lives consumed in that ruthless process that uses generations of effort to build a single cell. There was a dreary parallel between her grandfather's fruitless toil and her own unprofitable sacrifice. Each in turn had kept vigil by a corpse.

III.

THE BELL RANG—she remembered it afterward—with a loud thrilling note. It was what they used to call the "visitor's ring"; not the tentative tinkle of a neighbor dropping in to borrow a sauce-pan or discuss parochial incidents, but a decisive summons from the outer world.

Miss Anson put down her knitting and listened. She sat upstairs now, making her rheumatism an excuse for avoiding the rooms below. Her interests had insensibly adjusted themselves to the perspective of her neighbors' lives, and she wondered—as the bell re-echoed—if it could mean that Mrs. Heminway's baby had come. Conjecture had time to ripen into certainty, and she was limping toward the closet where her cloak and bonnet hung, when her little maid fluttered in with the announcement: "A gentleman to see the house."

"The *House*?"

"Yes, m'm. I don't know what he means," faltered the messenger, whose memory did not embrace the period when such announcements were a daily part of the domestic routine.

Miss Anson glanced at the proffered card. The name it bore—*Mr. George Corby*—was unknown to her, but the blood rose to her languid cheek. "Hand me my Mechlin cap, Katy," she said, trembling a little, as she laid aside her walking stick. She put her cap on before the mirror, with rapid unsteady touches. "Did you draw up the library blinds?'' she breathlessly asked.

She had gradually built up a wall of commonplace between herself and her illusions, but at the first summons of the past filial passion swept away the frail barriers of expediency.

She walked down-stairs so hurriedly that her stick clicked like a girlish heel; but in the hall she paused, wondering nervously if Katy had put a match to the fire. The autumn air was cold and she had the reproachful vision of a visitor with elderly ailments shivering by her inhospitable hearth. She thought instinctively of the stranger as a survivor of the days when such a visit was a part of the young enthusiast's itinerary.

The fire was unlit and the room forbiddingly cold; but the figure which, as Miss Anson entered, turned from a lingering scrutiny of the book-shelves, was that of a fresh-eyed sanguine youth clearly independent of any artificial caloric. She stood still a moment, feeling herself the victim of some anterior impression that made this robust presence an insubstantial thing; but the young man advanced with an air of genial assurance which rendered him at once more real and more reminiscent.

"Why this, you know," he exclaimed, "is simply immense!"

The words, which did not immediately present themselves as slang to Miss Anson's unaccustomed ear, echoed with an odd familiarity through the academic silence.

"The room, you know, I mean," he explained with a comprehensive gesture. "These jolly portraits, and the books—that's the old gentleman himself over the mantelpiece, I suppose?—and the elms outside, and—and the whole business. I do like a congruous background—don't you?"

His hostess was silent. No one but Hewlett Winsloe had ever spoken of her grandfather as "the old gentleman."

"It's a hundred times better than I could have

hoped," her visitor continued, with a cheerful disregard of her silence. "The seclusion, the remoteness, the philosophic atmosphere—there's so little of that kind of flavor left! I should have simply hated to find that he lived over a grocery, you know.—I had the deuce of a time finding out where he *did* live," he began again, after another glance of parenthetical enjoyment. "But finally I got on the trail through some old book on Brook Farm. I was bound I'd get the environment right before I did my article."

Miss Anson, by this time, had recovered sufficient self-possession to seat herself and assign a chair to her visitor.

"Do I understand," she asked slowly, following his rapid eye about the room, "that you intend to write an article about my grandfather?"

"That's what I'm here for," Mr. Corby genially responded; "that is, if you're willing to help me; for I can't get on without your help," he added with a confident smile.

There was another pause, during which Miss Anson noticed a fleck of dust on the faded leather of the writing-table and a fresh spot of discoloration in the right-hand upper corner of Raphael Morghen's "Parnassus."

"Then you believe in him?" she said, looking up. She could not tell what had prompted her; the words rushed out irresistibly.

"Believe in him?" Corby cried, springing to his feet. "Believe in Orestes Anson? Why, I believe he's simply the greatest—the most stupendous—the most phenomenal figure we've got!"

The color rose to Miss Anson's brow. Her heart was beating passionately. She kept her eyes fixed on the young man's face, as though it might vanish if she looked away.

"You—you mean to say this in your article?" she asked.

"Say it? Why, the facts will say it," he exulted. "The

baldest kind of a statement would make it clear. When a
man is as big as that he doesn't need a pedestal!''

Miss Anson sighed. "People used to say that when I
was young," she murmured. "But now—"

Her visitor stared. "When you were young? But how
did they know—when the thing hung fire as it did?
When the whole edition was thrown back on his
hands?''

"The whole edition—what edition?" It was Miss Anson's turn to stare.

"Why, of his pamphlet—*the* pamphlet—the one
thing that counts, that survives, that makes him what he
is! For heaven's sake," he tragically adjured her,
"don't tell me there isn't a copy of it left!''

Miss Anson was trembling slightly. "I don't think I
understand what you mean," she faltered, less
bewildered by his vehemence than by the strange sense
of coming on an unexplored region in the very heart of
her dominion.

"Why, his account of the *amphioxus*, of course! You
can't mean that his family didn't know about it—that
you don't know about it? I came across it by the merest
accident myself, in a letter of vindication that he wrote
in 1830 to an old scientific paper; but I understood there
were journals—early journals; there must be references
to it somewhere in the 'twenties. He must have been at
least ten or twelve years ahead of Yarrell; and he saw the
whole significance of it, too—he saw where it led to. As
I understand it, he actually anticipated in his pamphlet
Saint Hilaire's theory of the universal type, and supported the hypothesis by describing the notochord of
the *amphioxus* as a cartilaginous vertebral column. The
specialists of the day jeered at him, of course, as the specialists in Goethe's time jeered at the plant-metamor-
phosis. As far as I can make out, the anatomists and
zoologists were down on Dr. Anson to a man; that was
why his cowardly publishers went back on their bargain.
But the pamphlet must be here somewhere—he writes as
though, in his first disappointment, he had destroyed

the whole edition; but surely there must be at least one copy left?''

His scientific jargon was as bewildering as his slang; and there were even moments in his discourse when Miss Anson ceased to distinguish between them; but the suspense with which he continued to gaze on her acted as a challenge to her scattered thoughts.

"The *amphioxus*," she murmured, half-rising. "It's an animal, isn't it—a fish? Yes, I think I remember." She sank back with the inward look of one who retraces some lost line of association.

Gradually the distance cleared, the details started into life. In her researches for the biography she had patiently followed every ramification of her subject, and one of these overgrown paths now led her back to the episode in question. The great Orestes's title of "Doctor" had in fact not been merely the spontaneous tribute of a national admiration; he had actually studied medicine in his youth, and his diaries, as his granddaughter now recalled, showed that he had passed through a brief phase of anatomical ardor before his attention was diverted to supersensual problems. It had indeed seemed to Paulina, as she scanned those early pages, that they revealed a spontaneity, a freshness of feeling somehow absent from his later lucubrations—as though this one emotion had reached him directly, the others through some intervening medium. In the excess of her commemorative zeal she had even struggled through the unintelligible pamphlet to which a few lines in the journal had bitterly directed her. But the subject and the phraseology were alien to her and unconnected with her conception of the great man's genius; and after a hurried perusal she had averted her thoughts from the episode as from a revelation of failure. At length she rose a little unsteadily, supporting herself against the writing-table. She looked hesitatingly about the room; then she drew a key from her old-fashioned reticule and unlocked a drawer beneath one of the book-cases. Young Corby watched her breathlessly. With a tremulous hand she turned over the dusty documents that seemed to fill the drawer. "Is this it?" she said, holding out a thin discolored volume.

He seized it with a gasp. "Oh, by George," he said, dropping into the nearest chair.

She stood observing him strangely as his eye devoured the mouldy pages.

"Is this the only copy left?" he asked at length, looking up for a moment as a thirsty man lifts his head from his glass.

"I think it must be. I found it long ago, among some old papers that my aunts were burning up after my grandmother's death. They said it was of no use—that he'd always meant to destroy the whole edition and that I ought to respect his wishes. But it was something *he* had written; to burn it was like shutting the door against his voice—against something he had once wished to say, and that nobody had listened to. I wanted him to feel that I was always here, ready to listen, even when others hadn't thought it worth while; and so I kept the pamphlet, meaning to carry out his wish and destroy it before my death."

Her visitor gave a groan of retrospective anguish. "And but for me—but for to-day—you would have?"

"I should have thought it my duty."

"Oh, by George—by George," he repeated, subdued afresh by the inadequacy of speech.

She continued to watch him in silence. At length he jumped up and impulsively caught her by both hands.

"He's bigger and bigger!" he almost shouted. "He simply leads the field! You'll help me go to the bottom of this, won't you? We must turn out all the papers—letters, journals, memoranda. He must have made notes. He must have left some record of what led up to this. We must leave nothing unexplored. By Jove," he cried, looking up at her with his bright convincing smile, "do you know you're the granddaughter of a Great Man?"

Her color flickered like a girl's. "Are you—sure of him?" she whispered, as though putting him on his guard against a possible betrayal of trust.

"Sure! Sure! My dear lady—" he measured her again with his quick confident glance. "Don't *you* believe in him?"

She drew back with a confused murmur. "I—used to." She had left her hands in his: their pressure seemed to send a warm current to her heart. "It ruined my life!" she cried with sudden passion. He looked at her perplexedly.

"I gave up everything," she went on wildly, "to keep *him* alive. I sacrificed myself—others—I nursed his glory in my bosom and it died—and left me—left me here alone." She paused and gathered her courage with a gasp. "Don't make the same mistake!" she warned him.

He shook his head, still smiling. "No danger of that! You're not alone, my dear lady. He's here with you— he's come back to you to-day. Don't you see what's happened? Don't you see that it's your love that has kept him alive? If you'd abandoned your post for an in-stant—let things pass into other hands—if your won-derful tenderness hadn't perpetually kept guard—this might have been—must have been—irretrievably lost." He laid his hand on the pamphlet. "And then—then he *would* have been dead!"

"Oh," she said, "don't tell me too suddenly!" And she turned away and sank into a chair.

The young man stood watching her in an awed si-lence. For a long time she sat motionless, with her face hidden, and he thought she must be weeping.

At length he said, almost shyly: "You'll let me come back, then? You'll help me work this thing out?"

She rose calmly and held out her hand. "I'll help you," she declared.

"I'll come to-morrow, then. Can we get to work early?"

"As early as you please."

"At eight o'clock, then," he said briskly. "You'll have the papers ready?"

"I'll have everything ready." She added with a half-playful hesitancy: "And the fire shall be lit for you."

He went out with his bright nod. She walked to the window and watched his buoyant figure hastening down the elm-shaded street. When she turned back into the empty room she looked as though youth had touched her on the lips.

THE LAST ASSET

I.

"THE DEVIL!" Paul Garnett exclaimed as he re-read his note; and the dry old gentleman who was at the moment his only neighbour in the modest restaurant they both frequented, remarked with a smile: "You don't seem particularly disturbed at meeting him."

Garnett returned the smile. "I don't know why I apostrophised him, for he's not in the least present—except inasmuch as he may prove to be at the bottom of anything unexpected."

The old gentleman who, like Garnett, was an American, and spoke in the thin rarefied voice which seems best fitted to emit sententious truths, twisted his lean neck round to cackle out: "Ah, it's generally a woman who's at the bottom of the unexpected. Not," he added, leaning forward with deliberation to select a tooth-pick, "that that precludes the devil's being there too."

Garnett uttered the requisite laugh, and his neighbour, pushing back his plate, called out with a perfectly unbending American intonation: "Gassong! L'addition, silver play."

His repast, as usual, had been a simple one, and he

left only thirty centimes in the plate on which his account was presented; but the waiter, to whom he was evidently a familiar presence, received the tribute with Latin amenity, and hovered helpfully about the table while the old gentleman cut and lighted his cigar.

"Yes," the latter proceeded, revolving the cigar meditatively between his thin lips, "they're generally both in the same hole, like the owl and the prairie-dog in the natural history books of my youth. I believe it was all a mistake about the owl and the prairie-dog, but it isn't about the unexpected. The fact is, the unexpected *is* the devil—the sooner you find that out, the happier you'll be." He leaned back, tilting his bald head against the blotched mirror behind him, and rambling on with gentle garrulity while Garnett attacked his omelet.

"Get your life down to routine—eliminate surprises. Arrange things so that, when you get up in the morning, you'll know exactly what's going to happen to you during the day—and the next day and the next. I don't say it's funny—it ain't. But it's better than being hit on the head by a brickbat. That's why I always take my meals at this restaurant. I know just how much onion they put in things—if I went to the next place I shouldn't. And I always take the same streets to come here—I've been doing it for ten years now. I know at which crossing to look out—I know what I'm going to see in the shop-windows. It saves a lot of wear and tear to know what's coming. For a good many years I never *did* know, from one minute to another, and now I like to think that everything's cut-and-dried, and nothing unexpected can jump out at me like a tramp from a ditch."

He paused calmly to knock the ashes from his cigar and Garnett said with a smile: "Doesn't such a plan of life cut off nearly all the possibilities?"

The old gentleman made a contemptuous motion. "Possibilities of what? Of being multifariously miserable? There are lots of ways of being miserable, but there's only one way of being comfortable, and that is to stop running round after happiness. If you make up your mind not to be happy there's no reason why you shouldn't have a fairly good time.''

"That was Schopenhauer's idea, I believe," the young man said, pouring his wine with the smile of youthful incredulity.

"I guess he hadn't the monopoly," responded his friend. "Lots of people have found out the secret—the trouble is that so few live up to it."

He rose from his seat, pushing the table forward, and standing passive while the waiter advanced with his shabby overcoat and umbrella. Then he nodded to Garnett, lifted his hat to the broad-bosomed lady behind the desk, and passed out into the street.

Garnett looked after him with a musing smile. The two had exchanged views on life for two years without so much as knowing each other's names. Garnett was a newspaper correspondent whose work kept him mainly in London, but on his periodic visits to Paris he lodged in a dingy hotel of the Latin quarter, the chief merit of which was its nearness to the cheap and excellent restaurant where the two Americans had made acquaintance. But Garnett's assidulity in frequenting the place arose, in the end, less from the excellence of the food than from the enjoyment of his old friend's conversation. Amid the flashy sophistications of the Parisian life to which Garnett's trade introduced him, the American sage's conversation had the crisp and homely flavour of a native dish—one of the domestic compounds for which the exiled palate is suppose to yearn. It was a mark of the old man's impersonality that, in spite of the interest he inspired, Garnett had never got beyond idly wondering who he might be, where he lived, and what his occupations were. He was presumably a bachelor—a man of family ties, however relaxed, though he might have been as often absent from home would not have been as regularly present in the same place—and there was about him a boundless desultoriness which renewed Garnett's conviction that there is no one on earth as idle as an American who is not busy. From certain allusions it was plain that he had

lived many years in Paris, yet he had not taken the
trouble to adapt his tongue to the local inflections, but
spoke French with the accent of one who has formed his
notion of the language from a phrasebook.

The city itself seemed to have made as little impression on him as its speech. He appeared to have no
artistic or intellectual curiosities, to remain untouched
by the complex appeal of Paris, while preserving,
perhaps the more strikingly from his very detachment,
that odd American astuteness which seems the fruit of
innocence rather than of experience. His nationality
revealed itself again in a mild interest in the political
problems of his adopted country, though they appeared
to preoccupy him only as illustrating the boundless per-
versity of mankind. The exhibition of human folly never
ceased to divert him, and though his examples of it
seemed mainly drawn from the columns of one exiguous
daily paper, he found there matter for endless variations
on his favourite theme. If this monotony of topic did
not weary the younger man, it was because he fancied he
could detect under it the tragic note of the fixed
idea—of some great moral upheaval which had flung his
friend stripped and starving on the desert island of the
little restaurant where they met. He hardly knew
wherein he read this revelation—whether in the shabbiness of the sage's dress, the impersonal courtesy of his
manner, or the shade of apprehension which lurked in-
describably, in his guileless yet suspicious eye. There
were moments when Garnett could only define him by
saying that he looked like a man who had seen a ghost.

II.

AN APPARITION almost as startling had come to Garnett himself in the shape of the mauve note handed to him by his *concierge* as he was leaving the hotel for luncheon.

Not that, on the face of it, a missive announcing Mrs. Sam Newell's arrival at Ritz's, and her need of his presence there that day at five, carried any mark of the portentous. It was not her being at Ritz's that surprised him. The fact that she was chronically hard up, and had once or twice lately been so harshly confronted with the consequences as to accept—indeed solicit—a loan of five pounds from him: this circumstance, as Garnett knew, would never be allowed to affect the general tenor of her existence. If one came to Paris, where could one go but to Ritz's? Did he see her in some grubby hole across the river? Or in a family *pension* near the Place de l'Etoile? There was no affectation in her tendency to gravitate toward what was costliest and most conspicuous. In doing so she obeyed one of the profoundest instincts of her nature, and it was another instinct which taught her to gratify the first at any cost, even to that of dipping into the pocket of an impecunious journalist. It was a part of her strength—and of her charm, too—that she did such things naturally, openly, without any of the grimaces of dissimulation or compunction.

Her recourse to Garnett had of course marked a specially low ebb in her fortunes. Save in moments of exceptional dearth she had richer sources of supply; and he was nearly sure that by running over the "society column" of the Paris *Herald* he should find an explanation, not perhaps of her presence at Ritz's, but of her means of subsistence there. What perplexed him was not the financial but the social aspect of the case. When Mrs. Newell had left London in July she had told him that, between Cowes and Scotland, she and Hermy were provided for till the middle of October: after that, as she put it, they would have to look about. Why, then, when she had in her hand the opportunity of living for three

months at the expense of the British aristocracy, did she
rush off to Paris at heaven knew whose expense in the
beginning of September? She was not a woman to act
incoherently; if she made mistakes they were not of that
kind. Garnett felt sure she would never willingly relax
her hold on her distinguished friends—was it possible
that it was they who had somewhat violently let go of
her?

As Garnett reviewed the situation he began to see that
this possibility had for some time been latent in it. He
had felt that something might happen at any
moment—and was not this the something he had ob-
scurely foreseen? Mrs. Newell really moved too fast: her
position was as perilous as that of an invading army
without a base of supplies. She used up everything too
quickly—friends, credit, influence, forbearance. It was
so easy for her to acquire all these—what a pity she had
never learned to keep them! He himself, for instance—the most insignificant of her acquisitions—was
beginning to feel like a squeezed sponge at the mere
thought of her; and it was this sense of exhaustion, of
the inability to provide more, either materially or
morally, which had provoked his exclamation on
opening her note. From the first days of their acquaintance her prodigality had amazed him, but he had
believed it to be surpassed by the infinity of her resources. If she exhausted old supplies she always had new
ones to replace them. When one set of people began to
find her impossible, another was always beginning
to find her indispensable. Yes—but there were limits—
there were only so many sets of people, at least in her
classification, and when she came to an end of them,
what then? Was this flight to Paris a sign that she had
come to an end—was she going to try Paris because
London had failed her? The time of year precluded such
a conjecture. Mrs. Newell's Paris was non-existent in
September. The town was a desert of gaping trip-
pers—he could as soon think of her seeking social
restoration at Margate.

For a moment it occurred to him that she might have

come over to renew her wardrobe; but he knew her dates too well to dwell long on this. It was in April and December that she visited the dressmakers: before December, he had heard her explain, one got nothing but "the American fashions." Mrs. Newell's scorn of all things American was somewhat illogically coupled with the determination to use her own Americanism to the utmost as a means of social advance. She had found out long ago that, on certain lines, it paid in London to be American, and she had manufactured for herself a personality independent of geographical or social demarcations, and presenting that remarkable blend of plantation dialect, Bowery slang and hyperbolic statement, which expresses the British idea of an unadulterated Americanism. Mrs. Newell, for all her talents, was not by nature either humourous or hyperbolic, and there were times when it would doubtless have been a relief to her to be as stolid as some of the persons whose dulness it was her fate to enliven. It was perhaps the need of relaxing which had drawn her into her odd intimacy with Garnett, with whom she did not have to be either scrupulously English or artificially American, since the impression she made on him was of no more consequence than that which she produced on her footman. Garnett was aware that he owed his success to his insignificance, but the fact affected him only as adding one more element to his knowledge of Mrs. Newell's character. He was as ready to sacrifice his personal vanity in such a cause as he had been, at the outset of their acquaintance, to sacrifice his professional pride to the opportunity of knowing her.

When he had accepted the position of "London correspondent" (with an occasional side-glance at Paris) to the New York *Searchlight*, he had not understood that his work was to include the obligation of "interviewing"; indeed, had the possibility presented itself in advance, he would have met it by packing his valise and returning to the drudgery of his assistant-editorship in New York. But when, after three months in Europe, he received a letter from his chief, suggesting

that he should enliven the Sunday *Searchlight* by a series
of "Talks with Smart Americans in London" (beginning say, with Mrs. Sam Newell), the change of focus
already enabled him to view the proposal without
passion. For his life on the edge of the great world-
caldron of art, politics and pleasure—of that high-
spiced brew which is nowhere else so subtly and
variously compounded—had bred in him an eagerness
to taste of the heady mixture. He knew he should never
have the full spoon at his lips, but he recalled the
peasant-girl in one of Browning's plays, who boasts of
having eaten polenta cut with a knife which has carved
an ortolan. Might not Mrs. Newell, who had so suc-
cessfully cut a way into the dense and succulent mass of
English society, serve as the knife to season his polenta?

He had expected, as the result of the interview, to
which she promptly, almost eagerly, agreed, no more
than the glimpse of brightly lit vistas which a waiting
messenger may catch through open doors; but instead
he had found himself drawn at once into the inner sanctuary, not of London society, but of Mrs. Newell's
relation to it. She had been candidly charmed by the
idea of the interview: it struck him that she was conscious of the need of being freshened up. Her appearance was brilliantly fresh, with the inveterate
freshness of the toilet-table; her paint was as im-
penetrable as armour. But her personality was a little
tarnished: she was in want of social renovation. She had
been doing and saying the same things for too long a
time. London, Cowes, Homburg, Scotland, Monte
Carlo—that had been the round since Hermy was a
baby. Hermy was her daughter, Miss Hermione Newell,
who was called in presently to be shown off to the in-
terviewer and add a paragraph to the celebration of her
mother's charms.

Miss Newell's appearance was so full of an unassisted
freshness that for a moment Garnett made the mistake
of fancying that she could fill a paragraph of her own.
But he soon found that her vague personality was
merely tributary to her parent's; that her youth and

grace were, in some mysterious way, her mother's rather than her own. She smiled obediently on Garnett, but could contribute little beyond her smile, and the general sweetness of her presence, to the picture of Mrs. Newell's existence that it was the young man's business to draw. And presently he found that she had left the room without him noticing it.

He learned in time that this unnoticeableness was the most conspicuous thing about her. Burning at best with a mild light, she became invisible in the glare of her mother's personality. It was in fact only as a product of her environment that poor Hermione struck the imagination. With the smartest woman in London as her guide and example she had never developed a taste for dress, and with opportunities for enlightenment from which Garnett's fancy recoiled she remained simple, unsuspicious and tender, with an inclination to good works and afternoon church, a taste for the society of dull girls, and a clinging fidelity to old governesses and retired nurse-maids. Mrs. Newell, whose boast it was that she looked facts in the face, frankly owned that she had not been able to make anything of Hermione. "If she has a rôle I haven't discovered it," she confessed to Garnett. "I've tried everything, but she doesn't fit in anywhere."

Mrs. Newell spoke as if her daughter were a piece of furniture acquired without due reflection, and for which no suitable place could be found. She got, of course, what she could out of Hermione, who wrote her notes, ran her errands, saw tiresome people for her, and occupied an intermediate office between that of lady's maid and secretary; but such small returns on her investment were not what Mrs. Newell had counted on. What was the use of producing and educating a handsome daughter if she did not, in some more positive way, contribute to her parent's advancement?

III.

"IT'S ABOUT HERMY," Mrs. Newell said, rising from the heap of embroidered cushions which formed the background of her afternoon repose.

Her sitting-room at Ritz's was full of warmth and fragrance. Long-stemmed roses filled the vases on the chimney-piece, in which a fire sparkled with that effect of luxury which fires produce when the weather is not cold enough to justify them. On the writing table, among notes and cards, and signed photographs of celebrities, Mrs. Newell's gold inkstand, her jewelled penholder, her heavily monogrammed despatch-box, gave back from their expensive surfaces the glint of the flame, which sought out and magnified the orient of the pearls among the lady's laces and found a mirror in the pinky polish of her fingertips. It was just such a scene as a little September fire, lit for show and not for warmth, would delight to dwell on and pick out in all its opulent details; and even Garnett, inured to Mrs. Newell's capacity for extracting manna from the desert, reflected that she must have found new fields to glean.

"It's about Hermy," she repeated, making room for him at her side. "I had to see you at once. We came over yesterday from London."

Garnett, seating himself, continued his leisurely survey of the room. In the blaze of Mrs. Newell's refulgence Hermione, as usual, faded out of sight, and he hardly noticed her mother's allusion.

"I've never seen you more resplendent," he remarked.

She received the tribute with complacency. "The rooms are not bad, are they? We came over with the Woolsey Hubbards (you've heard of them, of course? —they're from Detroit), and really they do things very decently. Their motor met us at Boulogne, and the courier always wires ahead to have the rooms filled with flowers. This *salon* is really a part of their suite. I simply couldn't have afforded it myself."

She delivered these facts in a high decisive voice, which had a note like the clink of her many bracelets and the rattle of her ringed hands against the enamelled cigarette-case that she held out to Garnett after helping herself from its contents.

"You are always meeting such charming people," said the young man with mild irony; and, reverting to her first remark, he bethought himself to add: "I hope Miss Hermione is not ill?"

"Ill? She was never ill in her life," exclaimed Mrs. Newell, as though her daughter had been accused of an indelicacy.

"It was only that you said you had come over on her account."

"So I have. Hermione is to be married."

Mrs. Newell brought out the words impressively, drawing back to observe their effect on her visitor. It was such that he received them with a long silent stare, which finally passed into a cry of wonder. "Married? For heaven's sake, to whom?"

Mrs. Newell continued to regard him with a smile so serene and victorious that he saw she took his somewhat unseemly astonishment as a merited tribute to her genius. Presently she extended a glittering hand and took a sheet of note-paper from the blotter.

"You can have that put in to-morrow's *Herald*," she said.

Garnett, receiving the paper, read in Hermione's own finished hand: "A marriage has been arranged, and will shortly take place, between the Comte Louis du Trayas, son of the Marquis du Trayas de la Baume, and Miss Hermione Newell, daughter of Samuel C. Newell Esqre., of Elmira, N. Y. Comte Louis du Trayas belongs to one of the oldest and most distinguished families in France, and is equally well connected in England, being the nephew of Lord Saint Priscoe and a cousin of the Countess of Morningfield, whom he frequently visits at Adham and Portlow."

The perusal of this document filled Garnett with such deepening wonder that he could not, for the moment,

even do justice to the strangeness of its being written out
for publication in the bride's own hand. Hermione a
bride! Hermione a future countess! Hermione on the
brink of a marriage which would give her not only a
great "situation" in the Parisian world but a footing in
some of the best houses in England! Regardless of its
unflattering implications, Garnett prolonged his stare of
amazement till Mrs. Newell somewhat sharply exclaimed—"Well, didn't I always tell you she'd marry a
Frenchman?"

Garnett, in spite of himself, smiled at this revised version of his hostess's frequent assertion that Hermione
was too goody-goody to take in England, but that with
her little dowdy air she might very well "go off" in the
Faubourg if only a *dot* could be raked up—and the
recollection flashed a new light on the versatility of Mrs.
Newell's genius.

"But how did you do it—?" was on the tip of his
tongue; and he had barely time to give the query the
more conventional turn of: "How did it happen?"

"Oh, we were up at Glaish with the Edmund Fitz-
zarthurs. Lady Edmund is a sort of cousin of the Morningfields', who have a shooting-lodge near Glaish—a
place called Portlow—and young Trayas was there with
them. Lady Edmund, who is a dear, drove Hermy over
to Portlow, and the thing was done in no time. He
simply fell over head and ears in love with her. You
know Hermy is really very handsome in her peculiar
way. I don't think you've ever appreciated her," Mrs.
Newell summed up with a note of reproach.

"I've appreciated her, I assure you; but one somehow
didn't think of her marrying—so soon."

"Soon? She's three and twenty; but you've no
imagination," said Mrs. Newell; and Garnett inwardly
admitted that he had not enough to soar to the heights
of her invention. For the marriage, of course, was her
invention, a superlative stroke of business in which he
was sure the principal parties had all been passive
agents, in which every one, from the bankrupt and
disreputable Fitzarthurs to the rich and immaculate

Morningfields, had by some mysterious sleight of hand been made to fit into Mrs. Newell's designs. But it was not enough for Garnett to marvel at her work—he wanted to understand it, to take it apart, to find out how the trick had been done. It was true that Mrs. Newell had always said Hermy might go off in the Faubourg if she had a *dot*—but even Mrs. Newell's juggling could hardly conjure up a *dot*; such feats as she was able to perform in this line were usually made to serve her own urgent necessities. And besides, who was likely to take sufficient interest in Hermione to supply her with the means of marrying a French nobleman? The flowers ordered in advance by the Woolsey Hubbards' courier made Garnett wonder if that accomplished functionary had also wired over to have Miss Newell's settlements drawn up. But of all the comments hovering on his lips the only one he could decently formulate was the remark that he supposed Mrs. Newell and her daughter had come over to see the young man's family and make the final arrangements.

"Oh, they're made—everything's settled," said Mrs. Newell, looking him squarely in the eye. "You're wondering, of course, about the *dot*—Frenchmen never go off their heads to the extent of forgetting *that*; or at least their parents don't allow them to."

Garnett murmured a vague assent, and she went on without the least appearance of resenting his curiosity: "It all came about so fortunately. Only fancy, just the week they met I got a little legacy from an aunt in Elmira—a good soul I hadn't seen or heard of for years. I suppose I ought to have put on mourning for her, by the way, but it would have eaten up a good bit of the legacy, and I really needed it all for poor Hermy. Oh, it's not a fortune, you understand—but the young man is madly in love, and has always had his own way, so after a lot of correspondence it's been arranged. They saw Hermy this morning, and they're enchanted."

"And the marriage takes place very soon?"

"Yes, in a few weeks, here. His mother is an invalid and couldn't have gone to England. Besides, the French don't travel. And as Hermy has become a Catholic—''

"Already?"

Mrs. Newell stared. "It doesn't take long. And it suits Hermy exactly—she can go to church so much oftener. So I thought," Mrs. Newell concluded with dignity, "that a wedding at Saint Philippe du Roule would be the most suitable thing at this season."

"Dear me," said Garnett, "I am left breathless—I can't catch up with you. I suppose even the day is fixed, though Miss Hermione doesn't mention it," and he indicated the official announcement in his hand.

Mrs. Newell laughed. "Hermy had to write that herself, poor dear, because my scrawl's too hideous—but I dictated it. No, the day's not fixed—that's why I sent for you." There was a splendid directness about Mrs. Newell. It would never have occurred to her to pretend to Garnett that she had summoned him for the pleasure of his company.

"You've sent for me—to fix the day?" he enquired humourously.

"To remove the last obstacle to its being fixed."

"I? What kind of an obstacle could I have the least effect on?"

Mrs. Newell met his banter with a look which quelled it. "I want you to find her father."

"Her father? Miss Hermione's—?"

"My husband, of course. I suppose you know he's living."

Garnett blushed at his own clumsiness. "I—yes—that is, I really knew nothing—" he stammered, feeling that each word added to it. If Hermione was unnoticeable, Mr. Newell had always been invisible. The young man had never so much as given him a thought, and it was awkward to come on him so suddenly at a turn of the talk.

"Well, he is—living here in Paris," said Mrs. Newell, with a note of asperity which seemed to imply that her friend might have taken the trouble to post himself on this point.

"In Paris? But in that case isn't it quite simple—?"

"To find him? I dare say it won't be difficult, though he's rather mysterious. But the point is that I can't go to him—and that if I write to him he won't answer."

"Ah," said Garnett thoughtfully.

"And so you've got to find him for me, and tell him."

"Tell him what?"

"That he must come to the wedding—that we must show ourselves together at church and afterward in the sacristy."

She delivered the behest in her sharp imperative key, the tone of the born commander. But for once Garnett ventured to question her orders.

"And supposing he won't come?"

"He must if he cares for his daughter's happiness. She can't be married without him."

"Can't be married?"

"The French are like that—especially the old families. I was given to understand at once that my husband must appear—if only to establish the fact that we're not divorced."

"Ah—you're *not*, then?" escaped from Garnett.

"Mercy no! Divorce is stupid. They don't like it in Europe. And in this case it would have been the end of Hermy's marriage. They wouldn't think of letting their son marry the child of divorced parents."

"How fortunate, then—"

"Yes; but I always think of such things beforehand. And of course I've told them that my husband will be present."

"You think he will consent?"

"No; not at first; but you must make him. You must tell him how sweet Hermione is—and you must see Louis, and be able to describe their happiness. You must dine here to-night—he's coming. We're all dining with the Hubbards, and they expect you. They've given Hermy some very good diamonds—though I should have preferred a cheque, as she'll be horribly poor. But

I think Kate Hubbard means to do something about the trousseau—Hermy is at Paquin's with her now. You've no idea how delightful all our friends have been.—Ah, here is one of them now," she broke off smiling, as the door opened to admit, without preliminary announcement, a gentleman so glossy and ancient, with such a fixed unnatural freshness of smile and eye, that he gave Garnett the effect of having been embalmed and then enamelled. It needed not the exotic-looking ribbon in the visitor's buttonhole, nor Mrs. Newell's introduction of him as her friend Baron Schenkelderff, to assure Garnett of his connection with a race as ancient as his appearance.

Baron Schenkelderff greeted his hostess with paternal playfulness, and the young man with an ease which might have been acquired on the Stock Exchange and in the dressing-rooms of "leading ladies." He spoke a faultless colourless English, from which one felt he might pass with equal mastery to half a dozen other languages. He inquired patronisingly for the excellent Hubbards, asked his hostess if she did not mean to give him a drop of tea and a cigarette, remarked that he need not ask if Hermione was still closeted with the dressmaker, and, on the waiter's coming in answer to his ring, ordered the tea himself, and added a request for *fine champagne*. It was not the first time that Garnett had seen such minor liberties taken in Mrs. Newell's drawing-room, but they had hitherto been taken by persons who had at least the superiority of knowing what they were permitting themselves, whereas the young man felt almost sure that Baron Schenkelderff's manner was the most distinguished he could achieve; and this deepened the disgust with which, as the minutes passed, he yielded to the conviction that the Baron was Mrs. Newell's aunt.

IV.

GARNETT HAD always foreseen that Mrs. Newell might some day ask him to do something he should greatly dislike. He had never gone so far as to conjecture what it might be, but had simply felt that if he allowed his acquaintance with her to pass from spectatorship to participation he must be prepared to find himself, at any moment, in a queer situation.

The moment had come; and he was relieved to find that he could meet it by refusing her request. He had not always been sure that she would leave him this alternative. She had a way of involving people in her complications without their being aware of it; and Garnett had pictured himself in holes so tight that there might not be room for a wriggle. Happily in this case he could still move freely. Nothing compelled him to act as an intermediary between Mrs. Newell and her husband, and it was preposterous to suppose that, even in a life of such perpetual upheaval as hers, there were no roots which struck deeper than her casual intimacy with himself. She had simply laid hands on him because he happened to be within reach, and he would put himself out of reach by leaving for London on the morrow.

Having thus inwardly asserted his independence, he felt free to let his fancy dwell on the strangeness of the situation. He had always supposed that Mrs. Newell, in her flight through life, must have thrown a good many victims to the wolves, and had assumed that Mr. Newell had been among the number. That he had been dropped overboard at an early stage in the lady's career seemed probable from the fact that neither his wife nor his daughter ever mentioned him. Mrs. Newell was incapable of reticence, and if her husband had still been an active element in her life he would certainly have figured in her conversation. Garnett, if he thought of the matter at all, had concluded that divorce must long since have eliminated Mr. Newell; but he now saw how he had underrated his friend's faculty for using up the waste material of life. She had always struck him as the most extravagant of women, yet it turned out that by a miracle of thrift she had for years kept a superfluous husband on the chance that he might some day be useful. The day had come, and Mr. Newell was to be called from his obscurity. Garnett wondered what had become of him in the interval, and in what shape he would respond to the evocation. The fact that his wife feared he might not respond to it at all seemed to show that his exile was voluntary, or had at least come to appear preferable to other alternatives; but if that were the case it was curious he should not have taken legal means to free himself. He could hardly have had his wife's motives for wishing to maintain the vague tie between them; but conjecture lost itself in trying to picture what his point of view was likely to be, and Garnett, on his way to the Hubbards' dinner that evening, could not help regretting that circumstances denied him the opportunity of meeting so enigmatic a person. The young man's knowledge of Mrs. Newell's methods made him feel that her husband might be an interesting study. This, however, did not affect his resolve to keep clear of the business. He entered the Hubbards' dining-room with the firm intention of refusing to execute Mrs. Newell's commission, and if he changed his mind in the course of the evening it was not owing to that lady's persuasions.

Garnett's curiosity as to the Hubbards' share in Hermione's marriage was appeased before he had been five minutes at their table.

Mrs. Woolsey Hubbard was an expansive blonde, whose ample but disciplined outline seemed the result of a well-matched struggle between her cook and her corset-maker. She talked a great deal of what was appropriate in dress and conduct, and seemed to regard Mrs. Newell as a final arbiter on both points. To do or to wear anything inappropriate would have been extremely mortifying to Mrs. Hubbard, and she was evidently resolved, at the price of eternal vigilance, to prove her familiarity with what she frequently referred

to as "the right thing." Mr. Hubbard appeared to have
no such preoccupations. Garnett, if called on to
describe him, would have done so by saying that he was
the American who always pays. The young man, in the
course of his foreign wanderings, had come across many
fellow-citizens of Mr. Hubbard's type in the most di-
verse company and surroundings; and wherever they
were to be found, they always had their hands in their
pockets. Mr. Hubbard's standard of gentility was the
extent of a man's capacity to "foot the bill"; and as no
one but an occasional compatriot cared to dispute the
privilege with him he seldom had reason to doubt his
social superiority.

Garnett, nevertheless, did not believe that this lavish
pair were, as Mrs. Newell would have phrased it, "putting up" Hermione's *dot*. They would go very far in
diamonds but they would hang back from securities.
Their readiness to pay was indefinably mingled with a
dread of being expected to, and their prodigalities
would take flight at the first hint of coercion. Mrs.
Newell, who had had a good deal of experience in
managing this type of millionaire, could be trusted not
to arouse their susceptibilities, and Garnett was
therefore certain that the chimerical legacy had been extracted from other pockets. There were none in view but
those of Baron Schenkelderff, who, seated at Mrs. Hubbard's right, with a new order in his buttonhole, and a
fresh glaze upon his features, enchanted that lady by his
careless references to crowned heads and his con-
descending approval of the champagne. Garnett was
more than ever certain that it was the Baron who was
paying; and it was this conviction which made him suddenly resolve that, at any cost, Hermione's marriage
must take place. He had felt no special interest in the
marriage except as one more proof of Mrs. Newell's extraordinary capacity; but now it appealed to him from
the girl's own stand-point. For he saw, with a touch of
compunction, that in the mephitic air of her surroundings a love-story of miraculous freshness had
flowered. He had only to intercept the glances which the

young couple exchanged to find himself transported to
the candid region of romance. It was evident that Hermione adored and was adored; that the lovers believed
in each other and in every one about them, and that
even the legacy of the defunct aunt had not been too
great a strain on their faith in human nature.

His first glance at the Comte Louis du Trayas showed
Garnett that, by some marvel of fitness, Hermione had
happened on a kindred nature. If the young man's long
mild features and shortsighted glance revealed no
special force of character, they showed a benevolence
and simplicity as incorruptible as her own, and declared
that their possessor, whatever his failings, would never
imperil the illusions she had so wondrously preserved.
The fact that the girl took her good fortune naturally,
and did not regard herself as suddenly snatched from
the jaws of death, added poignancy to the situation; for
if she missed this way of escape, and was thrown back
on her former life, the day of discovery could not be
long deferred. It made Garnett shiver to think of her
growing old between her mother and Schenkelderff, or
such successors of the Baron's as might probably attend
on Mrs. Newell's waning fortunes; for it was clear to
him that the Baron marked the first stage in his friend's
decline. When Garnett took leave that evening he had
promised Mrs. Newell that he would try to find her
husband.

V.

IF MR. NEWELL read in the papers the announcement of
his daughter's marriage it did not cause him to lift the
veil of seclusion in which his wife represented him as
shrouded.

A round of the American banks in Paris failed to give Garnett his address, and it was only in chance talk with one of the young secretaries of the Embassy that he was put on Mr. Newell's track. The secretary's father, it appeared, had known the Newells some twenty years earlier. He had had business relations with Mr. Newell, who was then a man of property, with factories or something of the kind, the narrator thought, somewhere in Western New York. There had been at this period, for Mrs. Newell, a phase of large hospitality and showy carriages in Washington and at Narragansett. Then her husband had had reverses, had lost heavily in Wall Street, and had finally drifted abroad and disappeared from sight. The young man did not know at what point in his financial decline Mr. Newell had parted company with his wife and daughter; "though you may bet your hat," he philosophically concluded, "that the old girl hung on as long as there were any pickings." He did not himself know Mr. Newell's address, but opined that it might be extracted from a certain official of the Consulate, if Garnett could give a sufficiently good reason for the request; and here in fact Mrs. Newell's emissary learned that her husband was to be found in an obscure street of the Luxembourg quarter.

In order to be near the scene of action, Garnett went to breakfast at his usual haunt, determined to despatch his business as early in the day as politeness allowed. The head waiter welcomed him to a table near that of the transatlantic sage, who sat in his customary corner, his head tilted back against the blistered mirror at an angle suggesting that in a freer civilisation his feet would have sought the same level. He greeted Garnett affably and the two exchanged their usual generalisations on life till the sage rose to go; whereupon it occurred to Garnett to accompany him. His friend took the offer in good part, merely remarking that he was going to the Luxembourg gardens, where it was his invariable habit, on good days, to feed the sparrows with the remains of his breakfast roll; and Garnett replied that, as it happened, his own business lay in the same direction.

"Perhaps, by the way," he added, "you can tell me how to find the rue Panonceaux, where I must go presently. I thought I knew this quarter fairly well, but I have never heard of it."

His companion came to a halt on the narrow pavement, to the confusion of the dense and desultory traffic which flows through the old streets of the Latin quarter. He fixed his mild eye on Garnett and gave a twist to the cigar which lingered in the corner of his mouth.

"The rue Panonceaux? It *is* an out-of-the-way hole, but I can tell you how to find it," he answered.

He made no motion to do so, however, but continued to bend on the young man the full force of his interrogative gaze; then he added: "Would you mind telling me your object in going there?"

Garnett looked at him with surprise: a question so unblushingly personal was strangely out of keeping with his friend's usual attitude of detachment. Before he could reply, however, the other had continued: "Do you happen to be in search of Samuel C. Newell?"

"Why, yes, I am," said Garnett with a start of conjecture.

His companion uttered a sigh. "I supposed so," he said resignedly; "and in that case," he added, "we may as well have the matter out in the Luxembourg."

Garnett had halted before him with deepening astonishment. "But you don't mean to tell me—?" he stammered.

The little man made a motion of assent. "I am Samuel C. Newell," he said; "and if you have no objection, I prefer not to break through my habit of feeding the sparrows. We are five minutes late as it is."

He quickened his pace without awaiting a reply from Garnett, who walked beside him in unsubdued wonder till they reached the Luxembourg gardens, where Mr. Newell, making for one of the less frequented alleys, seated himself on a bench and drew the fragment of a roll from his pocket. His coming was evidently expected, for a shower of little dusky bodies at once descended on him, and the gravel fluttered with battling beaks and wings as he distributed his dole.

It was not till the ground was white with crumbs, and the first frenzy of his pensioners appeased, that he turned to Garnett and said: "I presume, sir, that you come from my wife."

Garnett coloured with embarrassment: the more simply the old man took his mission the more complicated it appeared to himself.

"From your wife—and from Miss Newell," he said at length. "You have perhaps heard that your daughter is to be married."

"Oh, yes—I read the *Herald* pretty faithfully," said Miss Newell's parent, shaking out another handful of crumbs.

Garnett cleared his throat. "Then you have no doubt thought it natural that, under the circumstances, they should wish to communicate with you."

The sage continued to fix his attention on the sparrows. "My wife," he remarked, "might have written to me."

"Mrs. Newell was afraid she might not hear from you in reply."

"In reply? Why should she? I suppose she merely wishes to announce the marriage. She knows I have no money left to buy wedding-presents," said Mr. Newell astonishingly.

Garnett felt his colour deepen: he had a vague sense of standing as the representative of something guilty and enormous, with which he had rashly identified himself.

"I don't think you understand," he said. "Mrs. Newell and your daughter have asked me to see you because they're anxious that you should consent to appear at the wedding."

Mr. Newell, at this, ceased to give his attention to the birds, and turned a compassionate gaze on Garnett.

"My dear sir—I don't know your name—" he remarked, "would you mind telling me how long you've been acquainted with Mrs. Newell?" And without waiting for an answer he added: "If you wait long enough she will ask you to do some very disagreeable things for her."

This echo of his own thoughts gave Garnett a twinge of discomfort, but he made shift to answer good-humouredly: "If you refer to my present errand, I must tell you that I don't find it disagreeable to do anything which may be of service to Miss Hermione."

Mr. Newell fumbled in his pocket, as though searching unavailingly for another morsel of bread; then he said: "From her point of view I shall not be the most important person at the ceremony."

Garnett smiled. "That is hardly a reason—" he began; but he was checked by the brevity of tone with which his companion replied: "I am not aware that I am called upon to give you my reasons."

"You are certainly not," the young man rejoined, "except in so far as you are willing to consider me as the messenger of your wife and daughter."

"Oh, I accept your credentials," said the other with his dry smile; "what I don't recognise is their right to send a message."

This reduced Garnett to silence, and after a moment's pause Mr. Newell drew his watch from his pocket.

"I am sorry to cut the conversation short, but my days are mapped out with a certain regularity, and this is the hour for my nap." He rose as he spoke and held out his hand with a glint of melancholy humour in his small clear eyes.

"You dismiss me, then? I am to take back a refusal?" the young man exclaimed.

"My dear sir, those ladies have got on very well without me for a number of years: I imagine they can put through this wedding without my help."

"You're mistaken, then; if it were not for that I shouldn't have undertaken this errand."

Mr. Newell paused as he was turning away. "Not for what?" he inquired.

"The fact that, as it happens, the wedding can't be put through without your help."

Mr. Newell's thin lips formed a noiseless whistle. "They've got to have my consent, have they? Well, is he a good young man?"

"The bridegroom?" Garnett echoed in surprise. "I hear the best accounts of him—and Miss Newell is very much in love."

Her parent met this with an odd smile. "Well, then, I give my consent—it's all I've got left to give," he added philosophically.

Garnett hesitated. "But if you consent—if you approve—why do you refuse your daughter's request?"

Mr. Newell looked at him a moment. "Ask Mrs. Newell!" he said. And as Garnett was again silent, he turned away with a slight gesture of leave-taking.

But in an instant the young man was at his side. "I will not ask your reasons, sir," he said, "but I will give you mine for being here. Miss Newell cannot be married unless you are present at the ceremony. The young man's parents know that she has a father living, and they give their consent only on condition that he appears at her marriage. I believe it is customary in old French families—"

"Old French families be damned!" said Mr. Newell. "She had better marry an American." And he made a more decided motion to free himself from Garnett's importunities.

But his resistance only strengthened the young man's. The more unpleasant the latter's task became, the more unwilling he grew to see his efforts end in failure. During the three days which had been consumed in his quest it had become clear to him that the bridegroom's parents, having been surprised to a reluctant consent, were but too ready to withdraw it on the plea of Mr. Newell's nonappearance. Mrs. Newell, on the last edge of tension, had confided to Garnett that the Morningfields were "being nasty"; and he could picture the whole powerful clan, on both sides of the Channel, arrayed in a common resolve to exclude poor Hermione from their ranks. The very inequality of the contest stirred his blood, and made him vow that in this case at

least the sins of the parents should not be visited on the
children. In his talk with the young secretary he had ob-
tained certain glimpses of Baron Schenkelderff's past
that fortified this resolve. The Baron, at one time a
familiar figure in a much-observed London set, had
been mixed up in an ugly money-lending business
ending in suicide, which had excluded him from the
society most accessible to his race. His alliance with
Mrs. Newell was doubtless a desperate attempt at
rehabilitation, a forlorn hope on both sides, but likely
to be an enduring tie because it represented, to both
partners, their last chance of escape from social ex-
tinction. That Hermione's marriage was a mere stake in
their game did not in the least affect Garnett's view of
its urgency. If on their part it was a sordid speculation,
to her it had the freshness of the first wooing. If it made
of her a mere pawn in their hands, it would put her, so
Garnett hoped, beyond farther risk of such base uses;
and to achieve this had become a necessity to him.

The sense that, if he lost sight of Mr. Newell, the latter might not easily be found again, nerved Garnett to
hold his ground in spite of the resistance he en-
countered; and he tried to put the full force of his plea
into the tone with which he cried: "Ah, you don't know
your daughter!"

VI.

MRS. NEWELL, that afternoon, met him on the
threshold of her sitting-room with a "Well?" of pent-up
anxiety.

In the room itself, Baron Schenkelderff sat with
crossed legs and head thrown back, in an attitude which
he did not see fit to alter at the young man's approach.

Garnett hesitated; but it was not the summariness of the Baron's greeting which he resented.

"You've found him?" Mrs. Newell exclaimed.

"Yes; but—"

She followed his glance and answered it with a slight shrug. "I can't take you into my room, because there's a dress-maker there, and she won't go because she's waiting to be paid. Schenkelderff," she exclaimed, "you're not wanted; please go and look out of the window."

The Baron rose, and lighting a cigarette, laughingly retired to the embrasure. Mrs. Newell flung herself down and signed to Garnett to take a seat at her side.

"Well—you've found him? You've talked with him?"

"Yes; I've talked with him—for an hour."

She made an impatient movement. "That's too long! Does he refuse?"

"He doesn't consent."

"Then you mean—?"

"He wants time to think it over."

"Time? There *is* no time—did you tell him so?"

"I told him so; but you must remember that he has plenty. He has taken twenty-four hours."

Mrs. Newell groaned. "Oh, that's too much. When he thinks things over he always refuses."

"Well, he would have refused at once if I had not agreed to the delay."

She rose nervously from her seat and pressed her hands to her forehead. "It's too hard, after all I've done! The trousseau is ordered—think how disgraceful! You must have managed him badly; I'll go and see him myself."

The Baron, at this, turned abruptly from his study of the Place Vendôme.

"My dear creature, for heaven's sake don't spoil everything!" he exclaimed.

Mrs. Newell coloured furiously. "What's the meaning of that brilliant speech?"

"I was merely putting myself in the place of a man on

whom you have ceased to smile.''

He picked up his hat and stick, nodded knowingly to Garnett, and walked toward the door with an air of creaking jauntiness.

But on the threshold Mrs. Newell waylaid him.

"Don't go—I must speak to you," she said, following him into the ante-chamber; and Garnett remembered the dress-maker who was not to be dislodged from her bedroom.

In a moment Mrs. Newell returned, with a small flat packet which she vainly sought to dissemble in an inaccessible pocket.

"He makes everything too odious!" she exclaimed; but whether she referred to her husband or the Baron it was left to Garnett to decide.

She sat silent, nervously twisting her cigarette-case between her fingers, while her visitor rehearsed the details of his conversation with Mr. Newell. He did not indeed tell her the arguments he had used to shake her husband's resolve, since in his eloquent sketch of Hermione's situation there had perforce entered hints unflattering to her mother; but he gave the impression that his hearer had in the end been moved, and for that reason had consented to defer his refusal.

"Ah, it's not that—it's to prolong our misery!" Mrs. Newell exclaimed; and after a moment she added drearily: "He's been waiting for such an opportunity for years."

It seemed needless for Garnett to protract his visit, and he took leave with the promise to report at once the result of his final talk with Mr. Newell. But as he was passing through the ante-chamber a side door opened and Hermione stood before him. Her face was flushed and shaken out of its usual repose, and he saw at once that she had been waiting for him.

"Mr. Garnett!" she said in a whisper.

He paused, considering her with surprise: he had never supposed her capable of such emotion as her voice and eyes revealed.

"I want to speak to you; we are quite safe here.

Mamma is with the dress-maker," she explained, closing the door behind her, while Garnett laid aside his hat and stick.

"I am at your service," he said.

"You have seen my father? Mamma told me that you were to see him to-day," the girl went on, standing close to him in order that she might not have to raise her voice.

"Yes; I've seen him," Garnett replied with increasing wonder. Hermione had never before mentioned her father to him, and it was by a slight stretch of veracity that he had included her name in her mother's plea to Mr. Newell. He had supposed her to be either unconscious of the transaction, or else too much engrossed in her own happiness to give it a thought; and he had forgiven her the last alternative in consideration of the abnormal character of her filial relations. But he now saw that he must readjust his view of her.

"You went to ask him to come to my wedding; I know about it," Hermione continued. "Of course it's the custom—people will think it odd if he does not come." She paused, and then asked: "Does he consent?"

"No; he has not yet consented."

"Ah, I thought so when I saw Mamma just now!"

"But he hasn't quite refused—he has promised to think it over."

"But he hated it—he hated the idea?"

Garnett hesitated. "It seemed to arouse painful associations."

"Ah, it would—it would!" she exclaimed.

He was astonished at the passion of her accent; astonished still more at the tone with which she went on, laying her hand on his arm: "Mr. Garnett, he must not be asked—he has been asked too often to do things that he hated!"

Garnett looked at the girl with a shock of awe. What abysses of knowledge did her purity hide?

"But, my dear Miss Hermione—" he began.

"I know what you are going to say," she interrupted

him. "It is necessary that he should be present at the marriage, or the du Trayas will break it off. They don't want it very much, at any rate," she added with a strange candour, "and they'll not be sorry, perhaps—for of course Louis would have to obey them."

"So I explained to your father," Garnett assured her.

"Yes—yes; I knew you would put it to him. But that makes no difference. He must not be forced to come unwillingly."

"But if he sees the point—after all, no one can force him!"

"No; but if it's painful to him—if it reminds him too much. . . . Oh, Mr. Garnett, I was not a child when he left us. . . . I was old enough to see . . . to see how it must hurt him even now to be reminded. Peace was all he asked for, and I want him to be left in peace!"

Garnett paused in deep embarrassment. "My dear child, there is no need to remind you that your own future—"

She had a gesture that recalled her mother. "My future must take care of itself; he must not be made to see us!" she said imperatively. And as Garnett remained silent she went on: "I have always hoped he didn't hate me, but he would hate me now if he were forced to see me."

"Not if he could see you at this moment!"

She lifted her face with swimming eyes.

"Well, go to him, then; tell him what I've said to you!"

Garnett continued to stand before her, deeply struck. "It might be the best thing," he reflected inwardly; but he did not give utterance to the thought. He merely put out his hand, holding Hermione's in a long pressure.

"I will do whatever you wish," he replied.

"You understand that I'm in earnest?" she urged.

"I'm quite sure of it."

"Then I want you to repeat to him what I've said—I want him to be left undisturbed. I don't want him ever to hear of us again!"

*   *   *

The next day, at the appointed hour, Garnett resorted
to the Luxembourg gardens, which Mr. Newell had
named as a meeting-place in preference to his own
lodgings. It was clear that he did not wish to admit the
young man any farther into his privacy than the occasion required, and the extreme shabbiness of his dress
hinted that pride might be the cause of his reluctance.

Garnett found him feeding the sparrows, but he
desisted at the young man's approach, and said at once:
"You won't thank me for bringing you all this distance."

"If that means that you're going to send me away
with a refusal, I have come to spare you the necessity,"
Garnett answered.

Mr. Newell turned on him a glance of undisguised
wonder, in which a tinge of disappointment might
almost have been detected.

"Ah—they've got no use for me, after all?" he said
ironically.

Garnett, in reply, related without comment his conversation with Hermione, and the message with which
she had charged him. He remembered her words exactly
and repeated them without modification, heedless of
what they implied or revealed.

Mr. Newell listened with an immovable face, oc-
casionally casting a crumb to his flock. When Garnett
ended he asked: "Does her mother know of this?"

"Assuredly not!" cried Garnett with a movement of
disgust.

"You must pardon me; but Mrs. Newell is a very
ingenious woman." Mr. Newell shook out his remaining crumbs and turned thoughtfully toward Garnett.

"You believe it's quite clear to Hermione that these
people will use my refusal as a pretext for backing out of
the marriage?"

"Perfectly clear—she told me so herself."

"Doesn't she consider the young man rather chicken-
hearted?"

"No; he has already put up a big fight for her, and you know the French look at these things differently. He's only twenty-three, and his marrying against his parents' approval is in itself an act of heroism."

"Yes; I believe they look at it that way," Mr. Newell assented. He rose and picked up the half-smoked cigar which he had laid on the bench beside him.

"What do they wear at these French weddings, anyhow? A dress-suit, isn't it?" he asked.

The question was such a surprise to Garnett that for the moment he could only stammer out—"You consent then? I may go and tell her?"

"You may tell my girl—yes." He gave a vague laugh and added: "One way or another, my wife always gets what she wants."

VII.

MR. NEWELL'S consent brought with it no accompanying concessions. In the first flush of his success Garnett had pictured himself as bringing together the father and daughter, and hovering in an attitude of benediction over a family group in which Mrs. Newell did not very distinctly figure.

But Mr. Newell's conditions were inflexible. He would "see the thing through" for his daughter's sake; but he stipulated that in the meantime there should be no meetings of further communications of any kind. He agreed to be ready when Garnett called for him, at the appointed hour on the wedding-day; but until then he begged to be left alone. To this decision he adhered immovably, and when Garnett conveyed it to Hermione she accepted it with a deep look of understanding. As for Mrs. Newell she was too much engrossed in the nup-

tial preparations to give her husband another thought.
She had gained her point, she had disarmed her foes,
and in the first flush of success she had no time to
remember by what means her victory had been won.
Even Garnett's services received little recognition,
unless he found them sufficiently compensated by the
new look in Hermione's eyes.

The principal figures in Mrs. Newell's foreground
were the Woolsey Hubbards and Baron Schenkelderff.
With these she was in hourly consultation, and Mrs.
Hubbard went about aureoled with the importance of
her close connection with an "aristocratic marriage,"
and dazzled by the Baron's familiarity with the in-
tricacies of the Almanach de Gotha. In his society and
Mrs. Newell's, Mrs. Hubbard evidently felt that she had
penetrated to the sacred precincts where "the right
thing" flourished in its native soil. As for Hermione,
her look of happiness had returned, but with it an un-
der-tint of melancholy, visible perhaps only to Garnett,
but to him always hauntingly present. Outwardly she
sank back into her passive self, resigned to serve as the
brilliant lay-figure on which Mrs. Newell hung the
trophies of conquest. Preparations for the wedding were
zealously pressed. Mrs. Newell knew the danger of
giving people time to think things over, and her fears
about her husband being allayed, she began to dread a
new attempt at evasion on the part of the bridegroom's
family.

"The sooner it's over the sounder I shall sleep!" she
declared to Garnett; and all the mitigations of art could
not conceal the fact that she was desperately in need of
that restorative. There were moments, indeed, when he
was sorrier for her than for her husband or her
daughter; so black and unfathomable appeared the
abyss into which she must slip back if she lost her hold
on this last spar of safety.

But she did not lose her hold; his own experience, as
well as her husband's declaration, might have told him
that she always got what she wanted. How much she
had wanted this particular thing was shown by the way

in which, on the last day, when all peril was over, she bloomed out in renovated splendour. It gave Garnett a shivering sense of the ugliness of the alternative which had confronted her.

The day came; the showy coupé provided by Mrs. Newell presented itself punctually at Garnett's door, and the young man entered it and drove to the rue Panonceaux. It was a little melancholy back street, with lean old houses sweating rust and damp, and glimpses of pit-like gardens, black and sunless, between walls bristling with iron spikes. On the narrow pavement a blind man pottered along led by a red-eyed poodle: a little farther on a dishevelled woman sat grinding coffee on the threshold of a *buvette*. The bridal carriage stopped before one of the doorways, with a clatter of hoofs and harness which drew the neighbourhood to its windows, and Garnett started to mount the ill-smelling stairs to the fourth floor, on which he learned from the *concierge* that Mr. Newell lodged. But half-way up he met the latter descending, and they turned and went down together.

Hermione's parent wore his usual imperturbable look, and his eye seemed as full as ever of generalisations on human folly; but there was something oddly shrunken and submerged in his appearance, as though he had grown smaller or his clothes larger. And on the last hypothesis Garnett paused—for it became evident to him that Mr. Newell had hired his dress-suit.

Seated at the young man's side on the satin cushions, he remained silent while the carriage rolled smoothly and rapidly through the net-work of streets leading to the Boulevard Saint-Germain; only once he remarked, glancing at the elaborate fittings of the coupé: "Is this Mrs. Newell's carriage?"

"I believe so—yes," Garnett assented, with the guilty sense that in defining that lady's possessions it was impossible not to trespass on those of her friends.

Mr. Newell made no farther comment, but presently requested his companion to rehearse to him once more the exact duties which were to devolve on him during the coming ceremony. Having mastered these he remained silent, fixing a dry speculative eye on the panorama of the brilliant streets, till the carriage drew up at the entrance of Saint Philippe du Roule.

With the same air of composure he followed his guide through the mob of spectators, and up the crimson velvet steps, at the head of which, but for a word from Garnett, a formidable Suisse, glittering with cocked hat and mace, would have checked the advance of the small crumpled figure so oddly out of keeping with the magnificence of the bridal party. The French fashion prescribing that the family *cortège* shall follow the bride to the altar, the vestibule of the church was thronged with the participators in the coming procession; but if Mr. Newell felt any nervousness at his sudden projection into this unfamiliar group, nothing in his look or manner betrayed it. He stood beside Garnett till a white-favoured carriage, dashing up to the church with a superlative glitter of highly groomed horse-flesh and silver-plated harness, deposited the snowy apparition of the bride, supported by her mother; then, as Hermione entered the vestibule, he went forward quietly to meet her.

The girl, wrapped in the haze of her bridal veil, and a little confused, perhaps, by the anticipation of the meeting, paused a moment, as if in doubt, before the small oddly-clad figure which blocked her path—a horrible moment to Garnett, who felt a pang of misery at this satire on the infallibility of the filial instinct. He longed to make some sign, to break in some way the pause of uncertainty; but before he could move he saw Mrs. Newell give her daughter a sharp push, he saw a blush of compunction flood Hermione's face, and the girl, throwing back her veil, bent her tall head and flung her arms about her father.

Mr. Newell emerged unshaken from the embrace: it seemed to have no effect beyond giving an odder twist to his tie. He stood beside his daughter till the church doors were thrown open; then, at a sign from the verger, he gave her his arm, and the strange couple, with the long train of fashion and finery behind them, started on their march to the altar.

Garnett had already slipped into the church and secured a post of vantage which gave him a side-view over the assemblage. The building was thronged—Mrs. Newell had attained her ambition and given Hermione a smart wedding. Garnett's eye travelled curiously from one group to another—from the numerous representatives of the bridegroom's family, all stamped with the same air of somewhat dowdy distinction, the air of having had their thinking done for them for so long that they could no longer perform the act individually, and the heterogeneous company of Mrs. Newell's friends, who presented, on the opposite side of the nave, every variety of individual conviction in dress and conduct. Of the two groups the latter was decidedly the more interesting to Garnett, who observed that it comprised not only such recent acquisitions as the Woolsey Hubbards and the Baron, but also sundry more important figures which of late had faded to the verge of Mrs. Newell's horizon. Hermione's marriage had drawn them back, had once more made her mother a social entity, had in short already accomplished the object for which it had been planned and executed.

And as he looked about him Garnett saw that all the other actors in the show faded into insignificance beside the dominant figure of Mrs. Newell, became mere marionettes pulled hither and thither by the hidden wires of her intention. One and all they were there to serve her ends and accomplish her purpose: Schenkelderff and the Hubbards to pay for the show, the bride and bridegroom to seal and symbolize her social rehabilitation, Garnett himself as the humble instrument adjusting the different parts of the complicated machinery, and her husband, finally, as the last stake in her game, the last asset on which she could draw to rebuild her fallen fortunes. At the thought Garnett was filled with deep disgust for what the scene signified, and for his own share in it. He had been her tool and dupe like the others; if he imagined that he was serving

Hermione, it was for her mother's ends that he had worked. What right had he to sentimentalise a marriage founded on such base connivances, and how could he have imagined that in so doing he was acting a disinterested part?

While these thoughts were passing through his mind the ceremony had already begun, and the principal personages in the drama were ranged before him in the row of crimson velvet chairs which fills the foreground of a Catholic marriage. Through the glow of lights and the perfumed haze about the altar, Garnett's eyes rested on the central figures of the group, and gradually the others disappeared from his view and his mind. After all, neither Mrs. Newell's schemes nor his own share in them could ever unsanctify Hermione's marriage. It was one more testimony to life's indefatigable renewals, to nature's secret of drawing fragrance from corruption; and as his eyes turned from the girl's illuminated presence to the resigned and stoical figure sunk in the adjoining chair, it occurred to him that he had perhaps worked better than he knew in placing them, if only for a moment, side by side.

AFTER HOLBEIN

I.

ANSON WARLEY had had his moments of being a rather
remarkable man; but they were only intermittent; they
recurred at ever-lengthening intervals; and between
times he was a small poor creature, chattering with cold
inside, in spite of his agreeable and even distinguished
exterior.

He had always been perfectly aware of these two sides
of himself (which, even in the privacy of his own mind,
he contemptuously refused to dub a dual personality);
and as the rather remarkable man could take fairly good
care of himself, most of Warley's attention was devoted
to ministering to the poor wretch who took longer and
longer turns at bearing his name, and was more and
more insistent in accepting the invitations which New
York, for over thirty years, had tirelessly poured out on
him. It was in the interest of this lonely fidgety unem-
ployed self that Warley, in his younger days, had
frequented the gaudiest restaurants and the most glittering Palace Hotels of two hemispheres, subscribed to
the most advanced literary and artistic reviews, bought
the pictures of the young painters who were being the
most vehemently discussed, missed few of the showiest

first nights in New York, London or Paris, sought the
company of the men and women—especially the
women—most conspicuous in fashion, scandal, or any
other form of social notoriety, and thus tried to warm
the shivering soul within him at all the passing bonfires
of success.

The original Anson Warley had begun by staying at
home in his little flat, with his books and his thoughts,
when the other poor creature went forth; but gradually—he hardly knew when or how—he had slipped into
the way of going too, till finally he made the bitter
discovery that he and the creature had become one, except on the increasingly rare occasions when, detaching
himself from all casual contingencies, he mounted to the
lofty water-shed which fed the sources of his scorn. The
view from there was vast and glorious, the air was icy
but exhilarating; but soon he began to find the place too
lonely, and too difficult to get to, especially as the lesser
Anson not only refused to go up with him but began to
sneer, at first ever so faintly, then with increasing in-
solence, at this affectation of a taste for the heights.

"What's the use of scrambling up there, anyhow? I
could understand it if you brought down anything
worth while—a poem or a picture of your own. But just
climbing and staring: what does it lead to? Fellows with
the creative gift have got to have their occasional Sinais;
I can see that. But for a mere looker-on like you, isn't
that sort of thing rather a pose? You talk awfully
well—brilliantly, even (oh, my dear fellow, no false
modesty between you and *me*, please!). But who the
devil is there to listen to you, up there among the
glaciers? And sometimes, when you come down, I
notice that you're rather—well, heavy and tongue-tied.
Look out, or they'll stop asking us to dine! And sitting
at home every evening—brr! Look here, by the way; if
you've got nothing better for tonight, come along with
me to Chrissy Torrance's—or the Bob Briggses'—or
Princess Kate's; anywhere where there's lots of racket
and sparkle, places that people go to in Rollses, and that
are smart and hot and overcrowded, and you have to

pay a lot—in one way or another—to get in.''

Once and again, it is true, Warley still dodged his double and slipped off on a tour to remote uncomfortable places, where there were churches or pictures to be seen, or shut himself up at home for a good bout of reading, or just, in sheer disgust at his companion's platitude, spent an evening with people who were doing or thinking real things. This happened seldomer than of old, however, and more clandestinely; so that at last he used to sneak away to spend two or three days with an archaeologically-minded friend, or an evening with a quiet scholar, as furtively as if he were stealing to a lover's tryst; which, as lovers' trysts were now always kept in the limelight, was after all a fair exchange. But he always felt rather apologetic to the other Warley about these escapades—and, if the truth were known, rather bored and restless before they were over. And in the back of his mind there lurked an increasing dread of missing something hot and noisy and overcrowded when he went off to one of his mountain-tops. "After all, that high-brow business has been awfully overdone—now hasn't it?" the little Warley would insinuate, rummaging for his pearl studs, and consulting his flat evening watch as nervously as if it were a railway time-table. "If only we haven't missed something really jolly by all this backing and filling . . .''

"Oh, you poor creature, you! Always afraid of being left out, aren't you? Well—just for once, to humour you, and because I happen to be feeling rather stale myself. But only to think of a sane man's wanting to go to places just because they're hot and smart and overcrowded!'' And off they would dash together . . .

II.

ALL THAT was long ago. It was years now since there had been two distinct Anson Warleys. The lesser one had made away with the other, done him softly to death without shedding of blood; and only a few people suspected (and they no longer cared) that the pale white-haired man, with the small slim figure, the ironic smile and the perfect evening clothes, whom New York still indefatigably invited, was nothing less than a murderer.

Anson Warley—Anson Warley! No party was complete without Anson Warley. He no longer went abroad now; too stiff in the joints; and there had been two or three slight attacks of dizziness . . . Nothing to speak of, nothing to think of, even; but somehow one dug one's self into one's comfortable quarters, and felt less and less like moving out of them, except to motor down to Long Island for weekends, or to Newport for a few visits in summer. A trip to the Hot Springs, to get rid of the stiffness, had not helped much, and the ageing Anson Warley (who really, otherwise, felt as young as ever) had developed a growing dislike for the promiscuities of hotel life and the monotony of hotel food.

Yes; he was growing more fastidious as he grew older. A good sign, he thought. Fastidious not only about food and comfort but about people also. It was still a privilege, a distinction, to have him to dine. His old friends were faithful, and the new people fought for him, and often failed to get him; to do so they had to offer very special inducements in the way of *cuisine*, conversation or beauty. Young beauty; yes, that would do it. He did like to sit and watch a lovely face, and call laughter into lovely eyes. But no dull dinners for *him*, not even if they fed you off gold. As to that he was as firm as the other Warley, the distant aloof one with whom he had—er, well, parted company, oh, quite amicably, a good many years ago . . .

On the whole, since that parting, life had been much easier and pleasanter; and by the time the little Warley was sixty-three he found himself looking forward with equanimity to an eternity of New York dinners.

Oh, but only at the right houses—always at the right houses; that was understood! The right people—the right setting—the right wines . . . He smiled a little over his perennial enjoyment of them; said "Nonsense, Filmore," to his devoted tiresome man-servant, who was beginning to hint that really, every night, sir, and sometimes a dance afterward, was too much, especially when you kept at it for months on end; and Dr. —

"Oh, damn your doctors!" Warley snapped. He was seldom ill-tempered; he knew it was foolish and upsetting to lose one's self-control. But Filmore began to be a nuisance, nagging him, preaching at him. As if he himself wasn't the best judge . . .

Besides, he chose his company. He'd stay at home any time rather than risk a boring evening. Damned rot, what Filmore had said about his going out every night. Not like poor old Mrs. Jaspar, for instance . . . He smiled self-approvingly as he evoked her tottering image. "That's the kind of fool Filmore takes me for," he chuckled, his good-humour restored by an analogy that was so much to his advantage.

Poor old Evelina Jaspar! In his youth, and even in his prime, she had been New York's chief entertainer— "leading hostess," the newspapers called her. Her big house in Fifth Avenue had been an entertaining machine. She had lived, breathed, invested and reinvested her millions, to no other end. At first her pretext had been that she had to marry her daughters and amuse her sons; but when sons and daughters had married and left her she had seemed hardly aware of it; she had just gone on entertaining. Hundreds, no, thousands of dinners (on gold plate, of course, and with orchids, and all the delicacies that were out of season), had been served in that vast pompous dining-room, which one had only to close one's eyes to transform into a railway buffet for millionaires, at a big junction, before the invention of restaurant trains . . .

Warley closed his eyes, and did so picture it. He lost

himself in amused computation of the annual number of guests, of saddles of mutton, of legs of lambs, of terrapin, canvas-backs, magnums of champagne and pyramids of hot-house fruit that must have passed through that room in the last forty years.

And even now, he thought—hadn't one of old Evelina's nieces told him the other day, half bantering, half shivering at the avowal, that the poor old lady, who was gently dying of softening of the brain, still imagined herself to be New York's leading hostess, still sent out invitations (which of course were never delivered), still ordered terrapin champagne and orchids, and still came down every evening to her great shrouded drawing-rooms, with her tiara askew on her purple wig, to receive a stream of imaginary guests?

Rubbish, of course—a macabre pleasantry of the extravagant Nelly Pierce, who had always had her joke at Aunt Evelina's expense . . . But Warley could not help smiling at the thought that those dull monotonous dinners were still going on in their hostess's clouded imagination. Poor old Evelina, he thought! In a way she was right. There was really no reason why that kind of standardized entertaining should ever cease; a performance so undiscriminating, so undifferentiated, that one could almost imagine, in the hostess's tired brain, all the dinners she had ever given merging into one Gargantuan pyramid of food and drink, with the same faces, perpetually the same faces, gathered stolidly about the same gold plate.

Thank heaven, Anson Warley had never conceived of social values in terms of mass and volume. It was years since he had dined at Mrs. Jaspar's. He even felt that he was not above reproach in that respect. Two or three times, in the past, he had accepted her invitations (always sent out weeks ahead), and then chucked her at the eleventh hour for something more amusing. Finally, to avoid such risks, he had made it a rule always to refuse her dinners. He had even—he remembered—been rather funny about it once, when someone had told him that Mrs. Jaspar couldn't understand . . . was a little

hurt . . . said it couldn't be true that he always had
another engagement the nights she asked him . . .
"*True?* Is the truth what she wants? All right! Then the
next time I get a 'Mrs. Jaspar requests the pleasure' I'll
answer it with a 'Mr. Warley declines the boredom.'
Think she'll understand that, eh?" And the phrase
became a catchword in his little set that winter. " 'Mr.
Warley declines the boredom'—good, good, *good!*"
"Dear Anson, I do hope you won't decline the boredom
of coming to lunch next Sunday to meet the new Hindu
Yoghi"—or the new saxophone soloist, or that genius
of a mulatto boy who plays Negro spirituals on a tooth-
brush; and so on and so on. He only hoped poor old
Evelina never heard of it . . .

"Certainly I shall *not* stay at home tonight—why,
what's wrong with me?" he snapped, swinging round
on Filmore.
The valet's long face grew longer. His way of answering such questions was always to pull out his face; it
was his only means of putting any expression into it. He
turned away into the bedroom; and Warley sat alone by
his library fire . . . Now what did the man see that was
wrong with him, he wondered? He had felt a little confusion that morning, when he was doing his daily sprint
around the Park (his exercise was reduced to that!); but
it had been only a passing flurry, of which Filmore
could of course know nothing. And as soon as it was
over his mind had seemed more lucid, his eye keener,
than ever; as sometimes (he reflected) the electric light in
his library lamps would blaze up too brightly after
a break in the current, and he would say to himself,
wincing a little at the sudden glare on the page he was
reading: "That means that it'll go out again in a
minute."
Yes; his mind, at that moment, had been quite pierc-
ingly clear and perceptive; his eye had passed with a
renovating glitter over every detail of the daily scene. He
stood still for a minute under the leafless trees of the
Mall, and looking about him with the sudden insight of

age, understood that he had reached the time of life when Alps and cathedrals become as transient as flowers.

Everything was fleeting, fleeting . . . yes, that was what had given him the vertigo. The doctors, poor fools, called it the stomach, or high blood-pressure; but it was only the dizzy plunge of the sands in the hour-glass, the everlasting plunge that emptied one of heart and bowels, like the drop of an elevator from the top floor of a sky-scraper.

Certainly, after that moment of revelation, he had felt a little more tired than usual for the rest of the day; the light had flagged in his mind as it sometimes did in his lamps. At Chrissy Torrance's, where he had lunched, they had accused him of being silent, his hostess had said that he looked pale; but he had retorted with a joke, and thrown himself into the talk with a feverish loquacity. It was the only thing to do; for he could not tell all these people at the lunch table that very morning he had arrived at the turn in the path from which mountains look as transient as flowers—and that one after another they would all arrive there too.

He leaned his head back and closed his eyes, but not in sleep. He did not feel sleepy, but keyed up and alert. In the next room he heard Filmore reluctantly, protestingly, laying out his evening clothes . . . He had no fear about the dinner tonight; a quiet intimate little affair at an old friend's house. Just two or three congenial men, and Elfmann, the pianist (who would probably play), and that lovely Elfrida Flight. The fact that people asked him to dine to meet Elfrida Flight seemed to prove pretty conclusively that he was still in the running! He chuckled softly at Filmore's pessimism, and thought: "Well, after all, I suppose no man seems young to his valet . . . Time to dress very soon," he thought; and luxuriously postponed getting up out of his chair . . .

III.

"SHE'S WORSE than usual tonight," said the day nurse, laying down the evening paper as her colleague joined her. "Absolutely determined to have her jewels out."

The night nurse, fresh from a long sleep and an afternoon at the movies with a gentleman friend, threw down her fancy bag, tossed off her hat and rumpled up her hair before old Mrs. Jaspar's tall toilet mirror. "Oh, I'll settle that—don't you worry," she said brightly.

"Don't you fret her, though, Miss Cress," said the other, getting wearily out of her chair. "We're very well off here, take it as a whole, and I don't want her pressure rushed up for nothing."

Miss Cress, still looking at herself in the glass, smiled reassuringly at Miss Dunn's pale reflection behind her. She and Miss Dunn got on very well together, and knew on which side their bread was buttered. But at the end of the day Miss Dunn was always fagged out and fearing the worst. The patient wasn't as hard to handle as all that. Just let her ring for her old maid, old Lavinia, and say: "My sapphire velvet tonight, with the diamond stars"—and Lavinia would know exactly how to manage her.

Miss Dunn had put on her hat and coat, and crammed her knitting, and the newspaper, into her bag, which, unlike Miss Cress's, was capacious and shabby; but she still loitered undecided on the threshold. "I could stay with you till ten as easy as not . . ." She looked almost reluctantly about the big high-studded dressing-room (everything in the house was high-studded), with its rich dusky carpet and curtains, and its monumental dressing-table draped with lace and laden with gold-backed brushes and combs, gold-stoppered toilet-bottles, and all the charming paraphernalia of beauty at her glass. Old Lavinia even renewed every morning the roses and carnations in the slim crystal vases between the powder boxes and the nail polishers. Since the family had shut down the hot-houses at the uninhabited country place on the Hudson, Miss Cress suspected that old Lavinia bought these flowers out of her own pocket.

"Cold out tonight?" queried Miss Dunn from the door.

"Fierce . . . Reg'lar blizzard at the corners. Say, shall I lend you my fur scarf?" Miss Cress, pleased with the memory of her afternoon (they'd be engaged soon, she thought), and with the drowsy prospect of an evening in a deep arm-chair near the warm gleam of the dressing-room fire, was disposed to kindliness toward that poor thin Dunn girl, who supported her mother, and her brother's idiot twins. And she wanted Miss Dunn to notice her new fur.

"My! Isn't it too lovely? No, not for worlds, thank you . . ." Her hand on the door-knob, Miss Dunn repeated: "Don't you cross her now," and was gone.

Lavinia's bell rang furiously, twice; then the door between the dressing-room and Mrs. Jaspar's bedroom opened, and Mrs. Jaspar herself emerged.

"Lavinia!" she called, in a high irritated voice; then, seeing the nurse, who had slipped into her print dress and starched cap, she added in a lower tone: "Oh, Miss Lemoine, good evening." Her first nurse, it appeared, had been called Miss Lemoine; and she gave the same name to all the others, quite unaware that there had been any changes in the staff.

"I heard talking, and carriages driving up. Have people begun to arrive?" she asked nervously. "Where is Lavinia? I still have my jewels to put on."

She stood before the nurse, the same petrifying apparition which always, at this hour, struck Miss Cress to silence. Mrs. Jaspar was tall; she had been broad; and her bones remained impressive though the flesh had withered on them. Lavinia had encased her, as usual, in her low-necked purple velvet dress, nipped in at the waist in the old-fashioned way, expanding in voluminous folds about the hips and flowing in a long train over the darker velvet of the carpet. Mrs. Jaspar's swollen feet could no longer be pushed into the high-heeled satin slippers which went with the dress; but her skirts were so long and spreading that, by taking short steps, she managed (so Lavinia daily assured her) entirely to conceal the broad round tips of her black orthopaedic shoes.

"Your jewels, Mrs. Jaspar? Why, you've got them on," said Miss Cress brightly.

Mrs. Jaspar turned her porphyry-tinted face to Miss Cress, and looked at her with a glassy incredulous gaze. Her eyes, Miss Cress thought, were the worst . . . She lifted one old hand, veined and knobbed as a raised map, to her elaborate purple-black wig, groped among the puffs and curls and undulations (queer, Miss Cress thought, that it never occurred to her to look into the glass), and after an interval affirmed: "You must be mistaken, my dear. Don't you think you ought to have your eyes examined?"

The door opened again, and a very old woman, so old as to make Mrs. Jaspar appear almost young, hobbled in with sidelong steps. "Excuse me, madam. I was downstairs when the bell rang."

Lavinia had probably always been small and slight; now, beside her towering mistress, she looked a mere feather, a straw. Everything about her had dried, contracted, been volatilized into nothingness, except her watchful gray eyes, in which intelligence and comprehension burned like two fixed stars. "Do excuse me, madam," she repeated.

Mrs. Jaspar looked at her despairingly. "I hear carriages driving up. And Miss Lemoine says I have my jewels on; and I know I haven't."

"With that lovely necklace!" Miss Cress ejaculated.

Mrs. Jaspar's twisted hand rose again, this time to her denuded shoulders, which were as stark and barren as the rock from which the hand might have been broken. She felt and felt, and tears rose in her eyes . . .

"Why do you lie to me?" she burst out passionately.

Lavinia softly intervened. "Miss Lemoine meant how lovely you'll be when you get the necklace on, madam."

"Diamonds, diamonds," said Mrs. Jaspar with an awful smile.

"Of course, madam."

Mrs. Jaspar sat down at the dressing-table, and Lavinia, with eager random hands, began to adjust the *point de Venise* about her mistress's shoulders, and to repair the havoc wrought in the purple-black wig by its wearer's gropings for her tiara.

"Now you do look lovely, madam," she sighed.

Mrs. Jaspar was on her feet again, stiff but incredibly active. ("Like a cat she is," Miss Cress used to relate.) "I do hear carriages—or is it an automobile? The Magraws, I know, have one of those new-fangled automobiles. And now I hear the front door opening. Quick, Lavinia! My fan, my gloves, my handkerchief . . . how often have I got to tell you? I used to have a *perfect* maid—"

Lavinia's eyes brimmed. "That was me, madam," she said, bending to straighten out the folds of the long purple velvet train. ("To watch the two of 'em," Miss Cress used to tell a circle of appreciative friends, "is a lot better than any circus.")

Mrs. Jaspar paid no attention. She twitched the train out of Lavinia's vacillating hold, swept to the door, and then paused there as if stopped by a jerk of her constricted muscles. "Oh, but my diamonds—you cruel woman, you! You're letting me go down without my diamonds!" Her ruined face puckered up in a grimace like a new-born baby's, and she began to sob despairingly. "Everybody . . . Every . . . body's . . . against me . . ." she wept in her powerless misery.

Lavinia helped herself to her feet and tottered across the floor. It was almost more than she could bear to see her mistress in distress. "Madam, madam—if you'll just wait till they're got out of the safe," she entreated.

The woman she saw before her, the woman she was entreating and consoling, was not the old petrified Mrs. Jaspar with porphyry face and wig awry whom Miss Cress stood watching with a smile, but a young proud creature, commanding and splendid in her Paris gown of amber *moiré*, who, years ago, had burst into just such furious sobs because, as she was sweeping down to

receive her guests, the doctor had told her that little
Grace, with whom she had been playing all the afternoon, had a diphtheritic throat, and no one must
be allowed to enter. "Everybody's against me, everybody . . ." she had sobbed in her fury; and the young
Lavinia, stricken by such Olympian anger, had stood
speechless, longing to comfort her, and secretly in-
dignant with little Grace and the doctor . . .

"If you'll just wait, madam, while I go down and ask
Munson to open the safe. There's no one come yet, I do
assure you . . ."

Munson was the old butler, the only person who knew
the combination of the safe in Mrs. Jaspar's bedroom.
Lavinia had once known it too, but now she was no
longer able to remember it. The worst of it was that she
feared lest Munson, who had been spending the day in
the Bronx, might not have returned. Munson was
growing old too, and he did sometimes forget about
these dinner-parties of Mrs. Jaspar's, and then the
stupid footman, George, had to announce the names;
and you couldn't be sure that Mrs. Jaspar wouldn't
notice Munson's absence, and be excited and angry.
These dinner-party nights were killing old Lavinia, and
she did so want to keep alive; she wanted to live long
enough to wait on Mrs. Jaspar to the last.

She disappeared, and Miss Cress poked up the fire,
and persuaded Mrs. Jaspar to sit down in an arm-chair
and "tell her who was coming." It always amused Mrs.
Jaspar to say over the long list of her guests' names, and
generally she remembered them fairly well, for they
were always the same—the last people, Lavinia and
Munson said, who had dined at the house, on the very
night before her stroke. With recovered complacency
she began, counting over one after another on her ring-
laden fingers: "The Italian Ambassador, the Bishop,
Mr. and Mrs. Torrington Bligh, Mr. and Mrs. Fred
Amesworth, Mr. and Mrs. Mitchell Magraw, Mr. and
Mrs. Torrington Bligh . . ." ("You've said them
before," Miss Cress interpolated, getting out her fancy

knitting—a necktie for her friend—and beginning to count the stitches.) And Mrs. Jasper, distressed and bewildered by the interruption, had to repeat over and over: "Torrington Bligh, Torrington Bligh," till the connection was re-established, and she went on again swimmingly with "Mr. and Mrs. Fred Amesworth, Mr. and Mrs. Mitchell Magraw, Miss Laura Ladew, Mr. Harold Ladew, Mr. and Mrs. Benjamin Bronx, Mr. and Mrs. Torrington Bl—no, I mean, Mr. Anson Warley. Yes, Mr. Anson Warley; that's it," she ended complacently.

Miss Cress smiled and interrupted her counting. "No, that's *not* it."

"What do you mean, my dear—not it?"

"Mr. Anson Warley. He's not coming."

Mrs. Jaspar's jaw fell, and she stared at the nurse's coldly smiling face. "Not coming?"

"No. He's not coming. He's not on the list." (That old list! As if Miss Cress didn't know it by heart! Everybody in the house did, except the booby, George, who heard it reeled off every other night by Munson, and who was always stumbling over the names, and having to refer to the written paper.)

"Not on the list?" Mrs. Jaspar gasped.

Miss Cress shook her pretty head.

Signs of uneasiness gathered on Mrs. Jaspar's face and her lip began to tremble. It always amused Miss Cress to give her these little jolts, though she knew Miss Dunn and the doctors didn't approve of her doing so. She knew also that it was against her own interests, and she did try to bear in mind Miss Dunn's oft-repeated admonition about not sending up the patient's blood pressure; but when she was in high spirits, as she was tonight (they would certainly be engaged), it was irresistible to get a rise out of the old lady. And she thought it funny, this new figure unexpectedly appearing among those time-worn guests. ("I wonder what the rest of 'em 'll say to him," she giggled inwardly.)

"No; he's not on the list." Mrs. Jaspar, after pondering deeply, announced the fact with an air of recovered composure.

"That's what I told you," snapped Miss Cress.

"He's not on the list; but he promised me to come. I saw him yesterday," continued Mrs. Jaspar, mysteriously.

"You *saw* him—where?"

She considered. "Last night, at the Fred Amesworths' dance."

"Ah," said Miss Cress, with a little shiver; for she knew that Mrs. Amesworth was dead, and she was the intimate friend of the trained nurse who was keeping alive, by dint of *piqûres* and high frequency, the inarticulate and inanimate Mr. Amesworth. "It's funny," she remarked to Mrs. Jaspar, "that you'd never invited Mr. Warley before."

"No, I hadn't; not for a long time. I believe he felt I'd neglected him; for he came up to me last night, and said he was so sorry he hadn't been able to call. It seems he's been ill, poor fellow. Not as young as he was! So of course I invited him. He was very much gratified."

Mrs. Jaspar smiled at the remembrance of her little triumph; but Miss Cress's attention had wandered, as it always did when the patient became docile and reasonable. She thought: "Where's old Lavinia? I bet she can't find Munson." And she got up and crossed the floor to look into Mrs. Jaspar's bedroom, where the safe was.

There an astonishing sight met her. Munson, as she had expected, was nowhere visible; but Lavinia, on her knees before the safe, was in the act of opening it herself, her twitching hand slowly moving about the mysterious dial.

"Why, I thought you'd forgotten the combination!" Miss Cress exclaimed.

Lavinia turned a startled face over her shoulder. "So I had, Miss. But I've managed to remember it, thank God. I *had* to, you see, because Munson's forgot to come home."

"Oh," said the nurse incredulously. ("Old fox," she thought, "I wonder why she's always pretended she'd forgotten it.") For Miss Cress did not know that the age of miracles is not yet past.

Joyous, trembling, her cheeks wet with grateful tears, the little old woman was on her feet again, clutching to her breast the diamond stars, the necklace of *solitaires*, the tiara, the earrings. One by one she spread them out on the velvet-lined tray in which they always used to be carried from the safe to the dressing-room; then, with rambling fingers, she managed to lock the safe again, and put the keys in the drawer where they belonged, while Miss Cress continued to stare at her in amazement. "I don't believe the old witch is as shaky as she makes out," was her reflection as Lavinia passed her, bearing the jewels to the dressing-room where Mrs. Jaspar, lost in pleasant memories, was still computing: "The Italian Ambassador, the Bishop, the Torrington Blighs, the Mitchell Magraws, the Fred Amesworths . . ."

Mrs. Jaspar was allowed to go down to the drawing-room alone on dinner-party evenings because it would have mortified her too much to receive her guests with a maid or a nurse at her elbow; but Miss Cress and Lavinia always leaned over the stair-rail to watch her descent, and make sure it was accomplished in safety.

"She do look lovely yet, when all her diamonds is on," Lavinia sighed, her purblind eyes bedewed with memories, as the bedizened wig and purple velvet disappeared at the last bend of the stairs. Miss Cress, with a shrug, turned back to the fire and picked up her knitting, while Lavinia set about the slow ritual of tidying up her mistress's room. From below they heard the sound of George's stentorian monologue: "Mr. and Mrs. Torrington Bligh, Mr. and Mrs. Mitchell Magraw . . . Mr. Ladew, Miss Laura Ladew . . ."

IV.

ANSON WARLEY, who had always prided himself on his
equable temper, was conscious of being on edge that
evening. But it was an irritability which did not frighten
him (in spite of what those doctors always said about
the importance of keeping calm) because he knew it was
due merely to the unusual lucidity of his mind. He was
in fact feeling uncommonly well, his brain clear and all
his perceptions so alert that he could positively hear the
thoughts passing through his man-servant's mind on the
other side of the door, as Filmore grudgingly laid out
the evening clothes.

Smiling at the man's obstinacy, he thought: "I shall
have to tell them tonight that Filmore thinks I'm no
longer fit to get into society." It was always pleasant to
hear the incredulous laugh with which his younger
friends received any allusion to his supposed senility.
"What, *you*? Well, that's a good one!" And he thought
it was, himself.

And then, the moment he was in his bedroom,
dressing, the sight of Filmore made him lose his temper
again. "No; *not* those studs, confound it. The black
onyx ones—haven't I told you a hundred times? Lost
them, I suppose? Sent them to the wash again in a soiled
shirt? That it?" He laughed nervously, and sitting down
before his dressing-table began to brush back his hair
with short angry strokes.

"Above all," he shouted out suddenly, "don't stand
there staring at me as if you were watching to see exactly
at what minute to telephone for the undertaker!"

"The under—? Oh, sir!" gasped Filmore.

"The—the—damn it, are you *deaf* too? Who said undertaker? I said *taxi*; can't you hear what I say?"

"You want me to call a taxi, sir?"

"No; I don't. I've already told you so. I'm going to
walk." Warley straightened his tie, rose and held out his
arms toward his dress-coat.

"It's bitter cold, sir; better let me call a taxi all the same."

Warley gave a short laugh. "Out with it, now! What you'd really like to suggest is that I should telephone to say I can't dine out. You'd scramble me some eggs instead, eh?"

"I wish you would stay in, sir. There's eggs in the house."

"My overcoat," snapped Warley.

"Or else let me call a taxi; now do, sir."

Warley slipped his arms into his overcoat, tapped his chest to see if his watch (the thin evening watch) and his note-case were in their proper pockets, turned back to put a dash of lavender on his handkerchief, and walked with stiff quick steps toward the front door of his flat.

Filmore, abashed, preceded him to ring for the lift; and then, as it quivered upward through the long shaft, said again: "It's a bitter cold night, sir; and you've had a good deal of exercise today."

Warley levelled a contemptuous glance at him. "Daresay that's why I'm feeling so fit," he retorted as he entered the lift.

It *was* bitter cold; the icy air hit him in the chest when he stepped out of the overheated building, and he halted on the doorstep and took a long breath. "Filmore's missed his vocation; ought to be nurse to a paralytic," he thought. "He'd love to have to wheel me about in a chair."

After the first shock of the biting air he began to find it exhilarating, and walked along at a good pace, dragging one leg ever so little after the other. (The *masseur* had promised him that he'd soon be rid of that stiffness.) Yes—decidedly a fellow like himself ought to have a younger valet; a more cheerful one, anyhow. He felt like a young'un himself this evening; as he turned into Fifth Avenue he rather wished he could meet some one he knew, some man who'd say afterward at his club: "Warley? Why, I saw him sprinting up Fifth Avenue the other night like a two-year-old; that night it was four or five below . . ." He needed a good counter-irritant for Filmore's gloom. "Always have young people about you," he thought as he walked along; and at the words his mind turned to Elfrida Flight, next to whom he would soon be sitting in a warm pleasantly lit dining-room—*where?*

It came as abruptly as that: the gap in his memory. He pulled up at it as if his advance had been checked by a chasm in the pavement at his feet. Where the dickens was he going to dine? And with whom was he going to dine? God! But things didn't happen in that way; a sound strong man didn't suddenly have to stop in the middle of the street and ask himself where he was going to dine . . .

"Perfect in mind, body and understanding." The old legal phrase bobbed up inconsequently into his thoughts. Less than two minutes ago he had answered in every particular to that description; what was he now? He put his hand to his forehead, which was bursting; then he lifted his hat and let the cold air blow for a while on his overheated temples. It was queer, how hot he'd got, walking. Fact was, he'd been sprinting along at a damned good pace. In future he must try to remember not to hurry . . . Hang it—one more thing to remember! . . . Well, but what was all the fuss about? Of course, as people got older their memories were subject to these momentary lapses; he'd noticed it often enough among his contemporaries. And, brisk and alert though he still was, it wouldn't do to imagine himself totally exempt from human ills . . .

Where was it he was dining? Why, somewhere farther up Fifth Avenue; he was perfectly sure of that. With that lovely . . . that lovely . . . No; better not make any effort for the moment. Just keep calm, and stroll slowly along. When he came to the right street corner of course he'd spot it; and then everything would be perfectly clear again. He walked on, more deliberately, trying to empty his mind of all thoughts. "Above all," he said to himself, "don't worry."

He tried to beguile his nervousness by thinking of

amusing things. "Decline the boredom—" He thought
he might get off that joke tonight. "Mrs. Jaspar
requests the pleasure—Mr. Warley declines the
boredom." Not so bad, really; and he had an idea he'd
never told it to the people . . . what in hell *was* their
name? . . . the people he was on his way to dine with . . .
Mrs. Jaspar requests the pleasure. Poor old Mrs.
Jaspar; again it occurred to him that he hadn't always
been very civil to her in old times. When everybody's
running after a fellow it's pardonable now and then to
chuck a boring dinner at the last minute; but all the
same as one grew older one understood better how an
unintentional slight of that sort might cause offense,
cause even pain. And he hated to cause people pain . . .
He thought perhaps he'd better call on Mrs. Jaspar
some afternoon. She'd be surprised! Or ring her up,
poor old girl, and propose himself, just informally, for
dinner. One dull evening wouldn't kill him—and how
pleased she'd be! Yes—he thought decidedly . . . When
he got to be her age, he could imagine how much he'd
like it if somebody still in the running should ring him
up unexpectedly and say—

He stopped, and looked up, slowly, wonderingly, at
the wide illuminated facade of the house he was approaching. Queer coincidence—it was the Jaspar house.
And all lit up; for a dinner evidently. And that was
queerer yet; almost uncanny; for here he was, in front
of the door, as the clock struck a quarter past eight; and
of course—he remembered it quite clearly now—it was
just here, it was with Mrs. Jaspar, that he was
dining . . . Those little lapses of memory never lasted
more than a second or two. How right he'd been not to
let himself worry. He pressed his hand on the door-bell.

"God," he thought, as the double doors swung open,
"but it's good to get in out of the cold."

V.

IN THAT hushed sonorous house the sound of the door-bell was as loud to the two women upstairs as if it had been rung in the next room.

Miss Cress raised her head in surprise, and Lavinia dropped Mrs. Jaspar's other false set (the more comfortable one) with a clatter on the marble wash-stand. She stumbled across the dressing-room, and hastened out to the landing. With Munson absent, there was no knowing how George might muddle things . . .

Miss Cress joined her. "Who is it?" she whispered excitedly. Below, they heard the sound of a hat and a walking stick being laid down on the big marble-topped table in the hall, and then George's stentorian drone: "Mr. Anson Warley."

"It is—it *is!* I can see him—a gentleman in evening clothes," Miss Cress whispered, hanging over the stair-rail.

"Good gracious—mercy me! And Munson not here! Oh, whatever, whatever shall we do?" Lavinia was trembling so violently that she had to clutch the stair-rail to prevent herself from falling. Miss Cress thought, with her cold lucidity: "She's a good deal sicker than the old woman."

"What shall we do, Miss Cress? That fool of a George—he's showing him in! Who could have thought it?" Miss Cress knew the images that were whirling through Lavinia's brain: the vision of Mrs. Jaspar's having another stroke at the sight of this mysterious intruder, of Mr. Anson Warley's seeing her there, in her impotence and her abasement, of the family's being summoned, and rushing in to exclaim, to question, to be horrified and furious—and all because poor old Munson's memory was going, like his mistress's, like Lavinia's, and because he had forgotten that it was one of the *dinner nights.* Oh, misery! . . . The tears were running down Lavinia's cheeks, and Miss Cress knew she was thinking: "If the daughters send him off—and they will—where's he going to, old and deaf as he is, and all his people dead? Oh, if only he can hold on till she dies, and get his pension . . ."

Lavinia recovered herself with one of her supreme efforts. "Miss Cress, we must go down at once, at once! Something dreadful's going to happen . . ." She began to totter toward the little velvet-lined lift in the corner of the landing.

Miss Cress took pity on her. "Come along," she said. "But nothing dreadful's going to happen. You'll see."

"Oh, thank you, Miss Cress. But the shock—the awful shock to her—of seeing that strange gentleman walk in."

"Not a bit of it." Miss Cress laughed as she stepped into the lift. "He's not a stranger. She's expecting him."

"Expecting him? Expecting Mr. Warley?"

"Sure she is. She told me so just now. She says she invited him yesterday."

"But, Miss Cress, what are you thinking of? Invite him—how? When you know she can't write nor telephone?"

"Well, she says she saw him; she saw him last night at a dance."

"Oh, God," murmured Lavinia, covering her eyes with her hands.

"At a dance at the Fred Amesworths'—that's what she said," Miss Cress pursued, feeling the same little shiver run down her back as when Mrs. Jaspar had made the statement to her.

"The Amesworths—oh, not the Amesworths?" Lavinia echoed, shivering too. She dropped her hands from her face, and followed Miss Cress out of the lift. Her expression had become less anguished, and the nurse wondered why. In reality, she was thinking, in a sort of dreary beautitude: "But if she's suddenly got as much worse as this, she'll go before me, after all, my poor lady, and I'll be able to see to it that she's properly laid out and dressed, and nobody but Lavinia's hands'll touch her."

"You'll see—if she was expecting him, as she says, it won't give her a shock, anyhow. Only, how did *he* know?" Miss Cress whispered, with an acuter renewal of her shiver. She followed Lavinia with muffled steps down the passage to the pantry, and from there the two women stole into the dining-room, and placed themselves noiselessly at its farther end, behind the tall Coromandel screen through the cracks of which they could peep into the empty room.

The long table was set, as Mrs. Jaspar always insisted that it should be on these occasions; but old Munson not having returned, the gold plate (which his mistress also insisted on) had not been got out, and all down the table, as Lavinia saw with horror, George had laid the coarse blue and white plates from the servants' hall. The electric wall-lights were on, and the candles lit in the branching Sèvres candelabra—so much at least had been done. But the flowers in the great central dish of Rose Dubarry porcelain, and in the smaller dishes which accompanied it—the flowers, oh, shame, had been forgotten! They were no longer real flowers; the family had long since suppressed that expense; and no wonder, for Mrs. Jaspar always insisted on orchids. But Grace, the youngest daughter who was the kindest, had hit on the clever device of arranging three beautiful clusters of artificial orchids and maiden hair, which had only to be lifted from their shelf in the pantry and set in the dishes—only, of course, that imbecile footman had forgotten, or had not known where to find them. And, oh, horror, realizing his oversight too late, no doubt to appeal to Lavinia, he had taken some old newspapers and bunched them up into something that he probably thought resembled a bouquet, and crammed one into each of the priceless Rose Dubarry dishes.

Lavinia clutched at Miss Cress's arm. "Oh, look—look what he's done; I shall die of the shame of it . . . Oh, Miss, hadn't we better slip around to the drawing-room and try to coax my poor lady upstairs again, afore she ever notices?"

Miss Cress, peering through the crack of the screen,

could hardly suppress a giggle. For at that moment the
double doors of the dining-room were thrown open, and
George, shuffling about in a baggy livery inherited from
a long-departed predecessor of more commanding
build, bawled out in his loud singsong: "Dinner is
served, madam."

"Oh, it's too late," moaned Lavinia. Miss Cress
signed to her to keep silent, and the two watchers glued
their eyes to their respective cracks of the screen.

What they saw, far off down the vista of empty
drawing-rooms, and after an interval during which (as
Lavinia knew) the imaginary guests were supposed to
file in and take their seats, was the entrance, at the end
of the ghostly cortège, of a very old woman, still tall and
towering on the arm of a man somewhat smaller than
herself, with a fixed smile on a darkly pink face, and a
slim erect figure clad in perfect evening clothes, who advanced with short measured steps, profiting (Miss Cress
noticed) by the support of the arm he was supposed to
sustain. "Well—I never!" was the nurse's inward comment.

The couple continued to advance, with rigid smiles
and eyes staring straight ahead. Neither turned to the
other, neither spoke. All their attention was concentrated on the immense, the almost unachievable effort of reaching that point, halfway down the long dinner table, opposite the big Dubarry dish, where George
was drawing back a gilt arm-chair for Mrs. Jaspar. At
last they reached it, and Mrs. Jaspar seated herself, and
waved a stony hand to Mr. Warley. "On my right." He
gave a little bow, like the bend of a jointed doll, and
with infinite precaution let himself down into his chair.
Beads of perspiration were standing on his forehead,
and Miss Cress saw him draw out his handkerchief and
wipe them stealthily away. He then turned his head
somewhat stiffly toward his hostess.

"Beautiful flowers," he said, with great precision and
perfect gravity, waving his hand toward the bunched-up
newspaper in the bowl of Sèvres.

Mrs. Jaspar received the tribute with complacency.

"So glad . . . orchards . . . From High Lawn . . . every morning," she simpered.

"Mar-vellous," Mr. Warley completed.

"I always say to the Bishop . . ." Mrs. Jaspar continued.

"Ha—of course," Mr. Warley warmly assented.

"Not that I don't think . . ."

"Ha—rather!"

George had reappeared from the pantry with a blue crockery dish of mashed potatoes. This he handed in turn to one after another of the imaginary guests, and finally presented to Mrs. Jaspar and her right-hand neighbour.

They both helped themselves cautiously, and Mrs. Jaspar addressed an arch smile to Mr. Warley. " 'Nother month—no more oysters."

"Ha—no more!"

George, with a bottle of Apollinaris wrapped in a napkin, was saying to each guest in turn: "Perrier-Jouet, 'ninety-five." (He had picked that up, thought Miss Cress, from hearing old Munson repeat it so often.)

"Hang it—well, then just a sip," murmured Mr. Warley.

"Old times," bantered Mrs. Jaspar; and the two turned to each other and bowed their heads and touched glasses.

"I often tell Mrs. Amesworth . . ." Mrs. Jaspar continued, bending to an imaginary presence across the table.

"Ha—*ha!*" Mr. Warley approved.

George reappeared and slowly encircled the table with a dish of spinach. After the spinach the Apollinaris also went the rounds again, announced successively as Château Lafite, 'seventy-four, and "the old Newbold Madeira." Each time that George approached his glass, Mr. Warley made a feint of lifting a defensive hand, and then smiled and yielded. "Might as well—hanged for a sheep . . ." he remarked gaily; and Mrs. Jaspar giggled.

Finally a dish of Malaga grapes and apples was

handed. Mrs. Jaspar, now growing perceptibly languid, and nodding with more and more effort at Mr. Warley's pleasantries, transferred a bunch of grapes to her plate, but nibbled only two or three. "Tired," she said suddenly, in a whimper like a child's; and she rose, lifting herself up by the arms of her chair, and leaning over to catch the eye of an invisible lady, presumably Mrs. Amesworth, seated opposite to her. Mr. Warley was on his feet too, supporting himself by resting one hand on the table in a jaunty attitude. Mrs. Jaspar waved to him to be reseated. "Join us—after cigars," she smilingly ordained; and with a great and concentrated effort he bowed to her as she passed toward the double doors which George was throwing open. Slowly, majestically, the purple velvet train disappeared down the long enfilade of illuminated rooms, and the last door closed behind her.

"Well, I do believe she's enjoyed it!" chuckled Miss Cress, taking Lavinia by the arm to help her back to the hall. Lavinia, for weeping, could not answer.

VI.

ANSON WARLEY found himself in the hall again, getting into his fur-lined overcoat. He remembered suddenly thinking that the rooms had been intensely over-heated, and that all the other guests had talked very loud and laughed inordinately. "Very good talk though, I must say," he had to acknowledge.

In the hall, as he got his arms into his coat (rather a job, too, after that Perrier-Jouet) he remembered saying to somebody (perhaps it was to the old butler): "Slipping off early—going on; 'nother engagement," and thinking to himself the while that when he got out into the fresh air again he would certainly remember where the other engagement was. He smiled a little while the servant, who seemed a clumsy fellow, fumbled with the fastening of the door. "And Filmore, who thought I wasn't well enough to dine out! Damned ass! What would he say if he knew I was going on?"

The door opened, and with an immense sense of exhilaration Mr. Warley issued forth from the house and drew in a first deep breath of night air. He heard the door closed and bolted behind him, and continued to stand motionless on the step, expanding his chest, and drinking in the icy draught.

" 'Spose it's about the last house where they give you 'ninety-five Perrier-Jouet," he thought; and then: "Never heard better talk either . . ."

He smiled again with satisfaction at the memory of the wine and the wit. Then he took a step forward, to where a moment before the pavement had been—and where now there was nothing.

AUTRES TEMPS . . .

I.

MRS. LIDCOTE, as the huge menacing mass of New York defined itself far off across the waters, shrank back into her corner of the deck and sat listening with a kind of unreasoning terror to the steady onward drive of the screws.

She had set out on the voyage quietly enough,—in what she called her "reasonable" mood,—but the week at sea had given her too much time to think of things and had left her too long alone with the past.

When she was alone, it was always the past that occupied her. She couldn't get away from it, and she didn't any longer care to. During her long years of exile she had made her terms with it, had learned to accept the fact that it would always be there, huge, obstructing, encumbering, bigger and more dominant than anything the future could ever conjure up. And, at any rate, she was sure of it, she understood it, knew how to reckon with it; she had learned to screen and manage and protect it as one does an afflicted member of one's family.

There had never been any danger of her being allowed to forget the past. It looked out at her from the face of every acquaintance, it appeared suddenly in the eyes of strangers when a word enlightened them: "Yes, *the* Mrs. Lidcote, don't you know?" It had sprung at her the first day out, when, across the dining-room, from the captain's table, she had seen Mrs. Lorin Boulger's revolving eye-glass pause and the eye behind it grow as blank as a dropped blind. The next day, of course, the captain had asked: "You know your ambassadress, Mrs. Boulger?" and she had replied that, No, she seldom left Florence, and hadn't been to Rome for more than a day since the Boulgers had been sent to Italy. She was so used to these phrases that it cost her no effort to repeat them. And the captain had promptly changed the subject.

No, she didn't, as a rule, mind the past, because she was used to it and understood it. It was a great concrete fact in her path that she had to walk around every time she moved in any direction. But now, in the light of the unhappy event that had summoned her from Italy,—the sudden unanticipated news of her daughter's divorce from Horace Pursh and remarriage with Wilbour Barkley—the past, her own poor miserable past, started up at her with eyes of accusation, became, to her disordered fancy, like the afflicted relative suddenly breaking away from nurses and keepers and publicly parading the horror and misery she had, all the long years, so patiently screened and secluded.

Yes, there it had stood before her through the agitated weeks since the news had come—during her interminable journey from India, where Leila's letter had overtaken her, and the feverish halt in her apartment in Florence, where she had had to stop and gather up her possessions for a fresh start—there it had stood grinning at her with a new balefulness which seemed to say: "Oh, but you've got to look at me *now*, because I'm not only your own past but Leila's present."

Certainly it was a master-stroke of those arch-ironists of the shears and spindle to duplicate her own story in her daughter's. Mrs. Lidcote had always somewhat grimly fancied that, having so signally failed to be of use to Leila in other ways, she would at least serve her as a warning. She had even abstained from defending herself, from making the best of her case, had stoically refused to plead extenuating circumstances, lest Leila's impulsive sympathy should lead to deductions that might react disastrously on her own life. And now that very thing had happened, and Mrs. Lidcote could hear the whole of New York saying with one voice: "Yes, Leila's done just what her mother did. With such an example what could you expect?"

Yet if she had been an example, poor woman, she had been an awful one; she had been, she would have supposed, of more use as a deterrent than a hundred blameless mothers as incentives. For how could any one who had seen anything of her life in the last eighteen years have had the courage to repeat so disastrous an experiment?

Well, logic in such cases didn't count, example didn't count, nothing probably counted but having the same impulses in the blood; and that was the dark inheritance she had bestowed upon her daughter. Leila hadn't consciously copied her; she had simply "taken after" her, had been a projection of her own long-past rebellion.

Mrs. Lidcote had deplored, when she started, that the *Utopia* was a slow steamer, and would take eight full days to bring her to her unhappy daughter; but now, as the moment of reunion approached, she would willingly have turned the boat about and fled back to the high seas. It was not only because she felt still so unprepared to face what New York had in store for her, but because she needed more time to dispose of what the *Utopia* had already given her. The past was bad enough, but the present and future were worse, because they were less comprehensible, and because, as she grew older, surprises and inconsequences troubled her more than the worst certainties.

There was Mrs. Boulger, for instance. In the light, or rather the darkness, of new developments, it might really be that Mrs. Boulger had not meant to cut her, but had simply failed to recognize her. Mrs. Lidcote had arrived at this hypothesis simply by listening to the conversation of the persons sitting next to her on deck—two lively young women with the latest Paris hats on their heads and the latest New York ideas in them. These ladies, as to whom it would have been impossible for a person with Mrs. Lidcote's old-fashioned categories to determine whether they were married or unmarried, "nice" or "horrid," or any one or other of the definite things which young women, in her youth and her society, were conveniently assumed to be, had revealed a familiarity with the world of New York that, again according to Mrs. Lidcote's traditions, should have implied a recognized place in it. But in the present fluid state of manners what did anything imply except what their hats implied—that no one could tell what was coming next?

They seemed, at any rate, to frequent a group of idle and opulent people who executed the same gestures and revolved on the same pivots as Mrs. Lidcote's daughter and her friends: their Coras, Matties and Mabels seemed at any moment likely to reveal familiar patronymics, and once one of the speakers, summing up a discussion of which Mrs. Lidcote had missed the beginning, had affirmed with headlong confidence: "Leila? Oh, *Leila's* all right."

Could it be *her* Leila, the mother had wondered, with a sharp thrill of apprehension? If only they would mention surnames! But their talk leaped elliptically from allusion to allusion, their unfinished sentences dangled over bottomless pits of conjecture, and they gave their bewildered hearer the impression not so much of talking only of their intimates, as of being intimate with everyone alive.

Her old friend Franklin Ide could have told her, perhaps; but here was the last day of the voyage, and she hadn't yet found courage to ask him. Great as had been the joy of discovering his name on the passenger-list and seeing his friendly bearded face in the throng against the taffrail at Cherbourg, she had as yet said nothing to him except, when they had met: "Of course I'm going out to Leila."

She had said nothing to Franklin Ide because she had always instinctively shrunk from taking him into her confidence. She was sure he felt sorry for her, sorrier perhaps than any one had ever felt; but he had always paid her the supreme tribute of not showing it. His attitude allowed her to imagine that compassion was not the basis of his feeling for her, and it was part of her joy in his friendship that it was the one relation seemingly unconditioned by her state, the only one in which she could think and feel and behave like any other woman.

Now, however, as the problem of New York loomed nearer, she began to regret that she had not spoken, had not at least questioned him about the hints she had gathered on the way. He did not know the two ladies next to her, he did not even, as it chanced, know Mrs. Lorin Boulger; but he knew New York, and New York was the sphinx whose riddle she must read or perish.

Almost as the thought passed through her mind his stooping shoulders and grizzled head detached themselves against the blaze of light in the west, and he sauntered down the empty deck and dropped into the chair at her side.

"You're expecting the Barkleys to meet you, I suppose?" he asked.

It was the first time she had heard any one pronounce her daughter's new name, and it occurred to her that her friend, who was shy and inarticulate, had been trying to say it all the way over and had at last shot it out at her only because he felt it must be now or never.

"I don't know. I cabled, of course. But I believe she's at—they're at—*his* place somewhere."

"Oh, Barkley's; yes, near Lenox, isn't it? But she's sure to come to town to meet you."

He said it so easily and naturally that her own constraint was relieved, and suddenly, before she knew what she meant to do, she had burst out: "She may dislike the idea of seeing people."

Ide, whose absent short-sighted gaze had been fixed on the slowly gliding water, turned in his seat to stare at his companion.

"Who? Leila?" he said with an incredulous laugh.

Mrs. Lidcote flushed to her faded hair and grew pale again. "It took *me* a long time—to get used to it," she said.

His look grew gently commiserating. "I think you'll find—" he paused for a word—"that things are different now—altogether easier."

"That's what I've been wondering—ever since we started." She was determined now to speak. She moved nearer, so that their arms touched, and she could drop her voice to a murmur. "You see, it all came on me in a flash. My going off to India and Siam on that long trip kept me away from letters for weeks at a time; and she didn't want to tell me beforehand—oh, I understand *that*, poor child! You know how good she's always been to me; how she's tried to spare me. And she knew, of course, what a state of horror I'd be in. She knew I'd rush off to her at once and try to stop it. So she never gave me a hint of anything, and she even managed to muzzle Susy Suffern—you know Susy is the one of the family who keeps me informed about things at home. I don't yet see how she prevented Susy's telling me; but she did. And her first letter, the one I got up at Bangkok, simply said the thing was over—the divorce, I mean—and that the very next day she'd—well, I suppose there was no use waiting; and *he* seems to have behaved as well as possible, to have wanted to marry her as much as—"

"Who? Barkley?" he helped her out. "I should say so! Why what do you suppose—" He interrupted himself. "He'll be devoted to her, I assure you."

"Oh, of course; I'm sure he will. He's written me—really beautifully. But it's a terrible strain on a man's devotion. I'm not sure that Leila realizes—"

Idle sounded again his little reassuring laugh. "I'm not sure that you realize. *They're* all right."

It was the very phrase that the young lady in the next

seat had applied to the unknown "Leila," and its recurrence on Ide's lips flushed Mrs. Lidcote with fresh courage.

"I wish I knew just what you mean. The two young women next to me—the ones with the wonderful hats—have been talking in the same way."

"What? About Leila?"

"About *a* Leila; I fancied it might be mine. And about society in general. All their friends seem to be divorced; some of them seem to announce their engagements before they get their decree. One of them—*her* name was Mabel—as far as I could make out, her husband found out that she meant to divorce him by noticing that she wore a new engagement-ring."

"Well, you see Leila did everything 'regularly,' as the French say," Ide rejoined.

"Yes; but are these people in society? The people my neighbours talk about?"

He shrugged his shoulders. "It would take an arbitration commission a good many sittings to define the boundaries of society nowadays. But at any rate they're in New York; and I assure you you're *not*; you're farther and farther from it."

"But I've been back there several times to see Leila." She hesitated and looked away from him. Then she brought out slowly: "And I've never noticed—the least change—in—in my own case—"

"Oh," he sounded deprecatingly, and she trembled with the fear of having gone too far. But the hour was past when such scruples could restrain her. She must know where she was and where Leila was. "Mrs. Boulger still cuts me," she brought out with an embarrassed laugh.

"Are you sure? You've probably cut *her;* if not now, at least in the past. And in a cut if you're not first you're nowhere. That's what keeps up so many quarrels."

The word roused Mrs. Lidcote to a renewed sense of realities. "But the Purshes," she said—"the Purshes are so strong! There are so many of them, and they all back each other up, just as my husband's family did. I know what it means to have a clan against one. They're stronger than any number of separate friends. The Purshes will *never* forgive Leila for leaving Horace. Why, his mother opposed his marrying her because of—of me. She tried to get Leila to promise that she wouldn't see me when they went to Europe on their honeymoon. And now she'll say it was my example.''

Her companion, vaguely stroking his beard, mused a moment upon this; then he asked, with seeming irrelevance, "What did Leila say when you wrote that you were coming?''

"She said it wasn't the least necessary, but that I'd better come, because it was the only way to convince me that it wasn't.''

"Well, then, that proves she's not afraid of the Purshes.''

She breathed a long sigh of remembrance. "Oh, just at first, you know—one never is.''

He laid his hand on hers with a gesture of intelligence and pity. "You'll see, you'll see,'' he said.

A shadow lengthened down the deck before them, and a steward stood there, proffering a Marconigram.

"Oh, now I shall know!'' she exclaimed.

She tore the message open, and then let it fall on her knees, dropping her hands on it in silence.

Ide's enquiry roused her: "It's all right?''

"Oh, quite right. Perfectly. She can't come; but she's sending Susy Suffern. She says Susy will explain.'' After another silence she added, with a sudden gush of bitterness: "As if I needed any explanation!''

She felt Ide's hesitating glance upon her. "She's in the country?''

"Yes. 'Prevented last moment. Longing for you, expecting you. Love from both.' Don't you *see*, the poor darling, that she couldn't face it?''

"No, I don't.'' He waited. "Do you mean to go to her immediately?''

"It will be too late to catch a train this evening; but I shall take the first to-morrow morning.'' She considered

a moment. "Perhaps it's better. I need a talk with Susy
first. She's to meet me at the dock, and I'll take her
straight back to the hotel with me."

As she developed this plan, she had the sense that Ide
was still thoughtfully, even gravely, considering her.
When she ceased, he remained silent a moment; then he
said almost ceremoniously: "If your talk with Miss Suffern doesn't last too late, may I come and see you when
it's over? I shall be dining at my club, and I'll call you
up at about ten, if I may, I'm off to Chicago on business
to-morrow morning, and it would be a satisfaction to
know, before I start, that your cousin's been able to
reassure you, as I know she will."

He spoke with a shy deliberateness that, even to Mrs.
Lidcote's troubled perceptions, sounded a long-silenced
note of feeling. Perhaps the breaking down of the
barrier of reticence between them had released unsuspected emotions in both. The tone of his appeal
moved her curiously and loosened the tight strain of her
fears.

"Oh, yes, come—do come," she said, rising. The
huge threat of New York was imminent now, dwarfing,
under long reaches of embattled masonry, the great
deck she stood on and all the little specks of life it
carried. One of them, drifting nearer, took the shape of
her maid, followed by luggage-laden stewards, and
signing to her that it was time to go below. As they
descended to the main deck, the throng swept her
against Mrs. Lorin Boulger's shoulder, and she heard
the ambassadress call out to some one, over the vexed
sea of hats: "So sorry! I should have been delighted, but
I've promised to spend Sunday with some friends at
Lenox."

II.

SUSY SUFFERN'S explanation did not end till after ten o'clock, and she had just gone when Franklin Ide, who, complying with an old New York tradition, had caused himself to be preceded by a long white box of roses, was shown into Mrs. Lidcote's sitting-room.

He came forward with his shy half-humorous smile and, taking her hand, looked at her for a moment without speaking.

"It's all right," he then pronounced.

Mrs. Lidcote returned his smile. "It's extraordinary. Everything's changed. Even Susy has changed; and you know the extent to which Susy used to represent the old New York. There's no old New York left, it seems. She talked in the most amazing way. She snaps her fingers at the Purshes. She told me—*me*, that every woman had a right to happiness and that self-expression was the highest duty. She accused me of misunderstanding Leila; she said my point of view was conventional! She was bursting with pride at having been in the secret, and wearing a brooch that Wilbour Barkley'd given her!"

Franklin Ide had seated himself in the arm-chair she had pushed forward for him under the electric chandelier. He threw back his head and laughed. "What did I tell you?"

"Yes; but I can't believe that Susy's not mistaken. Poor dear, she has the habit of lost causes; and she may feel that, having stuck to me, she can do no less than stick to Leila."

"But she didn't—did she?—openly defy the world for you? She didn't snap her fingers at the Lidcotes?"

Mrs. Lidcote shook her head, still smiling. "No. It was enough to defy *my* family. It was doubtful at one time if they would tolerate her seeing me, and she almost had to disinfect herself after each visit. I believe that at first my sister-in-law wouldn't let the girls come down when Susy dined with her."

"Well, isn't your cousin's present attitude the best

possible proof that times have changed?''

"Yes, yes; I know.'' She leaned forward from her sofa-corner, fixing her eyes on his thin kindly face, which gleamed on her indistinctly through her tears. "If it's true, it's—it's dazzling. She says Leila's perfectly happy. It's as if an angel had gone about lifting gravestones, and the buried people walked again, and the living didn't shrink from them.''

"That's about it,'' he assented.

She drew a deep breath, and sat looking away from him down the long perspective of lamp-fringed streets over which her windows hung.

"I can understand how happy you must be,'' he began at length.

She turned to him impetuously. "Yes, yes; I'm happy. But I'm lonely, too—lonelier than ever. I didn't take up much room in the world before; but now—where is there a corner for me? Oh, since I've begun to confess myself, why shouldn't I go on? Telling you this lifts a gravestone from *me!* You see, before this, Leila needed me. She was unhappy, and I knew it, and though we hardly ever talked of it I felt that, in a way, the thought that I'd been through the same thing, and down to the dregs of it, helped her. And her needing me helped *me.* And when the news of her marriage came my first thought was that now she'd need me more than ever, that she'd have no one but me to turn to. Yes, under all my distress there was a fierce joy in that. It was so new and wonderful to feel again that there was one person who wouldn't be able to get on without me! And now what you and Susy tell me seems to have taken my child from me; and just at first that's all I can feel.''

"Of course it's all you feel.'' He looked at her musingly. "Why didn't Leila come to meet you?''

"That was really my fault. You see, I'd cabled that I was not sure of being able to get off on the *Utopia*, and apparently my second cable was delayed, and when she received it she'd already asked some people over Sunday—one or two of her old friends, Susy says. I'm so glad they should have wanted to go to her at once; but naturally I'd rather have been alone with her."

"You still mean to go then?"

"Oh, I must. Susy wanted to drag me off to Ridgefield with her over Sunday, and Leila sent me word that of course I might go if I wanted to, and that I was not to think of her; but I know how disappointed she would be. Susy said she was afraid I might be upset at her having people to stay, and that, if I minded, she wouldn't urge me to come. But if *they* don't mind, why should I? And of course, if they're willing to go to Leila it must mean—"

"Of course. I'm glad you recognize that," Franklin Ide exclaimed abruptly. He stood up and went over to her, taking her hand with one of his quick gestures. "There's something I want to say to you," he began—

The next morning, in the train, through all the other contending thoughts in Mrs. Lidcote's mind there ran the warm undercurrent of what Franklin Ide had wanted to say to her.

He had wanted, she knew, to say it once before, when, nearly eight years earlier, the hazard of meeting at the end of a rainy autumn in a deserted Swiss hotel had thrown them for a fortnight into unwonted propinquity. They had walked and talked together, borrowed each other's books and newspapers, spent the long chill evenings over the fire in the dim lamplight of her little pitch-pine sitting-room; and she had been wonderfully comforted by his presence, and hard frozen places in her had melted, and she had known that she would be desperately sorry when he went. And then, just at the end, in his odd indirect way, he had let her see that it rested with her to have him stay. She could still relive the sleepless night she had given to that discovery. It was preposterous, of course, to think of repaying his devotion by accepting such a sacrifice; but how find reasons to convince him? She could not bear to let him think her less touched, less inclined to him than she was: the generosity of his love deserved that she should repay it with the truth. Yet how let him see what she felt, and yet refuse what he offered? How confess to him what had been on her lips when he made the offer: "I've seen what it did to one man; and there must never, never be another"? The tacit ignoring of her past had been the element in which their friendship lived, and she could not suddenly, to him of all men, begin to talk of herself like a guilty woman in a play. Somehow, in the end, she had managed it, had averted a direct explanation, had made him understand that her life was over, that she existed only for her daughter, and that a more definite word from him would have been almost a breach of delicacy. She was so used to behaving as if her life were over! And, at any rate, he had taken her hint, and she had been able to spare her sensitiveness and his. The next year, when he came to Florence to see her, they met again in the old friendly way; and that till now had continued to be the tenor of their intimacy.

And now, suddenly and unexpectedly, he had brought up the question again, directly this time, and in such a form that she could not evade it: putting the renewal of his plea, after so long an interval, on the ground that, on her own showing, her chief argument against it no longer existed.

"You tell me Leila's happy. If she's happy, she doesn't need you—need you, that is, in the same way as before. You wanted, I know, to be always in reach, always free and available if she should suddenly call you to her or take refuge with you. I understood that—I respected it. I didn't urge my case because I saw it was useless. You couldn't, I understood well enough, have felt free to take such happiness as life with me might give you while she was unhappy, and, as you imagined, with no hope of release. Even then I didn't feel as you did about it; I understood better the trend of things here. But ten years ago the change hadn't really come; and I had no way of convincing you that it was coming. Still, I always fancied that Leila might not think her case was closed, and so I chose to think that ours wasn't either. Let me go on thinking so, at any rate, till you've seen her, and confirmed with your own eyes what Susy Suffern tells you."

III.

ALL THROUGH what Susy Suffern told and retold during their four-hours' flight to the hills this plea of Ide's kept coming back to Mrs. Lidcote. She did not yet know what she felt as to its bearing on her own fate, but it was something on which her confused thoughts could stay themselves amid the welter of new impressions, and she was inexpressibly glad that he had said what he had, and said it at that particular moment. It helped her to hold fast to her identity in the rush of strange names and new categories that her cousin's talk poured out on her.

With the progress of the journey Miss Suffern's communications grew more and more amazing. She was like a cicerone preparing the mind of an inexperienced traveller for the marvels about to burst on it.

"You won't know Leila. She's had her pearls reset. Sargent's to paint her. Oh, and I was to tell you that she hopes you won't mind being the least bit squeezed over Sunday. The house was built by Wilbour's father, you know, and it's rather old-fashioned—only ten spare bedrooms. Of course that's small for what they mean to do, and she'll show you the new plans they've had made. Their idea is to keep the present house as a wing. She told me to explain—she's so dreadfully sorry not to be able to give you a sitting-room just at first. They're thinking of Egypt for next winter, unless, of course, Wilbour gets his appointment. Oh, didn't she write you about that? Why, he wants Rome, you know—the second secretaryship. Or, rather, he wanted England;

but Leila insisted that if they went abroad she must be near you. And of course what she says is law. Oh, they quite hope they'll get it. You see Horace's uncle is in the Cabinet,—one of the assistant secretaries,—and I believe he has a good deal of pull—''

"Horace's uncle? You mean Wilbour's, I suppose,'' Mrs. Lidcote interjected, with a gasp of which a fraction was given to Miss Suffern's flippant use of the language.

"Wilbour's? No, I don't. I mean Horace's. Theres no bad feeling between them, I assure you. Since Horace's engagement was announced—you didn't know Horace was engaged? Why, he's marrying one of Bishop Thorbury's girls: the red-haired one who wrote the novel that every one's talking about, 'This Flesh of Mine.' They're to be married in the cathedral. Of course Horace *can*, because it was Leila who—but, as I say, there's not the *least* feeling, and Horace wrote himself to his uncle about Wilbour.''

Mrs. Lidcote's thought fled back to what she had said to Ide the day before on the deck of the *Utopia*. "I didn't take up much room before, but now where is there a corner for me?" Where indeed in this crowded, topsy-turvey world, with its headlong changes and helter-skelter readjustments, its new tolerances and in-differences and accommodations, was there room for a character fashioned by slower sterner processes and a life broken under their inexorable pressure? And then, in a flash, she viewed the chaos from a new angle, and order seemed to move upon the void. If the old processes were changed, her case was changed with them; she, too, was a part of the general readjustment, a tiny fragment of the new pattern worked out in bolder freer harmonies. Since her daughter had no penalty to pay, was not she herself released by the same stroke? The rich arrears of youth and joy were gone; but was there not time enough left to accumulate new stores of happiness? That, of course, was what Franklin Ide had felt and had meant her to feel. He had seen at once what the change in her daughter's situation would make in

her view of her own. It was almost—wondrously
enough!—as if Leila's folly had been the means of vin-
dicating hers.

Everything else for the moment faded for Mrs. Lidcote in the glow of her daughter's embrace. It was unnatural, it was almost terrifying, to find herself standing
on a strange threshold, under an unknown roof, in a big
hall full of pictures, flowers, firelight, and hurrying servants, and in this spacious unfamiliar confusion to
discover Leila, bareheaded, laughing, authoritative,
with a strange young man jovially echoing her welcome
and transmitting her orders; but once Mrs. Lidcote had
her child on her breast, and her child's "It's all right,
you old darling!" in her ears, every other feeling was
lost in the deep sense of well-being that only Leila's hug
could give.

The sense was still with her, warming her veins and
pleasantly fluttering her heart, as she went up to her
room after luncheon. A little constrained by the presence of visitors, and not altogether sorry to defer for a
few hours the "long talk" with her daughter for which
she somehow felt herself tremulously unready, she had
withdrawn, on the plea of fatigue, to the bright
luxurious bedroom into which Leila had again and
again apologized for having been obliged to squeeze
her. The room was bigger and finer than any in her
small apartment in Florence; but it was not the standard
of affluence implied in her daughter's tone about it that
chiefly struck her, nor yet the finish and complexity of
its appointments. It was the look it shared with the rest
of the house, and with the perspective of the gardens
beneath its windows, of being part of an "establishment"—of something solid, avowed, founded on sacra-
ments and precedents and principles. There was nothing
about the place, or about Leila and Wilbour, that
suggested either passion or peril: their relation seemed
as comfortable as their furniture and as respectable as
their balance at the bank.

This was, in the whole confusing experience, the thing

that confused Mrs. Lidcote most, that gave her at once the deepest feeling of security for Leila and the strongest sense of apprehension for herself. Yes, there was something oppressive in the completeness and compactness of Leila's well-being. Ide had been right: her daughter did not need her. Leila, with her first embrace, had unconsciously attested the fact in the same phrase as Ide himself and as the two young women with the hats. "It's all right, you old darling!" she had said: and her mother sat alone, trying to fit herself into the new scheme of things which such a certainty betokened.

Her first distinct feeling was one of irrational resentment. If such a change was to come, why had it not come sooner? Here was she, a woman not yet old, who had paid with the best years of her life for the theft of the happiness that her daughter's contemporaries were taking as their due. There was no sense, no sequence, in it. She had had what she wanted, but she had had to pay too much for it. She had had to pay the last bitterest price of learning that love has a price: that it is worth so much and no more. She had known the anguish of watching the man she loved discover this first, and of reading the discovery in his eyes. It was a part of her history that she had not trusted herself to think of for a long time past: she always took a big turn about that haunted corner. But now, at the sight of the young man downstairs, so openly and jovially Leila's, she was overwhelmed at the senseless waste of her own adventure, and wrung with the irony of perceiving that the success or failure of the deepest human experiences may hang on a matter of chronology.

Then gradually the thought of Ide returned to her. "I chose to think that our case wasn't closed," he had said. She had been deeply touched by that. To everyone else her case had been closed so long! *Finis* was scrawled all over her. But here was one man who had believed and waited, and what if what he believed in and waited for were coming true? If Leila's "all right" should really foreshadow hers?

As yet, of course, it was impossible to tell. She had

fancied, indeed, when she entered the drawing-room before luncheon, that a too-sudden hush had fallen on the assembled group of Leila's friends, on the slender vociferous young women and the lounging golf-stockinged young men. They had all received her politely, with the kind of petrified politeness that may be either a tribute to age or a protest at laxity; but to them, of course, she must be an old woman because she was Leila's mother, and in a society so dominated by youth the mere presence of maturity was a constraint.

One of the young girls, however, had presently emerged from the group, and, attaching herself to Mrs. Lidcote, had listened to her with a blue gaze of admiration which gave the older woman a sudden happy consciousness of her long-forgotten social graces. It was agreeable to find herself attracting this young Charlotte Wynn, whose mother had been among her closest friends, and in whom something of the soberness and softness of the earlier manners had survived. But the little colloquy, broken up by the announcement of luncheon, could of course result in nothing more definite than this reminiscent emotion.

No, she could not yet tell how her own case was to be fitted into the new order of things; but there were more people—"older people" Leila had put it—arriving by the afternoon train, and that evening at dinner she would doubtless be able to judge. She began to wonder nervously who the new-comers might be. Probably she would be spared the embarrassment of finding old acquaintances among them; but it was odd that her daughter had mentioned no names.

Leila had proposed that, later in the afternoon, Wilbour should take her mother for a drive: she said she wanted them to have a "nice, quiet talk." But Mrs. Lidcote wished her talk with Leila to come first, and had, moreover, at luncheon, caught stray allusions to an impending tennis-match in which her son-in-law was engaged. Her fatigue had been a sufficient pretext for declining the drive, and she had begged Leila to think of her as peacefully resting in her room till such time as they could snatch their quiet moment.

"Before tea, then, you duck!" Leila with a last kiss had decided; and presently Mrs. Lidcote, through her open window, had heard the fresh loud voices of her daughter's visitors chiming across the gardens from the tennis-court.

IV.

LEILA HAD come and gone, and they had had their talk. It had not lasted as long as Mrs. Lidcote wished, for in the middle of it Leila had been summoned to the telephone to receive an important message from town, and had sent word to her mother that she couldn't come back just then, as one of the young ladies had been called away unexpectedly and arrangements had to be made for her departure. But the mother and daughter had had almost an hour together, and Mrs. Lidcote was happy. She had never seen Leila so tender, so solicitous. The only thing that troubled her was the very excess of this solicitude, the exaggerated expression of her daughter's annoyance that their first moments together should have been marred by the presence of strangers.

"Not strangers to me, darling, since they're friends of yours," her mother had assured her.

"Yes; but I know your feeling, you queer wild mother. I know how you've always hated people." (*Hated people!* Had Leila forgotten why?) "And that's why I told Susy that if you preferred to go with her to Ridgefield on Sunday I should perfectly understand, and patiently wait for our good hug. But you didn't really mind them at luncheon, did you, dearest?"

Mrs. Lidcote, at that, had suddenly thrown a startled look at her daughter. "I don't mind things of that kind any longer," she had simply answered.

"But that doesn't console me for having exposed you to the bother of it, for having let you come here when I ought to have *ordered* you off to Ridgefield with Susy. If Susy hadn't been stupid she'd have made you go there with her. I hate to think of you up here all alone."

Again Mrs. Lidcote tried to read something more than a rather obtuse devotion in her daughter's radiant gaze. "I'm glad to have had a rest this afternoon, dear; and later—"

"Oh, yes, later, when all this fuss is over, we'll more than make up for it, sha'n't we, you precious darling?" And at this point Leila had been summoned to the telephone, leaving Mrs. Lidcote to her conjectures.

These were still floating before her in cloudy uncertainty when Miss Suffern tapped at the door.

"You've come to take me down to tea? I'd forgotten how late it was," Mrs. Lidcote exclaimed.

Miss Suffern, a plump peering little woman, with prim hair and a conciliatory smile, nervously adjusted the pendent bugles of her elaborate black dress. Miss Suffern was always in mourning, and always commemorating the demise of distant relatives by wearing the discarded wardrobe of their next of kin. "It isn't *exactly* mourning," she would say; "but it's the only stitch of black poor Julia had—and of course George was only my mother's step-cousin."

As she came forward Mrs. Lidcote found herself humorously wondering whether she were mourning Horace Pursh's divorce in one of his mother's old black satins.

"Oh, *did* you mean to go down for tea?" Susy Suffern peered at her, a little fluttered. "Leila sent me up to keep you company. She thought it would be cozier for you to stay here. She was afraid you were feeling rather tired."

"I was; but I've had the whole afternoon to rest in. And this wonderful sofa to help me."

"Leila told me to tell you that she'd rush up for a minute before dinner, after everybody had arrived; but the train is always dreadfully late. She's in despair at not giving you a sitting-room; she wanted to know if I thought you really minded.''

''Of course I don't mind. It's not like Leila to think I should.'' Mrs. Lidcote drew aside to make way for the housemaid, who appeared in the doorway bearing a table spread with a bewildering variety of tea-cakes.

''Leila saw to it herself,'' Miss Suffern murmured as the door closed. ''Her one idea is that you should feel happy here.''

It struck Mrs. Lidcote as one more mark of the sub-verted state of things that her daughter's solicitude should find expression in the multiplicity of sandwiches and the piping-hotness of muffins; but then everything that had happened since her arrival seemed to increase her confusion.

The note of a motor-horn down the drive gave another turn to her thoughts. ''Are those the new arrivals already?'' she asked.

''Oh, dear, no; they won't be here till after seven.'' Miss Suffern craned her head from the window to catch a glimpse of the motor. ''It must be Charlotte leaving.''

''Was it the little Wynn girl who was called away in a hurry? I hope it's not on account of illness.''

''Oh, no; I believe there was some mistake about dates. Her mother telephoned her that she was expected at the Stepleys', at Fishkill, and she had to be rushed over to Albany to catch a train.''

Mrs. Lidcote meditated. ''I'm sorry. She's a charm-ing young thing. I hoped I should have another talk with her this evening after dinner.''

''Yes; it's too bad,'' Miss Suffern's gaze grew vague. ''You *do* look tired, you know,'' she continued, seating herself at the tea-table and preparing to dispense its delicacies. ''You must go straight back to your sofa and let me wait on you. The excitement has told on you more than you think, and you mustn't fight against it any longer. Just stay quietly up here and let yourself go. You'll have Leila to yourself on Monday.''

Mrs. Lidcote received the tea-cup which her cousin

proffered, but showed no other disposition to obey her injunctions. For a moment she stirred her tea in silence; then she asked: "Is it your idea that I should stay quietly up here till Monday?"

Miss Suffern set down her cup with a gesture so sudden that it endangered an adjacent plate of scones. When she had assured herself of the safety of the scones she looked up with a fluttered laugh. "Perhaps, dear, by to-morrow you'll be feeling differently. The air here, you know—"

"Yes, I know." Mrs. Lidcote bent forward to help herself to a scone. "Who's arriving this evening?" she asked.

Miss Suffern frowned and peered. "You know my wretched head for names. Leila told me—but there are so many—"

"So many? She didn't tell me she expected a big party."

"Oh, not big: but rather outside of her little group. And of course, as it's the first time, she's a little excited at having the older set."

"The older set? Our contemporaries, you mean?"

"Why—yes." Miss Suffern paused as if to gather herself up for a leap. "The Ashton Gileses," she brought out.

"The Ashton Gileses? Really? I shall be glad to see Mary Giles again. It must be eighteen years," said Mrs. Lidcote steadily.

"Yes," Miss Suffern gasped, precipitately refilling her cup.

"The Ashton Gileses; and who else?"

"Well, the Sam Fresbies. But the most important person, of course, is Mrs. Lorin Boulger."

"Mrs. Boulger? Leila didn't tell me she was coming."

"Didn't she? I suppose she forgot everything when she saw you. But the party was got up for Mrs. Boulger. You see, it's very important that she should—well, take a fancy to Leila and Wilbour; his being appointed to Rome virtually depends on it. And you know Leila insists on Rome in order to be near you. So she asked

Mary Giles, who's intimate with the Boulgers, if the visit couldn't possibly be arranged; and Mary's cable caught Mrs. Boulger at Cherbourg. She's to be only a fortnight in America; and getting her to come directly here was rather a triumph."

"Yes; I see it was," said Mrs. Lidcote.

"You know, she's rather—rather fussy; and Mary was a little doubtful if—"

"If she would, on account of Leila?" Mrs. Lidcote murmured.

"Well, yes. In her official position. But luckily she's a friend of the Barkleys. And finding the Gileses and Fresbies here will make it all right. The times have changed!" Susy Suffern indulgently summed up.

Mrs. Lidcote smiled. "Yes; a few years·ago it would have seemed improbable that I should ever again be dining with Mary Giles and Harriet Fresbie and Mrs. Lorin Boulger."

Miss Suffern did not at the moment seem disposed to enlarge upon this theme; and after an interval of silence Mrs. Lidcote suddenly resumed: "Do they know I'm here, by the way?"

The effect of her question was to produce in Miss Suffern an exaggerated access of peering and frowning. She twitched the tea-things about, fingered her bugles, and, looking at the clock, exclaimed amazedly: "Mercy! Is it seven already?"

"Not that it can make any difference, I suppose," Mrs. Lidcote continued. "But did Leila tell them I was coming?"

Miss Suffern looked at her with pain. "Why, you don't suppose, dearest, that Leila would do anything—"

Mrs. Lidcote went on: "For, of course, it's of the first importance, as you say, that Mrs. Lorin Boulger should be·favorably impressed, in order that Wilbour may have the best possible chance of getting Rome."

"I *told* Leila you'd feel that, dear. You see, it's actually on *your* account—so that they may get a post near you—that Leila invited Mrs. Boulger."

"Yes, I see that." Mrs. Lidcote, abruptly rising from her seat, turned her eyes to the clock. "But, as you say, it's getting late. Oughtn't we to dress for dinner?"

Miss Suffern, at the suggestion, stood up also, an agitated hand among her bugles. "I do wish I could persuade you to stay up here this evening. I'm sure Leila'd be happier if you would. Really, you're much too tired to come down."

"What nonsense, Susy!" Mrs. Lidcote spoke with sudden sharpness, her hand stretched to the bell. "When do we dine? At half-past eight? Then I must really send you packing. At my age it takes time to dress."

Miss Suffern, thus projected toward the threshold, lingered there to repeat: "Leila'll never forgive herself if you make an effort you're not up to." But Mrs. Lidcote smiled on her without answering, and the icy light-wave propelled her through the door.

V.

MRS. LIDCOTE, though she had made the gesture of ringing for her maid, had not done so.

When the door closed, she continued to stand motionless in the middle of her soft spacious room. The fire which had been kindled at twilight danced on the brightness of silver and mirrors and sober gilding; and the sofa toward which she had been urged by Miss Suffern heaped up its cushions in inviting proximity to a table laden with new books and papers. She could not recall having ever been more luxuriously housed, or having ever had so strange a sense of being out alone, under the night, in a wind-beaten plain. She sat down by the fire and thought.

A knock on the door made her lift her head, and she saw her daughter on the threshold. The intricate ordering of Leila's fair hair and the flying folds of her dressing-gown showed that she had interrupted her dressing to hasten to her mother; but once in the room she paused a moment, smiling uncertainly, as though she had forgotten the object of her haste.

Mrs. Lidcote rose to her feet. "Time to dress, dearest? Don't scold! I sha'n't be late."

"To dress?" Leila stood before her with a puzzled look. "Why, I thought, dear—I mean, I hoped you'd decided just to stay here quietly and rest."

Her mother smiled. "But I've been resting all the afternoon!"

"Yes, but—you know you *do* look tired. And when Susy told me just now that you meant to make the effort—"

"You came to stop me?"

"I came to tell you that you needn't feel in the least obliged—"

"Of course. I understand that."

There was a pause during which Leila, vaguely averting herself from her mother's scrutiny, drifted toward the dressing-table and began to disturb the symmetry of the brushes and bottles laid out on it.

"Do your visitors know that I'm here?" Mrs. Lidcote suddenly went on.

"Do they— Of course—why, naturally," Leila rejoined, absorbed in trying to turn the stopper of a salts-bottle.

"Then won't they think it odd if I don't appear?"

"Oh, not in the least, dearest. I assure you they'll *all* understand." Leila laid down the bottle and turned back to her mother, her face alight with reassurance.

Mrs. Lidcote stood motionless, her head erect, her smiling eyes on her daughter's. "Will they think it odd if I *do?*"

Leila stopped short, her lips half parted to reply. As she paused, the colour stole over her bare neck, swept up to her throat, and burst into flame in her cheeks.

Thence it sent its devastating crimson up to her very temples, to the lobes of her ears, to the edges of her eyelids, beating all over her in fiery waves, as if fanned by some imperceptible wind.

Mrs. Lidcote silently watched the conflagration; then she turned away her eyes with a slight laugh. "I only meant that I was afraid it might upset the arrangement of your dinner-table if I didn't come down. If you can assure me that it won't, I believe I'll take you at your word and go back to this irresistible sofa." She paused, as if waiting for her daughter to speak; then she held out her arms. "Run off and dress, dearest; and don't have me on your mind." She clasped Leila close, pressing a long kiss on the last afterglow of her subsiding blush. "I do feel the least bit overdone, and if it won't inconvenience you to have me drop out of things, I believe I'll basely take to my bed and stay there till your party scatters. And now run off, or you'll be late; and make my excuses to them all."

VI.

THE BARKLEYS' visitors had dispersed, and Mrs. Lidcote, completely restored by her two days' rest, found herself, on the following Monday alone with her children and Miss Suffern.

There was a note of jubilation in the air, for the party had "gone off" so extraordinarily well, and so completely, as it appeared, to the satisfaction of Mrs. Lorin Boulger, that Wilbour's early appointment to Rome was almost to be counted on. So certain did this seem that the prospect of a prompt reunion mitigated the distress with which Leila learned of her mother's decision to return almost immediately to Italy. No one understood this decision; it seemed to Leila absolutely unintelligible that Mrs. Lidcote should not stay on with them till their own fate was fixed, and Wilbour echoed her astonishment.

"Why shouldn't you, as Leila says, wait here till we can all pack up and go together?"

Mrs. Lidcote smiled her gratitude with her refusal. "After all, it's not yet sure that you'll be packing up."

"Oh, you ought to have seen Wilbour with Mrs. Boulger," Leila triumphed.

"No, you ought to have seen Leila with her," Leila's husband exulted.

Miss Suffern enthusiastically appended: "I *do* think inviting Harriet Fresbie was a stroke of genius!"

"Oh, we'll be with you soon," Leila laughed. "So soon that it's really foolish to separate."

But Mrs. Lidcote held out with the quiet firmness which her daughter knew it was useless to oppose. After her long months in India, it was really imperative, she declared, that she should get back to Florence and see what was happening to her little place there; and she had been so comfortable on the *Utopia* that she had a fancy to return by the same ship. There was nothing for it, therefore, but to acquiesce in her decision and keep her with them till the afternoon before the day of the *Utopia*'s sailing. This arrangement fitted in with certain projects which, during her two days' seclusion, Mrs. Lidcote had silently matured. It had become to her of the first importance to get away as soon as she could, and the little place in Florence, which held her past in every fold of its curtains and between every page of its books, seemed now to her the one spot where that past would be endurable to look upon.

She was not unhappy during the intervening days. The sight of Leila's well-being, the sense of Leila's tenderness, were, after all, what she had come for; and of these she had had full measure. Leila had never been happier or more tender; and the contemplation of her

bliss, and the enjoyment of her affection, were an absorbing occupation for her mother. But they were also a
sharp strain on certain overtightened chords, and Mrs.
Lidcote, when at last she found herself alone in the New
York hotel to which she had returned the night before
embarking, had the feeling that she had just escaped
with her life from the clutch of a giant hand.

She had refused to let her daughter come to town with
her; she had even rejected Susy Suffern's company. She
wanted no viaticum but that of her own thoughts; and
she let these come to her without shrinking from them as
she sat in the same high-hung sitting-room in which, just
a week before, she and Franklin Ide had had their
memorable talk.

She had promised her friend to let him hear from her,
but she had not kept her promise. She knew that he had
probably come back from Chicago, and that if he
learned of her sudden decision to return to Italy it would
be impossible for her not to see him before sailing; and
as she wished above all things not to see him she had
kept silent, intending to send him a letter from the
steamer.

There was no reason why she should wait till then to
write it. The actual moment was more favorable, and
the task, though not agreeable, would at least bridge
over an hour of her lonely evening. She went up to the
writing-table, drew out a sheet of paper and began to
write his name. And as she did so, the door opened and
he came in.

The words she met him with were the last she could
have imagined herself saying when they had parted.
"How in the world did you know that I was here?"

He caught her meaning in a flash. "You didn't want
me to, then?" He stood looking at her. "Suppose I
ought to have taken your silence as meaning that. But I
happened to meet Mrs. Wynn, who is stopping here,
and she asked me to dine with her and Charlotte, and
Charlotte's young man. They told me they'd seen you
arriving this afternoon, and I couldn't help coming
up."

There was a pause between them, which Mrs. Lidcote at last surprisingly broke with the exclamation: "Ah, she *did* recognize me, then!"

"Recognize you?" He stared. "Why—"

"Oh, I saw she did, though she never moved an eyelid. I saw it by Charlotte's blush. The child has the prettiest blush. I saw that her mother wouldn't let her speak to me."

Ide put down his hat with an impatient laugh. "Hasn't Leila cured you of your delusions?"

She looked at him intently. "Then you don't think Margaret Wynn meant to cut me?"

"I think your ideas are absurd."

She paused for a perceptible moment without taking this up; then she said, at a tangent: "I'm sailing tomorrow early. I meant to write to you—there's the letter I'd begun."

Ide followed her gesture, and then turned his eyes back to her face. "You didn't mean to see me, then, or even to let me know that you were going till you'd left?"

"I felt it would be easier to explain to you in a letter—"

"What in God's name is there to explain?" She made no reply, and he pressed on: "It can't be that you're worried about Leila, for Charlotte Wynn told me she'd been there last week, and there was a big party arriving when she left: Fresbies and Gileses, and Mrs. Lorin Boulger—all the board of examiners! If Leila has passed *that*, she's got her degree."

Mrs. Lidcote had dropped down into a corner of the sofa where she had sat during their talk of the week before. "I was stupid," she began abruptly. "I ought to have gone to Ridgefield with Susy. I didn't see till afterward that I was expected to."

"You were expected to?"

"Yes. Oh, it wasn't Leila's fault. She suffered—poor darling; she was distracted. But she'd asked her party before she knew I was arriving."

"Oh, as to that—" Ide drew a deep breath of relief. "I can understand that it must have been a disappointment not to have you to herself just at first. But, after all, you were among old friends or their children: the Gileses and Fresbies—and little Charlotte Wynn.'' He paused a moment before the last name, and scrutinized her hesitatingly. ''Even if they came at the wrong time, you must have been glad to see them all at Leila's.''

She gave him back his look with a faint smile. ''I didn't see them.''

''You didn't see them?''

''No. That is, excepting little Charlotte Wynn. That child is exquisite. We had a talk before luncheon the day I arrived. But when her mother found out that I was staying in the house she telephoned her to leave immediately, and so I didn't see her again.''

The colour rushed to Ide's sallow face. ''I don't know where you get such ideas!''

She pursued, as if she had not heard him: ''Oh, and I saw Mary Giles for a minute too. Susy Suffern brought her up to my room the last evening, after dinner, when all the others were at bridge. She meant it kindly—but it wasn't much use.''

''But what were you doing in your room in the evening after dinner?''

''Why, you see, when I found out my mistake in coming,—how embarrassing it was for Leila, I mean—I simply told her I was very tired, and preferred to stay upstairs till the party was over.''

Ide, with a groan, struck his hand against the arm of his chair. ''I wonder how much of all this you simply imagined!''

''I didn't imagine the fact of Harriet Fresbie's not even asking if she might see me when she knew I was in the house. Nor of Mary Giles's getting Susy, at the eleventh hour, to smuggle her up to my room when the others wouldn't know where she'd gone; nor poor Leila's ghastly fear lest Mrs. Lorin Boulger, for whom the party was given, should guess I was in the house, and prevent her husband's giving Wilbour the second secretaryship because she'd been obliged to spend a night under the same roof with his mother-in-law!''

Ide continued to drum on his chair-arm with exasperated fingers. "You don't *know* that any of the acts you describe are due to the causes you suppose.''

Mrs. Lidcote paused before replying, as if honestly trying to measure the weight of this argument. Then she said in a low tone: "I know that Leila was in an agony lest I should come down to dinner the first night. And it was for me she was afraid, not for herself. Leila is never afraid for herself.''

"But the conclusions you draw are simply preposterous. There are narrow-minded women everywhere, but the women who were at Leila's knew perfectly well that their going there would give her a sort of social sanction, and if they were willing that she should have it, why on earth should they want to withhold it from you?''

"That's what I told myself a week ago, in this very room, after my first talk with Susy Suffern.'' She lifted a misty smile to his anxious eyes. "That's why I listened to what you said to me the same evening, and why your arguments half convinced me, and made me think that what had been possible for Leila might not be impossible for me. If the new dispensation had come, why not for me as well as for the others? I can't tell you the flight my imagination took!''

Franklin Ide rose from his seat and crossed the room to a chair near her sofa-corner. "All I cared about was that it seemed—for the moment—to be carrying you toward me,'' he said.

"I cared about that, too. That's why I meant to go away without seeing you.'' They gave each other grave look for look. "Because, you see, I was mistaken,'' she went on. "We were both mistaken. You say it's preposterous that the women who didn't object to accepting Leila's hospitality should have objected to meeting me under her roof. And so it is; but I begin to understand why. It's simply that society is much too busy to revise its own judgments. Probably no one in the house with me stopped to consider that my case and

Leila's were identical. They only remembered that I'd done something which, at the time I did it, was condemned by society. My case has been passed on and classified: I'm the woman who has been cut for nearly twenty years. The older people have half forgotten why, and the younger ones have never really known: it's simply become a tradition to cut me. And traditions that have lost their meaning are the hardest of all to destroy."

Ide sat motionless while she spoke. As she ended, he stood up with a short laugh and walked across the room to the window. Outside, the immense black prospect of New York, strung with its myriad lines of light, stretched away into the smoky edges of the night. He showed it to her with a gesture.

"What do you suppose such words as you've been using—'society,' 'tradition,' and the rest—mean to all the life out there?"

She came and stood by him in the window. "Less than nothing, of course. But you and I are not out there. We're shut up in a little tight round of habit and association, just as we're shut up in this room. Remember, I thought I'd got out of it once; but what really happened was that the other people went out, and left me in the same little room. The only difference was that I was there alone. Oh, I've made it habitable now, I'm used to it; but I've lost any illusions I may have had as to an angel's opening the door."

Ide again laughed impatiently. "Well, if the door won't open, why not let another prisoner in? At least it would be less of a solitude—"

She turned from the dark window back into the vividly lighted room.

"It would be more of a prison. You forget that I know all about that. We're all imprisoned, of course—all of us middling people, who don't carry our freedom in our brains. But we've accommodated ourselves to our different cells, and if we're moved suddenly into new ones we're likely to find a stone wall where we thought there was thin air, and to knock ourselves senseless against it. I saw a man do that once.''

Ide, leaning with folded arms against the window-frame, watched her in silence as she moved restlessly about the room, gathering together some scattered books and tossing a handful of torn letters into the paper-basket. When she ceased, he rejoined: ''All you say is based on preconceived theories. Why didn't you put them to the test by coming down to meet your old friends? Don't you see the inference they would naturally draw from your hiding yourself when they arrived? It looked as though you were afraid of them—or as though you hadn't forgiven them. Either way, you put them in the wrong instead of waiting to let them put you in the right. If Leila had buried herself in a desert do you suppose society would have gone to fetch her out? You say you were afraid for Leila and that she was afraid for you. Don't you see what all these complications of feeling mean? Simply that you were too nervous at the moment to let things happen naturally, just as you're too nervous now to judge them rationally.'' He paused and turned his eyes to her face. ''Don't try to just yet. Give yourself a little more time. Give *me* a little more time. I've always known it would take time.''

He moved nearer, and she let him have her hand. With the grave kindness of his face so close above her she felt like a child roused out of frightened dreams and finding a light in the room.

''Perhaps you're right—'' she heard herself begin; then something within her clutched her back, and her hand fell away from him.

''I know I'm right: trust me,'' he urged. ''We'll talk of this in Florence soon.''

She stood before him, feeling with despair his kindness, his patience and his unreality. Everything he said seemed like a painted gauze let down between herself and the real facts of life; and a sudden desire seized her to tear the gauze into shreds.

She drew back and looked at him with a smile of superficial reassurance. ''You *are* right—about not talking any longer now. I'm nervous and tired, and it would do no good. I brood over things too much. As you say, I must try not to shrink from people.'' She turned away and glanced at the clock. ''Why, it's only ten! If I send you off I shall begin to brood again; and if you stay we shall go on talking about the same thing. Why shouldn't we go down and see Margaret Wynn for half an hour?''

She spoke lightly and rapidly, her brilliant eyes on his face. As she watched him, she saw it change, as if her smile had thrown a too vivid light upon it.

''Oh, no—not to-night!'' he exclaimed.

''Not to-night? Why, what other night have I, when I'm off at dawn? Besides, I want to show you at once that I mean to be more sensible—that I'm not going to be afraid of people any more. And I should really like another glimpse of little Charlotte.'' He stood before her, his hand in his beard, with the gesture he had in moments of perplexity. ''Come!'' she ordered him gaily, turning to the door.

He followed her and laid his hand on her arm. ''Don't you think—hadn't you better let me go first and see? They told me they'd had a tiring day at the dressmaker's. I daresay they have gone to bed.''

''But you said they'd a young man of Charlotte's dining with them. Surely he wouldn't have left by ten? At any rate, I'll go down with you and see. It takes so long if one sends a servant first.'' She put him gently aside, and then paused as a new thought struck her. ''Or wait; my maid's in the next room. I'll tell her to go and ask if Margaret will receive me. Yes, that's much the best way.''

She turned back and went toward the door that led to her bedroom; but before she could open it she felt Ide's quick touch again.

''I believe—I remember now—Charlotte's young man was suggesting that they should all go out—to a music-hall or something of the sort. I'm sure—I'm positively sure that you won't find them.''

Her hand dropped from the door, his dropped from

her arm, and as they drew back and faced each other she saw the blood rise slowly through his sallow skin, redden his neck and ears, encroach upon the edges of his beard, and settle in dull patches under his kind troubled eyes. She had seen the same blush on another face, and the same impulse of compassion she had then felt made her turn her gaze away again.

A knock on the door broke the silence, and a porter put his head into the room.

"It's only just to know how many pieces there'll be to go down to the steamer in the morning."

With the words she felt that the veil of painted gauze was torn in tatters, and that she was moving again among the grim edges of reality.

"Oh, dear," she exclaimed, "I never *can* remember! Wait a minute; I shall have to ask my maid."

She opened her bedroom door and called out: "Annette!"

About the Author

Born in 1862 into the New York society that she was to portray so scathingly, Edith Wharton abandoned her role to write and publish the novels that were to establish her as America's first major woman novelist. *The House of Mirth*, first published in 1905, was followed by *Ethan Frome*, *Summer* and *The Age of Innocence*. In addition to these classics, Edith Wharton was the author of several volumes of short stories and plays before her death in 1937.

EDITH WHARTON

Edith Wharton's novels about turn-of-the-century American society have long been acclaimed as literary classics. Berkley is proud to offer these unique editions with special introductions by Marilyn French, one of today's most popular writers.

__THE CUSTOM OF THE COUNTRY	04608-7/$3.50
__THE HOUSE OF MIRTH	04611-7/$2.95
__SUMMER	04610-9/$2.75
__ROMAN FEVER AND OTHER STORIES	04609-5/$2.95